# Night Visions

D0067328

# Thomas Fahy

DARK ALLEY

An Imprint of HarperCollinsPublishers

NIGHT VISIONS. Copyright © 2004 by Thomas Fahy. All rights reserved. Printed in the United States of America. No part of this book may be used or reproduced in any manner whatsoever without written permission except in the case of brief quotations embodied in critical articles and reviews. For information address HarperCollins Publishers Inc., 10 East 53rd Street, New York, NY 10022.

HarperCollins books may be purchased for educational, business, or sales promotional use. For information please write: Special Markets Department, HarperCollins Publishers Inc., 10 East 53rd Street, New York, NY 10022.

FIRST EDITION

Dark Alley is a federally registered trademark of HarperCollins Publishers Inc.

*Designed by Leah Carlson-Stanisic*

Printed on acid-free paper

Library of Congress Cataloging-in-Publication Data

Fahy, Thomas Richard.
  Night visions / Thomas Fahy.—1st ed.
     p.   cm.
  ISBN 0-06-059462-4 (acid-free paper)
  1. Dreams—Fiction. I. Title.

PS3606.A269N54 2004
813'.6—dc22                                        2003068774

04   05   06   07   08   WBC/RRD   10   9   8   7   6   5   4   3   2   1

# Contents

# Night Visions

# Parasomnia

*Simon the Sorcerer flew.*

*It was an ancient story that came to Butner Creedmoor in his dreams. Simon, a man consumed by his need for power, used magic and illusion to convince the people to worship him as God. Even Emperor Nero believed Simon's trickery. He sought his counsel in matters of the empire, built monuments in his honor, and proclaimed him guardian of the city.*

*When Peter heard this, he traveled to Rome and publicly challenged this self-proclaimed deity. He exposed Simon's lies, and in the name of the Lord he raised a man from the dead. The people who had believed in Simon were enraged and drove him from the city. For months, he lived among the shadows and beasts of the hills. Outcast. Forgotten.*

*One day, he returned to Rome in secret, asking the emperor to gather crowds on his behalf in a large piazza near the capi-*

tol. *Hundreds watched, including Peter, as Simon climbed a tower, leaped off, and began to fly.*

*Nero turned to Peter. "It is you who are the deceiver!"*

*With these words, Peter looked into the gray sky and cried out: "Angels of Satan, who keep Simon aloft, carry him no longer. Let him fall!"*

*Simon dropped to the ground, his screams filling the square until his neck snapped against the earth. Grieved and outraged, Nero condemned Peter to death.*

*Crowds surged as the executioners brought him to the cross. They wanted to intervene, but Peter begged them not to act, not to hinder his martyrdom. He then asked to be crucified upside down, saying that he was not worthy of dying like Christ.*

*Nero nodded in approval and watched as they nailed his feet above his head.*

Years ago, Butner's mother told him this story, and he can still hear the cadence of her voice. He had forgotten it until recently, but now it seems to be the only story he knows.

In the quiet, he breathes deeply and knocks on the apartment door, wearing his old UPS uniform and carrying a heavy rectangular box.

"Package for Miss Erin Winesburg."

She peers through the opening of the chained door. "A delivery on New Year's Eve?"

"Yes, Miss. UPS doesn't believe in holidays." He makes his voice sound strained, suggesting the weight of the package, and she opens the door quickly, smiling at the joke.

"Just grab the clipboard on top and sign by your name. Where do you want me to put this?"

"Oh . . . on the table over there. Thanks."

Butner steps inside the sparsely but stylishly furnished apartment. A black coat and a bottle of white wine have been

placed on a midnight-blue armchair. Erin is wearing an elegant black dress with crimson flowers; it stops a few inches
above her knees. She has long, slender legs and wavy chestnut-
brown hair. The mark under her chin suggests that she plays
the violin or viola, as his mother did for years, and he imagines
Erin onstage—the audience torn between listening and watching her statuesque figure. As she hands him the clipboard, he
wants to hear her play, to touch the soft material of her dress.
He wants a choice.

Tightening his right hand, he strikes her across the jaw. The
force of the blow knocks her against the wall, spraying blood on
the door.

Butner closes the blinds, then the front door. The dead bolt
locks with a hollow clap, and the phone starts ringing. He
opens the package, pulling out a strand of wire, two long
spikes, and a hammer.

Erin lies crumpled on the floor, blood on her chin and cheek.

Part of him doesn't want any of this, but he knows it's the
only way. He hasn't slept in over a month.

While dragging her body to the bathroom, he hears the
answering machine beep.

"Hey, girl, you're probably on your way. If not, get a move on.
We're waitin' for you. And guess who's here? Josh, the man of
your dreams. Anyway, I'll see you soon. Bye!"

The machine beeps again. The outgoing message rewinds.

Erin begins to moan.

JANUARY 1, 1990
5:53 P.M.

Officer Jennings knew it wouldn't be like television, but he has
secretly hoped for something more all along. Traffic tickets,

*drunken college students, paperwork, and more paperwork. No, law enforcement isn't a glamorous life, but as his sister reminds him after every complaint: "At least you're not being shot at by some crackhead serial killer!"*

*True enough, but he secretly hopes for something more.*

*After responding to several calls about flat tires and stalled engines, he and Officer Bland fill out a report for a stolen car that "reappeared" after the owner sobered up and remembered where he parked it. Now, off to an apartment on the west side of town. Apparently a young woman never showed up for a party yesterday evening. Her friends can't reach her by phone, and she isn't answering the door—even though her blue Saturn is parked out front.*

*It's going to be one of those days, Jennings thinks.*

*He knocks again and sends Bland to get a key from the manager. While waiting on the porch, he imagines breaking down the door and yelling, "Chapel Hill Police Department. We are entering under exigent circumstances!" His gun carefully poised in front of him as he peers into the dark corners of the home. "Clear!"*

*"Hey, Bob. Bob? We have to remember to leave this in the drop box." Officer Bland hands him the key.*

*"Sure." He unlocks the door, and they enter.*

*"Hello? Miss Winesburg? This is the police. Hello?"*

*The room feels hot. Jennings notices a bottle of wine on the armchair. Their footsteps echo loudly against the hardwood floors, and a glass bowl on the living room table rattles with each step. Jennings signals Bland to check out the kitchen while he walks into the bedroom. The door creaks as he slowly pushes it open. Someone is in bed, curled on top of the comforter, facing away from the door.*

*"Miss Winesburg?" he asks. Muted sunlight passes through the closed blinds, and the haze makes it difficult to see. "Miss*

Winesburg, are you all right?" Jennings takes a tentative step toward the bed, and the figure rocks slightly. He stops.

There is a sudden crash behind him as Officer Bland stumbles backward into the room and bumps into a dresser.

Jennings turns, startled. "What the hell?"

Bland's lower lip trembles. "She's . . . she's in the bath— WATCH OUT!"

Officer Jennings spins around, and the figure on the bed slices an upward arc into his chest. He falls back with a yell, and the entire room shudders when he hits the floor. In two quick motions, the attacker tears down the blinds and opens the window. He vanishes through the opening before Officer Bland can unlatch his gun.

Jennings winces as he gets to his feet and follows.

Garbage cans and boxes clutter the narrow, grassy alleyway. Jennings is panting now, and his temples throb rhythmically with each footstep. In the sunlight, he sees the man's all-brown outfit; it looks like a uniform of some kind. The suspect's lead increases, and he leaps over a fence like a track-and-field athlete. For Jennings, the climb is more labored. The chain-link rattles and bends under the weight of his body. One. Two. Three. Over.

Nothing.

Dogs bark wildly along the fence behind him. He pulls out his gun again and edges forward slowly. His shirt sticks to the blood on his chest, and he wipes sweat from his forehead. A few more steps until a clearing. Closer. He tries to breathe steadily, waiting and gripping the gun with both hands. He leans against the large brown Dumpster.

Go.

He spins into an open field, panning with his gun, looking for a target. Rusty iron pipes, scattered trash, a dilapidated wooden shed. No movement. He can hear sirens getting closer, and the throbbing in his head almost blinds him.

*   *   *

A few minutes later, Jennings returns to the apartment and walks to the bathroom with deliberate, heavy steps. His face shines with sweat, and his lower lip starts to quiver when he sees what terrified Officer Bland—Erin Winesburg's body hanging upside down at the back end of a bathtub. Wire cutting into her ankles, fastening them to a metallic towel rack at eye level. Her head and shoulders against the incline of the tub. Each hand elevated and positioned—the right nailed into the porcelain tiles, the left into the Plexiglas shower door. A circle has been carved into her torso, and bloods drips from the gash across her neck.

"What the hell happened here, Jennings? Bland said you went after the suspect."

He turns to see Detective Hicks standing behind him. "A man was asleep in the bed when we arrived."

"Asleep?"

"Yeah. I woke him when I entered her room. Then, before I knew what was going on, he attacked me with a knife and jumped through the window. He was wearing a brown uniform."

Detective Hicks looks at Jennings quizzically. "Get the paramedics to check you out." He turns, barking orders to no one in particular about searching the area.

Jennings lowers his eyes, then walks outside.

A small crowd of neighbors has gathered, wondering what has happened. They look at the officers for reassurance. They want to hear that everything will be all right, that they don't have to be afraid.

Jennings turns from them.

They should be afraid, he thinks. They all should.

# 1
## *Night Terrors*

**THURSDAY**

*H*er eyes open suddenly in the darkness. At first there is only panicked breathing and the tympani of a pounding heart. She struggles to lift her arms and legs but can't move. Car tires screech on the street below, and she turns her head toward the window. Moisture beads on the inside of the pane. She tries again to move, straining until her body rises like an anchor from deep waters. One at a time, her feet touch the floor, and she begins to feel safe. Sweat bleeds through both sides of her T-shirt.

The bedside clock reads 3:20.

That night, she isn't focused on the match. Her opponent, a beginner, hopes to win by brute force, but fencing is about refinement, strategy, precision. *En garde.* Relying on strength slows him down, and his body telegraphs each move. Once again, he overcommits to the attack, lunging too hard with little sense of timing or distance. Her right arm feels heavy, slow. She blinks twice, trying to ease the sting of her tired eyes. Foils clash around them, and she glances at a nearby duel. Each movement there seems choreographed, almost rhythmic.

Suddenly, she sees the metallic masks as cold and tortured. The fencers look like the faceless men who come for her in dreams. Coal-black eyes and bodies without shape. Her arm stiffens and her rhythm falters. A brute force punches through.

He scores a point.

"Gotcha, Sam." He smiles arrogantly through the wire mesh.

The masks return to normal.

Other than giving her a few bruises, he hasn't accomplished much in the last five minutes. Now, with this point, he can feel less embarrassed about losing to a woman. *En garde.* It's time to finish the match and go home. She attacks on his preparation, lunges, and parries for a quick point. Match.

"Damn!" He yanks off his mask and glares.

"Maybe next time, Jim." Samantha tries to sound encouraging but is too exhausted from her sleepless nights to really care.

"Yeah, yeah . . ." He hesitates, and Samantha wonders if he is going to ask her out for a drink. Again. She has used a string of unimaginative excuses to dodge his advances in the last few months, and she senses his growing resentment about her lack of interest.

They shake hands, and instead of speaking, he turns abruptly.

She can't be bothered with his bruised ego, she thinks. He's a poor fencer and a sore loser. She walks to the locker room with her head down.

Samantha undresses slowly. Her white cotton T-shirt is damp and heavy with sweat. Standing before a full-length mirror, she notices the way the light seems to reflect off the crescent-shaped scar on her abdomen. Its pallor disrupts the brown planes of her skin.

An image suddenly appears. A blade slicing through her yellow shirt into the skin. Her attacker's hand steady, the motion even and smooth.

She blinks, moving her head quickly from side to side.

She pulls a loose gray sweatshirt over her head, then frees the back of her shoulder-length hair from the collar. She grabs the gym bag at her feet and looks again in the mirror. Her thin body seems frail in the reflection. Dark circles have formed underneath her deep brown eyes.

She leaves the club without saying good-bye to anyone.

A cold, steady wind pours honey-thick fog over the hills of San Francisco. Samantha wraps a thin coat around her body and hurries past the vacant shops and dark office buildings. Even in a city this large, the streets can feel empty. Shadows from trees and parking signs quiver under the yellow streetlights, and her footsteps ricochet against the brick and plaster walls. At times she changes the rhythm of her steps to hear the sounds shift. It makes her feel less alone.

Samantha parked near her favorite church in the city. It's a few blocks out of the way, but she likes listening to the choir that rehearses on Thursday evenings. In the vestibule, she picks up the program for Sunday Mass, then steps into the nave. Dozens of candles glow peacefully in front of an altar to the Blessed Virgin Mary. Some of her white toes have turned flesh-colored from the hands and lips of the faithful. Her outstretched arms point downward.

Samantha has often considered lighting candles in a gesture of prayer but can't bring herself to worship. Instead, she sits in one of the back pews. It smells like dry leather and incense.

Inhaling deeply, she thinks about the long-ago Sunday mornings with her family. While Father slept, Mother would get her and Rachel ready for church. Then after dressing in their nicest outfits—faces shiny with makeup and hair brushed back and clipped—the sisters sprang into action. They pulled hair and tugged at clothes. They yelped and screeched while chasing each other through the house, dodging precariously close to end tables and floor lamps. Invariably someone fell. Invariably some-one cried for Mother. A few scratches and quickly forgotten tears later, they were out the door at 8:40. Mother in the middle. One girl clinging to her right hand, the other to her left.

All of this while Father slept.

The brisk walk in the cool air never failed to restore peace. Mother smelled like orange blossoms and lilacs, and her long, soft dress moved in waves as she walked. Samantha remem-bers thinking she wanted to smell that way when she grew up. She wanted to take long strides and wink while smiling. A few minutes before Mass, they climbed up the wide marble stairs, dipped their fingers into a bowl of holy water, and slid into a hard wooden pew. They fidgeted and half-listened as the priest started muttering in Latin that couldn't drown out a chorus of crying babies. The mixture of colognes, perfumes, and sweat made her dizzy. The air felt like a skin-tight sweater. Hot. Uncomfortable. She leaned closer to Mother and inhaled.

Samantha can't fully recall Mother's smell or even the touch of her hand. Sometimes a stray scent—a waft of perfume or springtime flower—brings back a gesture or expression. But it's never quite right. That is the worst part—not forgetting but not being able to remember either.

She was twelve when her mother died in a car accident. Her father, who slept on Sundays and preferred silence to the clamor in church, was too devastated to comfort anyone else. It was the first time she realized that some wounds were too deep to heal.

She looks at the cross hanging above the altar. The hands of Christ crushed, pierced. Did he ever forgive his father for allow-ing such suffering? The bass soloist starts singing an aria from

Bach's cantata *Ich habe genug,* and she follows the English trans-
lation as he sings in German:

> *Let them doze, your weary eyes,*
> *sink gently, blessedly to a close.*
>
> *Here I must live in misery;*
> *but I will look away, away,*
> *Toward sweet peace, quiet rest.*

He holds the word *rest* until the violins and cellos take over.
She closes her eyes, which burn from not sleeping for months,
and she listens. . . .

Outside, the final notes fade as the door closes behind her. It
feels darker now, and she wishes her car were here instead of
around the corner. She walks faster, and the city sounds play
tricks with her imagination. Car horns, the murmur of television
sets, voices, barking dogs. They seem near and far away at the
same time.

Then she hears another set of footsteps growing louder, moving faster and faster against the pavement. She looks behind her
but can't see anyone. Her name echoes off the walls.

"Sam—Samantha—"

Strong hands grab her shoulders suddenly. She runs into a
rock-hard chest, turning too late to see who's in front of her. His
coat whips around her with the wind, and she only has time for
one thought.

*I must act now, before he—before the darkness—*

# 2

# *The Return*

Samantha twists to the left and thrusts her right palm into his chest, bracing herself as she steps back.

"Hey, hey! Easy there."

"Frank? *Frank!* What the hell are you doing here?"

"It's good to see you too."

She watches him touch the spot where she pushed him. The dim streetlight turns his emerald eyes and sandy-blond hair to gray. As his hands disappear into the deep pockets of his long coat, she notices the familiar way it hangs from his shoulders, bringing out the muscular lines of his nearly six-foot frame.

"So . . . how are you?" His words sound tentative, unsteady.

"*How am I?* What the hell are you doing here?"

"I just flew in and wanted to see you. It's been a while."

"Most people call first. How did you know where—"

"You seem a little jumpy. Is everything all right?"

"I'm not jumpy," Samantha snaps, feeling another flash of anger. This type of presumption has always been his most irritating quality. While dating in law school, they rarely fought, and when they did, it was mostly about words. Frank needed words to explain what they had. Words to clarify and shape, define and solidify. Words to make her accountable. He wanted to be confident in their love, to know it was real, so he pushed too hard for assurances she couldn't give. And when she retreated further into silence, he talked as if he knew her better than she knew herself. Predicting when she would be late, angry, ecstatic, distant. As if he could fill in the words she refused to speak.

"So how did you know where to find me?" she continues.

"It's Thursday night. That means fencing practice, then choir. I assume you were fencing before this, right?" He points to her gym bag.

Samantha moves past him without answering and continues to her car. Her heart is still pounding loudly, and she hopes he can't hear it. She is relieved when he falls in step beside her.

"So, other than stalking me, what are you doing back in San Francisco? I can't believe your new firm is already giving you vacation time."

"Well, it's not exactly a firm. It's more like a corporation with a legal and investigative department." He pauses momentarily, looking down at the pavement as they walk. "That's why I'm here. I'm investigating a case."

"Wow, a real live crime fighter! Did they give you a cape and a utility belt?" Her smile takes the edge off the words.

"Funny. Actually, it involves a missing woman. I'd like to get your take on a few things, if you don't mind."

She doesn't respond. Only the sound of their syncopated footsteps and her thudding heart fill the silence between them.

"Well, here we are," she says. Standing in front of her once-red, now faded-orange Volvo, she searches through her bag for keys.

"Look, can we get coffee or something? I'd really appreciate—"

"I haven't heard from you in six months, Frank. What am I

supposed to do, drop everything just because you're back in town for a few days? If I'm so damn predictable, you should know better than—"

"I'm talking about a woman's life, Sam. I just want an hour of your time. Then, if you don't want to have anything to do with me, fine."

She looks at him, surprised by his words. She doesn't want him out of her life. She just doesn't know where he fits in anymore.

"Well, in that case, you're treating."

# 3
# *Missing Pieces*

*F*rank insists on driving his car because the radio in Sam's doesn't work. It hasn't worked in almost three years, another point of contention between them. As far back as he can remember, Frank has surrounded himself with sound. Most of the time, it doesn't matter what—talk radio, television shows, music. He needs something to fill the silence. For Frank, background noise makes the stillness in his apartment less lonely and pauses in conversation less sad.

He thinks he must have inherited this need for sound from his father, who lifted heavy boxes for a freight forwarding company. It was hard, loud work. Every day Mr. Bennett heard the din of forklifts, truck engines, and power tools while loading and unloading large aluminum containers. His thick, twisted knuckles looked like those of an arthritic puppeteer, and Frank can still see them clasped in front of his face at dinner. Elbows on the table, his fingers poised over a plate of colorless chicken and peas, dangling invisible strings. But after a glass of wine, when Frank and his sister went to their rooms, Mr. Bennett became an inventor. In the middle of their cluttered garage floor, his work-bench rested precariously on two cracked cement slabs, and a naked bulb glowed from the ceiling overhead. The bench's black-brown wood looked as if it came from the deck of a nineteenth-century whaling ship. And there, in that dimly lit place, where the bench would rock under the work of his hard hands, Frank's father must have felt like a sailor traveling to new lands.

He kept a radio next to the bench and listened to jazz or classical music. He especially loved the sound of wind instruments—trumpets, saxophones, clarinets. He liked to feel musical rhythms while working. Frank always thought that this must have been his father's favorite time of day, because he could control the sounds around him. Whatever noises he made with hammers and saws were accompanied by Cole Porter, George Gershwin, Aaron Copland. These were *his* sounds.

On most nights, Frank could peer out his bedroom window and see the garage. This was the way he liked to remember his father. Watching him work as the hum of a hacksaw and the folk tunes of Copland gradually lulled Frank to sleep.

He glances at Samantha, who has been changing radio stations absentmindedly. Her raven hair cascades over the side of her face until she instinctively hooks it behind her ear. He studies the gentle slope of her nose, her slightly parted lips, and remembers tracing them with his fingertip many months ago. Even though they are the same age, she seems much older than twenty-seven now. There is a weariness to her face that worries him.

She turns and asks about his new job. As Frank talks, he can faintly hear a woman's voice on the radio and the pulse of a song. He notices Sam fidgeting in the seat as if it is too small for her body. Her gym bag crowds the floor at her feet, and she leans forward to move it. Or is she straining to hear the music?

He can't tell. Her smell fills the car, and Frank inhales quietly. Being near her like this feels comforting, safe.

He talks about his job with unnecessary evasiveness. The Palici Corporation mostly specializes in investigative work for high-profile clients. The kind of people who can afford to pay for silence and minimal exposure. It is staffed by people who have worked in the legal system, law enforcement, criminology, psychology, technological sciences, and scientific research.

"We either get results faster than local law enforcement—and more discreetly—or we succeed where others have failed," he continues. "It's really amazing, Sam. I've been training with investigators at Quantico—"

"What are you doing with these people, Frank? Helping the wealthy get around the law because they can afford it?" She feels dizzy and slightly nauseated. Her voice doesn't disguise her disappointment. "You were one of the best law students to come out of Stanford—a shoe-in for assistant district attorney in San Francisco. A job where you could do something important."

"Something important? I'm searching for a missing woman." In truth, the corporation gave him the assignment because no one else wanted it. The director had called it an exercise in futility. "No one rents her own car before disappearing," he'd said. "She'll probably return home any day now."

That was over two weeks ago, and she was still missing.

Frank had researched the case and come up with more questions than answers. Following several leads, he took a 747 to San Francisco. To Sam.

"Oh, come on. Who's looking for her? A psycho boyfriend? Rich parents?"

He is annoyed that she guessed right. "The fact that her family has money doesn't make this case less important, less noble than the ones you deal with. You actually *were* Stanford's best, and now you're essentially a social worker for the Oakland Legal Clinic, helping 'the disadvantaged' get away scot-free." He pauses only to catch his breath, not to quell his anger. "Sure, some of them deserve it. Some of them need it. But how many really are criminals? How many do you defend under the banners of discrimination and social injustice? They take advantage of the system, Sam. You know it as well as I do."

"At least I don't check their bank accounts first. The system doesn't give a shit about the poor because it's easier to let them slip through the cracks. They can't protect themselves from wrongful evictions, discrimination on the job, police brutality. They can't afford it, and no one else cares—"

Frank brakes suddenly for a red light, and Sam presses hard against the dashboard.

"Sorry," he mutters unconvincingly. "Her parents may be rich, but they're also terrified." This is Frank's way of changing the subject. He doesn't want to fight, and he senses that she doesn't either.

"Sorry."

"Don't be."

The light turns green.

The Starbucks is crowded with lone college students, couples holding hands as they sip coffee, and single men pretending to read while checking out women at nearby tables. Frank and Sam find a corner booth that is somewhat private.

"Get me something decaffeinated," she says.

"In a coffee shop?"

He smiles and puts his satchel on the table before heading to the counter. He takes long, confident strides and says something that makes the cashier giggle. Samantha watches with a mixture of desire and envy. She has always admired his self-assurance and ease around strangers, but it makes her uncomfortable.

Communication should be earned. It shouldn't happen in line at fast-food restaurants and coffee shops. It should take time. It should take something more than words and a smile. Frank pays for the order, and the cashier giggles again.

Samantha wonders how Frank and the other men in the room see her. A tired woman with baggy sweatpants and a frayed sweatshirt? Or is there something enticing about a body masked with shapeless clothes? As Frank walks back to the table, she suddenly feels self-conscious about her empty hands. She reaches up and touches her hair, still damp and sticky with sweat. *I must look terrible,* she thinks as he places the coffee in front of her.

She doesn't want to think about her body or his exchange with the cashier, so she quickly turns to the case.

"What about this missing woman?"

Her abruptness makes Frank noticeably uncomfortable, uncertain about seeing her after so much time. Pulling out a file, he hands her two pictures and begins talking about Catherine Anne Weber. His tone is serious, more professional now.

"Until a month ago, Catherine was a victim's advocate for the Durham Police Department. She had that job for over two years, handling mostly domestic violence and child abuse cases. Apparently she was very good at it. She has lots of friends in the area, and her parents live in Raleigh."

Samantha looks at the first photograph while Frank talks. It was taken with a group of friends at an upscale bar. They are celebrating something—happy to be there, to be together. Catherine stands in the middle, smiling radiantly. Arms hidden, wrapped behind the girls beside her. She has a tall, slender body.

"As part of a short vacation, she went to visit a college girlfriend in Memphis, Tennessee, but she missed her return flight five days later. Her friend drove Catherine to the airport, even walked her to the security checkpoint. Ten minutes later, Catherine made two calls with a calling card—the first to her answering machine, the second to another friend in Boulder, Colorado. Then she rented a car and drove to Kansas City, where she stayed at a Lucky 8 motel. Late the following evening, she arrived in Boulder. According to this friend, Catherine only told her that she was coming the day before."

In the second photograph, Catherine sits by a lake, looking wistfully at the water. It's a quiet, solitary moment, and she must have been unaware of the camera. She has a striking face with small, perfectly proportioned features. Her short black hair brings out the delicate quality of her white skin. Any man could fall in love with this face, Samantha thinks, and she wonders if Frank has.

"She left Boulder exactly three weeks ago, and a series of credit-card charges leads to California: a motel the following night in Salt Lake City, including several drinks and dinner for two at Lucci's; then a motel in Reno; lunch in Davis, California; and dinner later that night at the Silver Dragon in San Francisco."

"She certainly was in a hurry." Samantha looks up. "Who'd she have dinner with in Salt Lake?"

"I don't know. Catherine never mentioned anyone from Salt Lake to her friends or family." He takes a sip of his caffè mocha. "She may have been picked up or something."

"Then she wouldn't have paid for dinner."

"Don't be sexist." He smiles at his own joke and continues. "In any case, the motel manager in Reno remembers her clearly because she complained about a leaky faucet in the bathroom. She demanded a room change at two in the morning, claiming that she couldn't sleep with all the noise."

"Was she alone?"

"She rented a single. The manager didn't mention anyone else. Why?"

"I'm just wondering about the dinner. She could have met someone who traveled with her or followed her to Reno."

"Possible." He pauses to consider this, looking away from her and the table for a moment. "In any case, she just disappears after that. The rental car hasn't been returned. No credit or calling card activity since then. Nothing."

"And you spoke with the restaurant here?"

"Yeah, but no one recognized her picture. It's a busy place with lots of solo customers."

Samantha lays the pictures on the table between them. "So what's the deal with her parents? They must be wealthy or you wouldn't be involved, right?"

"Yes," he answers, ignoring the jab.

"Let me guess, tobacco?"

"Actually they own the largest surgical equipment company in the United States, Precision Medical Supplies. They sell EKG monitors, fiberoptic tools for cardiac procedures, ultrasonic cutting systems, polymer ligation clips, surgical lighting."

"Do you even know what any of that stuff is?"

"I have a pretty good idea about the lights, but other than that, no."

They both laugh, then become silent.

"So what do you think happened?"

"I'm not sure. She was alone. She has no friends here that we know of."

Samantha recognizes the evasiveness. "And?"

His face falls to the left, avoiding her eyes. "I think she's dead—that her body and the car will turn up somewhere in the city."

"Wait a minute." Samantha doesn't want to accept this—not with Catherine's face staring up at her from the table. "What if she's running away? What if she wants to be missing?"

"Why leave such a clear trail? She could have paid for the dinners and hotels with cash. Why keep the rental car?"

"Maybe at first she wasn't sure if she wanted to disappear. Maybe she didn't have the courage until she got here."

"According to her friends and family, she has no reason to run."

"Unless she's running from them."

"Well, that still leaves the million-dollar question. Why come to San Francisco?" Frank notices Samantha's long fingers wrapping around the cup in front of her. "And that's where I need your help."

"How so?"

"If she did come here to start over, my guess is that she would try finding a job in social services. She was very committed to her work in North Carolina, and even though she doesn't need the money, she might be volunteering or working with some victims' advocacy group. Could you find out if any organization you work with has recently hired someone or received an application?"

"I thought you said she was probably dead."

"I did." He looks at the pictures lying in front of her. "But I know you'd rather prove me wrong about this." He smiles faintly. "I want to be sure, Sam. What do you say?"

"Of course." Catherine's smile seems sad and somewhat artificial to her now. The kind of smile that looks cracked from being used too often to make people think everything is all right. The kind of smile that flight attendants wear, strained and weary.

"Of course I will."

# Parasomnia

*Christina Castinella hastily clears away her makeshift dinner, then stands aside as the client walks into her kitchen. He tries to get comfortable in the hard, boxy chair, but his lanky body won't fit. Something about him makes the entire apartment feel small. Looking at his watery eyes and worn black clothes, she wonders if this part-time job reading people's fortunes is worth dealing with all the wackos in D.C.*

*She has a gift, and with that gift comes responsibility, Grandmama still tells her. Every summer, when visiting Calabria, Christina spends most afternoons in Grandmama's kitchen, listening to the townswomen talk about family fortunes, sickness, and shiftless men. They gesture emphatically with each word and wear faded one-piece sundresses to hide their tired bodies.*

*As the sun sets, Grandmama's house becomes quiet, and*

*that's when the men start coming. They bring their sorrow, uncertainty, pain, confusion—asking these women to uncover answers with each card. Most find hope in their prognostications, believing with almost unquestioned faith. Even the parish priest, Father Grigio, who grumbles about these women in private and earnestly advises his congregation to find answers through God, never questions their readings. Rumor has it that he seeks their advice from time to time, but no one at the table mentions this.*

*When Christina was twelve, they taught her to use a deck. "It will guide you and others through hardship and loss," they promised. Very quickly they realized that she was different. Her visions clearer, her predictions more profound. Soon the cards were almost incidental to her insights.*

*For her, the tarot is no more than a pastime, but a few months ago, she decided to advertise her fortune-telling skills in several local papers. She still has one year left at George-town, and her part-time job as a tutor doesn't even cover her long-distance phone bill, let alone tuition. So she turned to the cards.*

*Some of her clients are more interested in her long legs and tight button-down shirts than the future. But most are desperate for answers—needing them the way some need love. They are obsessed with a future they can't grasp or control, and Christina uses the Calabria deck for them.*

*Looking at this man, she decides to do the same. She doesn't usually make appointments on Sunday, but he was so insistent on the phone that she couldn't say no.* Anyway, *she thought after hanging up,* I really want tickets for the Police concert next month.

*He quietly watches her shuffle and place the deck in front of him.*

*"Cut them with your left hand."*

*He does so, and she begins turning them over. The Hanged Man, an inverse Wheel of Fortune, the four of swords—cards that speak of anguish and torment—the ten of swords, the Tower, Death . . .*

*The room gets darker as the sun sets, and the customer's still body and expressionless face blend into the growing blackness. She doesn't see him now as she's caught up in a series of images ignited by the cards. Music playing on a harpsichord, a stable smelling of hay and horse dung, a weathered statue casting its shadow over a tombstone, damp alleyways, thick fog, a sudden piercing scream.*

*Her breathing quickens.*

*"You're running through the dark. Your eyes burn, and you see some kind of light—silver flashes. Voices cry out in front of you, beneath you. Without stopping, you move. You're afraid to rest, because something is following you. No, it moves with you, with the rhythm of your footsteps, pushing against you. You turn to face it . . . but nothing is there. Well, not exactly, a feeling is, but it—I'm . . . I'm not sure. . . ."*

*"Go on!"*

*"I can't. It doesn't make sense."*

*"It does!" His voice sounds harsh. Then he softens it, as if to explain himself. "I have trouble sleeping."*

*She pauses, confused. "Okay?"*

*"When I wake up, I can't remember things. I just feel tired from dreaming. That's why I came here. To find out if you could see what I see—to help me understand."*

*"I just told you. I don't understand."*

*"But you do. You're not like the others. You see these things too."*

*She wants him to leave so she can get back to her frozen din-*

*ner and glass of cheap wine. Putting her hands on top of the cards, she starts to gather them up and end the session—even if he doesn't pay. Who cares.*

*"Please. Just tell me what else you see. That's all I want." He pulls out a hundred-dollar bill. "Just finish the reading," he pleads.*

*She looks at him skeptically, then at the neatly folded bill on the table. "All right."*

*He settles back into the chair with a strained smile and motions to the deck.*

*She passes her hands over the upturned cards and closes her eyes. Part of her is afraid of returning to the darkness, but she wants to get this over with quickly.*

*"The thing following you is very old. And there is a smell . . . something rotten." She winces from the stench, then starts seeing faces—each twisted by fear. Tears falling up from their eyes. One after another, they rush forward with muffled cries. She doesn't know whether or not she is talking anymore. Her body seems to be moving through an unfamiliar hallway. She is in someone's home—blood splattered in arcs on the walls, across family photos, a light switch, a child's crayon drawing of a purple tree and two stick figures holding hands. She stops to unlock the entryway door. Light reflects in a mirror to the left, and she turns. It's not her. It's him, the customer, in the mirror looking back at her. She hears heavy breathing and distant notes struck on a piano.*

*Lost in these visions, she doesn't see the customer turning his head away from the cards and reaching into his black coat. He pulls out two long knives. Lurching out of the chair, he extends his arms across the table and tries to slice an oval-shaped mark into her chest. The knives pierce the skin of her breasts, pushing her backward. She feels her body hit the floor. With his left hand, he flips the table sideways and towers above her.*

*He leans down, as if to whisper something, and his face becomes feral. Teeth bared. Eyes bulging with intensity and saliva stringing from his mouth. He sucks in his breath with a hiss. Wildly, instinctively, she kicks her legs out, hitting his left shin and knee. He falls on top of her. Air explodes out of his mouth—his lips almost touching her ear and his coarse, unshaven face scraping against her cheek. He is still.*

*She can feel the sticky warmth of his blood seeping through her shirt and mixing with her blood. She turns her head and vomits. The apartment is almost entirely dark now, and through the pounding in her temples, she listens to the night-time noises of the street outside. Car engines and loud conversations, bicycle bells and jackhammers. They seem far away. She thinks about calling the police, getting help. But not yet, she tells herself. I need rest.*

*I need sleep.*

OCTOBER 4, 1982

3:20 P.M.

*She doesn't remember calling the police—only that they are in her apartment when she wakes. The skin on the customer's face looks like an ancient slab of marble, and one of the coroners touches it before zipping up the body bag.*

*Detective Jacobs scribbles something in his notepad, then asks for the discarded clothes. She leads him to the bedroom, where he lifts them off the floor with latex gloves and places them in a plastic bag. She doesn't recognize her white top, which is still damp with blood.*

*"Chris . . . tina" He writes slowly and with strained concentration. "C-a-s-t-i-n-e-l-l-a. You must be Italian."*

"How could you tell." She leans back on the couch and looks at the poster of Italy hanging on the wall behind him. Her head is still throbbing, and she worries about passing out. "I feel dizzy."

"The paramedics are going to take you to the hospital now. You hit your head pretty hard in the struggle, but the wound on your chest is superficial."

The taped bandages above her chest itch, and she looks down at the front of her shirt. No blood seeps through the white gauze.

"I'm still unclear," Jacobs continues, "as to how you stabbed him."

"I . . . I didn't. He fell, I think. I'm not sure."

He waits for her to say more, but she simply lowers her head.

"You need some rest, Miss Castinella. Hopefully, you'll be able to remember more about what happened later this afternoon." He stands. "I'll stop by the hospital in a few hours."

"Who is he?" she asks, her voice shaking.

"We're fairly certain he's responsible for six murders in this area since September. You're lucky to be alive." The EMT walks over to Christina and helps her up.

"Six murders?" The number seems wrong somehow.

Detective Jacobs watches her leave, then returns to the investigators, who are taking photographs and collecting evidence in the kitchen.

7:12 P.M.

She gets out of the cab and decides to walk up M Street before going back to her place. The sidewalks are damp from a light rain that is still falling from the charcoal-gray sky. After being questioned by Detective Jacobs at the hospital, she started to remember more. The hallway with those blood-stained pictures. And that music, haunting, calm, insistent.

As Christina thinks more about the man in her kitchen, she wonders whether he was really trying to kill her. After throwing her to the floor, he leaned close as if to whisper. Maybe he said something that she didn't hear. Were his lips moving? Then he fell on top of her—on top of his knife. He tried to hold her still with the weight of his body and one free hand. The other gripped the knife. She could feel his closed fist against her sternum. But he didn't try to get up. He didn't strike or stab her again. He only struggled to keep their bodies together, holding himself against her until he died.

At the hospital, the doctor took some of her blood to run tests, and for the first time she started worrying about AIDS. What if he was sick? What if some disease will kill her after all? She won't know until the police conduct an autopsy on the killer. Even then, will she really be sure?

She stops in front of a newsstand, looking at the rows of shiny magazine covers. A new image comes to her, one she has not seen before. A woman surrounded by withered trees that are upside down. No. She is upside down, hanging by her feet, each arm stretched out by rope attached to other trees. Thick, arthritic branches twist above her, dangling her body like a puppet. Her legs are crossed, suspended from a single rope, and her back is torn from being dragged across the ground. On her front, blood drains slowly from a circle carved into her torso. Her body sways slightly.

Christina's eyes tear up. "What's wrong with me?" she mutters. Then she hears a man's voice—the vendor has turned on a shortwave radio. It's a news update on NPR.

"Pianist Glenn Gould died today at the age of fifty. A controversial artist, Gould was perhaps most famous for his recordings of Bach's Goldberg Variations, which he recorded twice—at both the beginning and the end of his career. . . ."

An excerpt from one of these recordings begins playing, and Christina immediately feels numb. A wave of nausea passes over her as she recognizes the music from her vision.

"Goldberg," she says aloud, and the vendor turns to her, puzzled. Suddenly, she feels the need to run—from the images, the sounds, the rainwater. Along the brick sidewalks leading back to her apartment, the name Goldberg repeats in her head, and the music follows her like her own shadow on a sunny afternoon.

# 4
# *Lost and Found*

The doorbell rings, followed by two quick knocks. Samantha knows immediately that it is Frank. The heaviness of his knuckles against the thin plywood door—it's a sound she has been waiting to hear for months. Too many times she mistook the footsteps of a neighbor or a knock on the door across the hall for him. Sometimes she just opened the door, as if he would be standing there one day, penitent and miserable without her. Instead, he found her on a street corner, right where he expected her. And so the knock this morning comes as no surprise.

She looks at the clock: 6:45 A.M.

Samantha closes her book and places it on the bedside table. She can feel the heat from the lamp that has been glowing for hours. She knows better than to read in bed, but last night she couldn't stop thinking about Frank after their conversation, about Catherine.

Her body feels weary, in part from yesterday's workout, but mostly from months of sleeplessness and nightmares. She had hoped that working longer hours, not eating after 6:00 P.M., and using her bed exclusively for sleep would help. But she can't stop mulling over her problems and getting so anxious that her eyes won't shut. She still worries about her father's health, about her clients at the legal clinic, about Frank's move to Washington. And the man who attacked her over two years ago seems to linger at the edge of every dream. Watching. Waiting to strike again.

Sometimes she wonders if loneliness is to blame. If she never stops being lonely, then what?

She opens the door.

"Hi, Sam. Sorry to come by so early. I just got a call from the San Francisco PD. They found Catherine's rental car in a parking lot along the Presidio. And a body."

"Is it hers?" she asks without being sure if she really wants the answer.

"No, it's someone else's—a man's. I'm on my way there now." He pauses, looking down at his black leather shoes. "Can you come?"

Nothing at first, then disbelief. "Why would I want to do that?"

"You might be right about her—that she's alive somewhere in the city. This is our best chance of finding her, Sam. We can go over there, take a quick look at the scene.... You might see something I'd miss."

"I doubt it." Another pause. Her head falls to the right, and she folds her arms in front of her chest. "Besides, I have an appointment this morning. I can't miss it."

"I'll get you there. I promise." His voice softens, and he looks directly into her eyes. "Look, this is the first physical evidence in the case, and I could really use some help." He runs his right hand through his pale hair, then looks away. "I've never done this before."

She watches his body. The fine hair on his forearms, the thick wrists. She remembers the contours of his chest, hidden now beneath a white dress shirt with rolled-up sleeves, but once suspended above her in the dark. Solid and strong. She searched for his face with her hands. A groan—the sound of pleasure without words—guided her lips to his.

No.

She wants to say no. She wants to say, *You can't just pick and choose when you want me in your life.* She wants to shut him out—treat him as he has treated her for the last six months. But she isn't ready for that, not yet. She can still see Catherine's face watching from the photos.

"I'll grab my coat."

Catherine's rental car, a black Pontiac Sunfire, was left at the edge of a parking lot with the passenger door facing the rough waters of the bay. Pairs of joggers run along the coast toward Fort Point, and a handful of fishermen stand on a short L-shaped pier. They mostly concentrate on the fishing lines that tug and sway against the current, but every few minutes, one looks at the gathering of police. Only fragments of the Golden Gate Bridge are visible through the fog. Its peaks jut above the clouds like shark fins.

The thick, moist air dampens Samantha's face as soon as she steps out of the car. She can see a few officers working closely on the Sunfire, taking photographs and spreading dust to lift fingerprints. As she and Frank move closer, a man with dark skin and gapped front teeth orders the others to get back to work. They have been standing around a body a few feet from the car. The body is a uniformed officer.

"What happened?" Frank asks.

The dark-skinned man turns. "Oh, him. That's Officer Kincaid. He . . . passed out."

"Passed out?"

"Yeah, he's new on the job. Who are you?"

"Frank Bennett. This is Samantha Ranvali. We're investigators with the Palici Corporation."

"Detective Snair." He shakes Frank's hand indifferently. "I was under the impression that you'd be alone." While waiting for an answer, he looks over Samantha's body with an obvious mixture of disapproval and desire. He notices the rum-colored skin of her neck, and the silver necklace dangling between her small breasts.

"Well, I'm not. May we?" Frank glances at the empty car.

"By all means."

"What about the body? On the phone, you said there was a body."

"Yeah, underneath." Snair coughs. His eyes never lift to Samantha's face.

A thick rope runs through the open windows of the backseat and wraps underneath the car. Samantha steps ahead of Frank and squats, placing both hands on the damp asphalt. She looks under the car between the tires. A man's body hangs there, unevenly, like a discarded marionette. His arms have been stretched out at ninety-degree angles from his torso—each wrist tied to part of the car's frame. Another rope dangles from the front end, where his feet have been bound together and fastened to part of the engine. His hands are bluish from the lack of circulation, and his forehead appears burrowed in the asphalt. The dark shadow of the car and lack of sunlight distort his face. Only his bright-white jawbone is clearly visible. She turns away abruptly, wondering if she is ready for this. Then she notices a small, oddly shaped object by the rear tire. Putting her left knee on the ground for balance, she looks closer.

It takes her only a few moments to recognize it. She stands abruptly.

"Sam," Frank says tentatively, "what is it?"

"A tooth," she whispers.

A trail leads from the car to the parking lot entrance—not from leaky oil or transmission fluid, but from the body being dragged against the cement. She closes her eyes and breathes deeply, hoping the cold air will keep her from being nauseated.

She should have said no.

# 5
# Endymion's Circle

*O*fficer Kincaid wakes up shortly after Samantha looks under the car. She sees the relief in his face when Detective Snair tells him to escort her from the crime scene. Once inside the squad car, he sucks deeply from his inhaler, holding himself inflated so the medicine can work. *Hssst.* His bulging stomach almost touches the steering wheel, and he tries adjusting the seat.

"It sticks—" He laughs nervously, and his breathing becomes strained as if he were lifting a heavy object. The seat rocks forward, then back. If in the end it has moved at all, Samantha can't tell.

"Damn it!" He looks over sheepishly and starts the car.

She senses his desire to talk, to share in the fact that neither or them did very well back there. Sure, she didn't pass out, but after seeing the body, she couldn't stay. Frank knew immediately that she had seen enough. He asked Detective Snair to have someone take her to an appointment across town. Samantha didn't object.

From the squad car, she can see Frank standing by the Sunfire, staring at the seats, the rope, everything but the body underneath.

As they drive away, she realizes that Officer Kincaid is talking, but she hasn't heard a word. "I'm sorry. What were you saying?"

He looks hurt, but not enough to stay quiet. "It looks like some kind of ritual."

"Ritual?"

He shifts in his seat. "Yeah, being tied up like that." He reaches for his inhaler. "It seems like a lot of trouble to go to— just to kill someone."

*Hssst.*

Samantha nods. "It does."

The only sign for the sleep clinic is a small brass plaque by the door. Otherwise the building looks like the other apartment houses on the street. Through the now steady rain, Samantha waves one last time to Officer Kincaid, who seems reluctant to leave her here, and walks inside. An apathetic receptionist with dirty blond hair and thick, unflattering makeup directs her to the third floor. "Conference Room Two."

Samantha shakes some of the rainwater off her coat and enters the elevator.

The corridor leading to the room smells like toast. She isn't surprised by the unimaginative decor: uniform light fixtures, pearl-white walls with forest-green trim, and a smattering of framed floral prints. She has never seen a well-decorated doctor's office—as if bright colors and real art might distract patients from their illnesses. The door to the small conference room is open. Two people, sitting quietly in chairs, look up as she walks in. Five chairs form a circle in the middle, and oak bookshelves filled with journals and rows of identically bound texts line the back wall. Above the dark green couch to her left, a print hangs in the center of the wall: A woman slides a thick curtain across the sky, bringing sleep to those in its shadow. Four horses pull a chariot through the sun-soaked clouds, and a young man kneels before a goddess with an arrow in her right hand and a cherub on her shoulder.

"Hi," Samantha says, and the people sitting down muddle through introductions—each of them talking to fill the awkward silences until Dr. Clay arrives.

Phebe, a cellist and music teacher for the Bay Area Youth Symphony, looks hyper and disheveled thanks to her damp, curly hair. She touches her face nervously and straightens her full-length dress as she talks of rain, rehearsals, and the rising cost of artichoke hearts in the same breath. She seems to smile perpetually, even while talking, and Samantha starts feeling somewhat dizzy from listening.

When Phebe stops, the man next to her grumbles, "Artemus Beecher. Arty for short." He extends his long, thin arm, gripping hers firmly, but he doesn't look directly at her. Both Samantha and Phebe wait, expecting him to say more, but he sits in silence, staring at the floor. After a few moments, Samantha introduces herself and talks about her job as a lawyer but not her troubles with sleep. They all avoid this topic, and whether it's shame or fear that keeps them silent, she can't tell.

She remembers the first time she called Dr. Clay. She was already getting treatment at the Oakland Sleep Institute when she heard about his study. The institute's staff told her of his reputation as one of the best sleep disorder specialists in the country. An award-winning researcher and prolific writer, Dr. Clay had helped hundreds of patients in the last ten years, and he was about to start a small experimental trial. She had spoken with him only twice before her appointment today. Both times on the phone. She didn't ask many questions then. In truth, she's willing to try almost anything.

Samantha still doesn't think of herself as the kind of person who asks for help. She can't remember the last time she saw a doctor before her troubles with sleeping. She is even wary of taking Advil for headaches and cramps. So at first she tried to handle insomnia like a cold, but instead of drinking lots of orange juice and resting, she tried common remedies—exercising (in her case taking up fencing again) and cutting out caffeine from her diet. But nothing seemed to help.

For three months, she slept only a few hours a night and felt as if she was sleepwalking through work. She didn't tell friends or colleagues, because she didn't want sympathy and uninformed advice. She wanted sleep.

Gradually, nighttime changed for her. She started waking up in different places—on the bathroom floor, underneath the kitchen table, on the futon couch. She could distinctly remember going to bed, but after that, nothing. Then about ten weeks ago, she awoke violently from a nightmare—as if jolted by electricity—and found she was sitting in her car. The windshield was misty from her breath. She clung to the steering wheel like a drowning swimmer to a life raft and watched the blood flow out of her swollen knuckles. She had three long scratches on her right forearm. Somehow she had driven to church, parked in front of it, and turned off the engine. Her pajama top was spattered with the blood from her arm, and she could feel a stinging cold in her bare feet. She drove home, shaking more from fear than the temperature. It was 4:19 when she got back into bed, cowering under her comforter and shivering until dawn.

A few hours later, she called the Oakland Sleep Institute.

She never figured out how she hurt her arm, and for weeks, those wounds were the only thing convincing her that the entire incident wasn't a dream.

\* \* \*

With no introduction and no reassuring smile, Dr. Clay begins talking as soon as he enters the room. His brown socks don't quite match the color of his pants or tweed jacket, and his striped tie is as interesting as the hallway. He reminds Samantha of a college English professor, but instead of dog-eared novels, he carries files and a yellow notepad.

"You are all here because everything else has failed." His voice is neither loud nor soft, but the intensity of it gives him tremendous authority. He speaks with a kind of reverence for what he's saying, like a man who values the power of words and expects others to do the same.

"Each of you suffers from chronic forms of insomnia and parasomnia—a state in which people can act out their dreams. As you know, parasomnias are manifested in various ways, depending on what stage of sleep you're in. The most severe and potentially dangerous type is the night terror. In its early stages, this disorder disrupts sleep and leads to behaviors in both semisleep and sleeping states—mostly sleepwalking, grinding your teeth, that kind of thing. Over a longer period of time, as with all of you, the symptoms become more acute. You wake up screaming and frightened—unable to remember what you dreamed about, how you ended up outside one morning, how you got cut or bruised.

"In its most advanced stages, this disorder can cause seizures or lead to physical violence against yourself and others." He pauses to look at each of them. "This is why we're here—to get control of this before it gets control over you."

Samantha's isn't sure whether he has made her feel better or worse, but he has convinced her to trust him. Something about the dry conviction of his words wins her over. He looks down at his notepad and reads each of their names aloud.

"One other person is supposed to be here." He writes something about this, then looks back at the group. "For the next week, you'll be sleeping here—in individual rooms on the fifth floor. We'll start treatment tonight at nine. Bring whatever makes you most comfortable—a favorite blanket, pillow—"

Arty interrupts, his voice tight and frustrated. "What exactly *is* the treatment?"

"It's a form of electrohypnosis. You'll wear lightweight goggles that emit flashes of light and an earpiece that produces synchronized harmonic tones. This will induce a kind of trance state to relax your body and promote sleep."

"Hypnosis?" Sam asks.

He must hear the waning confidence in her voice, but he doesn't seem concerned. He answers with absolute conviction, as if she had asked him the answer for two plus two. "Yes."

*Perhaps it doesn't matter,* she thinks. He knows that they're exhausted from fighting a losing battle, that they'll try anything to keep hoping.

"When you get here tonight," he continues, "tell the receptionist that you're part of Endymion's Circle."

Feeling the need to say more but afraid to ask the question on all of their minds (*What if it doesn't work?*), Samantha opens her mouth. "Why did you choose that name?" Unsteady and faint, she sounds like a high school student who gets called on in class when she hasn't done her homework.

"Oh." He points to the painting. "That is Nicolas Poussin's *Selene and Endymion*. According to Greek mythology, Selene—the personification of the moon—fell madly in love with Endymion, a carefree, handsome young shepherd. And on her behalf, Zeus granted him one wish. With all the possibilities in the world—love, happiness, power, wealth—Endymion asked for the same thing you all want." Dr. Clay looks around the incomplete circle. "Sleep. Of course, for him it was a way to preserve his beauty and youth for all time. That's what he wanted more than anything else, and Zeus gave him the gift of eternal sleep." He looks at Samantha. "That's why I chose the name."

"So, does that make you Zeus?"

She can't tell if he resents the question or not, but for the first time he seems unsure of what to say.

"We'll see."

She looks back at the painting, then notices the empty chair once again. For some reason, the break in their circle makes her anxious, as if something is about to go horribly wrong.

# 6
# *Martyrdom*

Slightly winded from running up three flights of stairs, Frank pauses in front of Sam's door. He still has a copy of the key in his wallet and wonders, after all this time, if he should return it. He rings the bell, following with two quick knocks.

She opens the door. Her eyes widen with surprise.

"I wasn't sure if you'd be home," he says, standing with his hands in his pockets.

"I took the day off. I didn't know how long my appointment would be."

Frank enters tentatively, looking for all the changes she's made since his move to Washington. It's like his first visit home after college; everything appears the same yet different. Rooms feel smaller. New picture frames hang on the walls. The artifacts of the past—picture albums, forgotten trinkets—have been boxed up and placed in a closet. Even the smallest change is a reminder of the way life has moved on without him. There is no history of their love.

The way she stands now, arms dangling at her sides, heightens his sense of loss. That is how she stood in their last weeks together. Away from him, without desire or passion. Always occupying other rooms, making conversation about furniture, the weather, television, food. About anything but them.

It was her gradual indifference, her silent detachment without words, that left him gasping for air. They could still be together, he pleaded. He wasn't choosing his job over her. He loved her. But no explanation worked. Something in her changed, as if she had decided overnight that loving him came at too high a price. Their sex became desperate. Physical without tenderness, rough without play. She left their bed quickly in the half-awake hours of morning. By sunrise the sheets were colder than the empty room.

He never believed that it was about his job. Another man? Doubtful. They were still spending too much time together. About the man who assaulted her in the law library over two years ago? The man who threw her to the floor and cut her? He didn't think so. She survived. *They* survived—staying together long after that night. He remembers sitting beside her bed in the hospital, holding her hand and trying not to look at the bandages taped across her stomach. But despite their history together, it was all ending, not with a bang but with a whimper. They didn't yell or say hurtful things. No dishes were broken or chairs knocked over. Just Sam and her goddamn silence.

He felt more relief than sadness on the day he left. She drove him to the airport in quiet agitation, as if there were no more words left to speak. The gray sky hung low like damp sheets from a clothesline, and the tires pulsed at regular intervals across the uneven surface of the bridge. *Th-thump. Th-thump. Th-thump.*

Maybe she'd never loved him at all.

*Th-thump.*

The possibility terrified him more than her silence.

*Th-thump. Th-thump.*

"I love you." He blurted.

She smiled uneasily as they pulled up to the terminal.

Faster than God created the world, their love was over. And six months later, he was still wandering in the desert looking for answers.

"Sorry about this morning," he says now. "I had no idea what we were going to see out there."

"No, it was my fault. I shouldn't have gone."

"That's not true."

"Really, it's no big deal. I'm fine."

Frank sits on her futon couch as she pulls up a desk chair. In the awkward silence, he tries to decide if he should say anything else about the morning, but she doesn't give him a chance.

"I made a few calls to social services and victims' advocacy groups, like you asked. They've had no new hires or volunteers in the last three weeks. I want to try a few more places, and I'm still waiting to hear from a friend at the San Francisco AIDS Foundation. I probably won't know anything more till Monday."

"After the car this morning, I'm not too hopeful."

"Well, I'll keep trying. What did you find out?"

"Unfortunately, not much. The victim had no ID. No match on his fingerprints in any criminal or federal employee database." He pulls out a file from his satchel. "Let's see. The corporation sent a pathologist to help with the preliminary medical exam. It looks like the victim was killed by a knife wound to the neck. There were also rope burns at two different angles on his wrists and ankles, suggesting that he was tied up somewhere else before being moved to the car."

"Why do that?"

"To make it more difficult to identify the body. To torture him—assuming he wasn't dead. To test out new shocks." Frank laughs at his own sarcasm. "I don't know."

She likes the sound of that laugh in her apartment but tries not to enjoy it.

"Well," she adds, "did you find anything else?"

"Inside the car there were two sets of fingerprints—Catherine's and the victim's—keys in the ignition, an empty bag of pretzels, three cigarette butts in the ashtray, and a tape of classical music in the deck."

"What tape?"

"You always were a fan." He looks down at his notes. "It was a Glenn Gould recording of Bach's *Goldberg Variations.*"

"Was it playing when they found the car?"

"I don't know. There wasn't any mention of it."

"The car was twenty feet from the water." She leans forward with upturned palms. "Why not dump it and get rid of the evidence altogether? Someone wanted the body and that tape to be found. Why?"

"And who? As far as the police are concerned, Catherine has moved from victim to prime suspect."

"Maybe she's neither."

They sit quietly for a moment, watching the light in the room change with the dying sun.

Frank sits up and moves to the edge of the couch. "I've been thinking about something you said the other day. The person she had dinner with in Salt Lake. What if he's the one who was under the car?"

"It's possible. Do you think Catherine killed him?"

"Can't rule it out. I'm going to get in touch with the police in Utah about any recent missing persons. Maybe someone's looking for him." He stands and adjusts his jacket slightly. Samantha rises at the same time, then turns on the light. It feels too bright in the small room. She isn't sure what to say next, so she looks aimlessly at the papers on her desk.

"Sam, do you want to have dinner?"

"Um, I can't. Not tonight."

She doesn't want to tell him about the night terrors, the

clinic, Dr. Clay, or any of it. She's not ready for this return of inti-macy. She doesn't want be a martyr to the past, to a love she can't trust.

Frank picks up his bag. "All right. Well, thanks again for your help." He walks to the door. "I'll be in touch. Good night."

"Good night."

# *Parasomnia*

*For over two weeks, the Georgetown skies have been thick with brown-gray clouds. The absence of color makes Christina feel uneasy, as if she needs to check her watch to know whether the day is just beginning or ending. She enters the basement library of the music building and is relieved to be indoors, away from crowded classrooms and loud students.*

*Dozens of different-sized water pipes hang overhead, and the entire room feels cramped by the low ceiling. It is dimly lit, with cold, metallic gray shelves and narrow passageways. She hunts for several call numbers and finds more volumes than she can carry easily to a cubicle. The books smell of dust and stale cigarette smoke.*

*Since October she hasn't been able to sleep for more than an hour or two each night. That relentless circular melody keeps pushing its way into her thoughts, as if it's trying to make her remember something already forgotten. Every week the school psychologist, whose degree in human resources hangs on the wall behind her desk, tells Christina that she is suffering from post-traumatic stress disorder. The attack was violent and life-threatening. It's only natural to have trouble sleeping now, to feel anxiety and fear.*

*To feel anger.*

A few weeks ago, while standing in a music store, she heard the piece again and decided to buy a recording. She didn't want to listen at first and left it unopened on the kitchen table throughout the afternoon. But at 3:16 in the morning—her eyes tearful with frustration and burning from the steady glow of television—she opened the tape, grabbed her Walkman, and climbed into bed. The notes progressed slowly, almost sluggishly, as if she were walking barefoot in wet sand. The physical sounds appeased some longing or craving in her memory.

She felt calm. She fell asleep.

Then the sudden flash of a body writhing upside down in the dark. Torn, damaged hands reaching up, grasping for the rope tied tightly around his ankles. Blood spilling unevenly from a gash across the neck. There was only a frantic gasping sound. No voice.

Christina woke up startled and out of breath, hair matted against her forehead with sweat. She looked at the clock: 8:36. In disbelief, she reached for her wristwatch on the cluttered bedside table: 8:36. She had slept just over five hours. With tears of relief in her eyes, she got out of bed and dressed as quickly as possible. There wasn't time to celebrate. She was about to miss sociology class.

*She started repeating the same ritual every night, using the* Goldberg Variations *as a kind of lullaby. At first, she put on her Walkman tentatively, like a swimmer testing water with her toes. The visions terrified her, but she accepted them as part of the price she would have to pay for sleeping again. Even though the music's effects were only temporary, never lasting more than five or six hours, they were better than nothing.*

*But why? She had listened to music before, and nothing ever helped her sleep. Why the* Goldberg Variations?

*Christina peruses several Bach biographies in the tiny cubicle. After a few minutes, water rushes through the pipes overhead, and she remembers that the men's restroom is directly overhead.*

*"Nasty," she mutters.*

*She can't find much information on Goldberg, but one story in* The Life and Works of J. S. Bach *catches her attention:*

*On a late summer afternoon in Dresden, Germany, Johann Sebastian Bach was approached by a sickly man wearing black clothes, a red silk scarf, and a circular pendant around his neck. He introduced himself as Count Hermann Carl von Keyserlingk and invited the composer for supper.*

*Bach arrived under a crepuscular sky that made the dirt roads shimmer with red and gold. Keyserlingk Castle was at the bottom of a steep hill, and moss covered much of the shadowy exterior. Bach paused briefly at the entryway to concentrate on the faint sounds of a harpsichord. The melody was dissonant, unfamiliar. The interior had a mausoleum-like stillness, and Bach couldn't remember ever feeling so cold in the summer. A servant led him down a corridor with eight faded tapestries that looked like distant memories. Orange-brown fields. Colorless skies. Faded-red sunsets. Bach was surprised that he* could only hear the sound of his footsteps as they walked. All of the count's servants seemed to float, moving about the castle in long gowns that hid their noiseless feet. None of them spoke or smiled. They communicated with mechanical gestures and nods.

Bach was led to a sparsely furnished room where he was greeted warmly. The count had not changed clothes after his midday ride, and he smelled of hay and horse dung. He sat in a chair directly across from the composer.

The count explained that for years he had suffered from sleepless nights. His eyes burned, and his body had become thin from nerves. At most, he slept one or two hours a night, and when he did, he experienced the most horrible visions. His wife, who had developed a nervous condition from his pacing and mad talk of dreams, had recently left for the spas in Baden-Baden. His servants were miserable from being summoned at all hours. They knew no rest— particularly the harpsichordist, Johann Goldberg, who was often required to play throughout the night.

The count spoke of Bach's reputation and the remarkable power of his music. He had been following the composer's career for quite some time. Then the count pleaded—begged—Bach to write some keyboard music to help him sleep. He was convinced that such a genius could help him somehow. He would pay well.

Flattered and in need of money, Bach agreed to try.

The count did not want to waste any time. He showed Bach out without serving supper. "Please, hurry."

Soon after Bach began the piece, he received an earnest letter from his eldest son:

*7 NOVEMBER 1742*

*Dearest Father,*

*You have no doubt heard the rumors buzzing about Dresden? This count from whom you have taken a commission is a notorious drinker and gambler. He lurks about the streets like a madman, and people say that he practices alchemy—that his servants do not dare leave the castle for fear of his magic.*

*I know such matters do not concern you. "People will always talk, regardless of truth," you are fond of saying. But perhaps this is a work best left unfinished.*

*Do not be angry, Father, but I have written to Goldberg. I met him in Berlin years ago, and I know him to be an honest, good man. His recent letter makes me fearful for you. He too describes the count as an alchemist and tells me that for decades he has been searching for the secret to immortality!*

*Even if these are only the ravings of a madman, is it not better to have nothing to do with this count? Please, Father, do not partake in this.*

*Your son,*
*Wilhelm Friedemann*

Bach did not take these concerns too seriously. He finished the piece and gave it to the count as promised. There is no record of the count's response to it—whether or not it broke the spell and helped him sleep again.

No matter, Christina thinks. She knows one thing that these historians don't.

*It works.*

*Even though she can't read music, she takes a copy off the shelf and starts looking through it. The lines and circles on the score appear encoded, leaving her disoriented and frustrated. She feels their meaning but doesn't know how to interpret them. As she flips through the pages, the notes blend together, forming shapes, and she remembers a game that she and her sister played as children. With a stack of scrap paper, they created moving pictures by drawing individual frames and fanning through them like a deck of cards. Christina's favorite was the swing. She would draw a little girl on a swing, then the same picture at a different angle on another sheet, and so on. Eventually, she could fan through them and the girl moved, as if she were swinging up and down.*

*She starts seeing the music this way. Picking up the score, she holds the binding in one hand and quickly moves through the pages with her thumb. The notes become images. The images form a picture. They seem to communicate something. The light around her fades.*

FEBRUARY 17, 1983
4:32 A.M.

*Staring down at the dark waters of the muddy Potomac, she notices that her hands have turned white from gripping the icy green rail of Key Bridge. She rocks her body back and forth, trying to remember how she got here and what she is doing.*

*. . . There is a room without floors and a man in black who floats toward her. He wears a red scarf and a shiny circular pendant around his neck. His mouth moves without making sounds. . . .*

Several cars pass behind her, and a flash of headlights breaks the trance. She looks at her watch.

"I need to go home," she says aloud, looking again at the waters that call to her like a siren song. She turns and hails a cab.

"Where to?" The driver looks over his shoulder.

She thinks for a moment. "I don't know."

# 7
# Light Without Shadows

When Samantha steps off the elevator onto the fifth floor of the clinic, she collides with Phebe, who mutters an apology and something about the bathroom. Samantha watches Phebe scurry down the hall, stunned less by the physical jolt than by her outfit—two frog hairclips that seem to be drowning in her waterfall of hair, a huge smiling frog on her T-shirt, green sweatpants, and slippers in the shape of frogs that squeak with every step.

Samantha turns and walks past an empty nursing station. Except for the gray carpet and dim lighting, the corridor looks like a hospital floor. Sterile and nondescript—but at least it doesn't smell like antiseptic. She inhales again and recognizes the scent of grassy fields after a long rain.

Both Phebe and Arty have already chosen rooms, and Samantha feels like a latecomer at summer camp who doesn't show up early enough to pick a good bunk. She walks down the hall, looking for a room. On the walls outside of each door, there are two screens. The top one is familiar to her; it displays both an electroencephalogram and an electrocardiogram. She has seen her brain wave and heart rate activity measured like this at the institute. The bottom screen shows a video feed of the bed inside, allowing Dr. Clay and the attending nurse to watch patients' faces and bodies during sleep.

Samantha steps into a small, empty room and places her overnight bag on the only chair. Nothing hangs on the walls. The muted lighting shows the room to be monochromatic. The bedside table, mattress frame, and chair are the same off-white color. They match the walls. She changes into shorts and a loose T-shirt, then sits on the firm bed.

She doesn't have time to begin worrying about whether this treatment will work before she hears Phebe scurrying down the hall.

*Squeak, squeak, squeak, squeak. Squeak, squeak, squeak, squeak.*

Phebe peers into the room and says "Good night" cheerfully, without waiting for a response. Samantha smiles at the sound of the slippers as Phebe continues to her room.

The hall becomes quiet again, and Dr. Clay steps inside. He half smiles, nodding his head and looking more at the clipboard in his hands than at Samantha.

"Shall we start," he says without making it sound like a question.

The plastic goggles feel cold around her eyes, and wires run from her chest and forehead to the wall. Dr. Clay speaks softly from the chair next to her bed. "Try to relax. Once you put the earpieces on, I want you to breathe deeply and concentrate on the sequence of flashing lights and sounds. Are you ready?"

"I think so."

The lights and sounds begin steadily. A deep *boom* like a bass drum or heartbeat. Red light flashes with each sound. New colors gradually overlap with the sound, and the tones become richer, more full. Yellows and blues merge with momentary bursts of red. The colors spray like water from a garden hose against her eyes. The sounds syncopate, becoming gradually faster and higher pitched. She imagines driving over yellow lines on a two-lane highway.... Gradually the images and harmonies begin moving away, farther and farther into the distant blackness, while the heartbeat still echoes steadily. The colors suddenly bleach, and everything becomes white—light without shadows, the lonely absence of color....

Then a new sound. It's barely audible. The soft and steady footsteps of a familiar visitor who doesn't need to knock before entering. All other sounds are gone except a deep baritone. The light around her changes into a hazy gray, and she vaguely recognizes a man's voice.

Dr. Clay has removed Samantha's earpieces and is still sitting in the chair. As her eyes readjust, she thinks that something has gone wrong, that she has failed; her first attempt at hypnosis didn't work. She must not have been susceptible or willing. Now he has to tell her to leave. She'll have to deal with the problem on her own. She is no Endymion.

"Sorry," she says. "I guess I wasn't relaxed enough."

"Quite the contrary. You did very well. It's time to get up."

"What time—"

"Six A.M. You went to sleep shortly after ten last night. We want to get your body used to an eight-hour sleep cycle."

"I was asleep for *eight hours*?" Tears well up in Samantha's eyes. For the first time since Frank left, she feels relieved, happy. Happy with the hope of regaining control.

"Yes." His manner is much less formal this morning, and Samantha can tell that he is pleased. "See you tonight at nine." Dr. Clay walks to the door, then turns. "By the way, you snore." His smile makes him look tired and older than she first suspected.

"What about Phebe and Arty?"

"They're fine."

"And the other person?"

"Still a no-show." He pauses, then looks at his watch. "I have to go, Sam. So far, so good. See you tonight."

Before leaving, Samantha wants to see Phebe to compare experiences. She gets out of bed and hurries next door. The room is empty. She turns and finds Arty watching her from the doorway. His mouth opens slightly, and for the first time she notices that one of his front teeth is chipped. He wears dark blue jeans and a wrinkled T-shirt. The overnight bag in his right hand dangles close to the floor.

"Have you seen Phebe this morning?" Her voice is slightly hoarse at first.

"She left already." He looks at her legs when he speaks. "She seemed upset. I don't think she slept last night."

"Do you think she's all right?"

He shrugs.

Samantha suddenly feels light-headed and unsteady. She touches her face to see if she is still wearing the goggles. Then a series of images—uneven hardwood floors, open boxes of Chinese takeout, a well-worn black book. Another flash, more visceral than the first. A black mirror hanging above a sink stained yellow-brown. A blade dripping red into a dirty porcelain basin. Her stomach turns, and she falls to the floor.

Dr. Clay is standing above her when she opens her eyes. Arty watches over the doctor's shoulder, and the room seems to vibrate like a fluorescent light.

Dr. Clay checks her pulse. "What happened?"

"I saw things. A house, I think. I don't know." She covers her eyes with her right hand. The left rests on her stomach. "It was cold. No, the bathroom tiles were cold, and there was a mirror with no reflection." She sits up suddenly. "What the hell is happening to me?"

"Relax. There's nothing to worry about. Spontaneous hallucinations are a common side effect of hypnosis, especially in conjunction with sleep deprivation."

"Nothing to worry about! If they're so damn common, why didn't you tell me?"

Dr. Clay flinches, then speaks with a soft sternness. "Sleep-wake cycles are like fingerprints—they're different for everyone. So just as it's impossible to predict how someone will respond to prolonged deprivation, it's also difficult to know how she will be affected by certain treatments, particularly hypnosis. Like dreams, hallucinations are a way of processing anxieties and fears. You haven't been sleeping well for months, Samantha, and this can cause chemical changes in your brain and body. In some cases, prolonged deprivation releases a chemical into the bloodstream similar to LSD, leading to altered states. That seems to be what's happening to you."

He touches her right hand, which now rests on her thigh, and says, "Trust me. Your brain is just trying to make sense of this new neural activity."

"But I didn't just see things. I *felt* them."

"As I said, extraordinary hypnotic experiences can create an altered state—some scientists even associate it with psychic phenomena such as ESP and clairvoyance. But the truth is that these hallucinations are a result of modified perception. They make you believe that what you're seeing is real. You think you felt something, but you didn't. It wasn't real."

"Oh, no problem then. I can just get a part-time job with the Psychic Network," she says with anxious sarcasm.

"I'll prove there's nothing supernatural about it. What am I thinking right now?"

"That I'm being a pain in the ass?" She tries to play along.

"Hey, maybe you're psychic after all."

He laughs halfheartedly, and Samantha smiles. She feels somewhat relieved, but not entirely convinced.

"Is this going to keep happening to me? What about when I'm driving to work or walking down the street?"

"Not likely. This state was induced by hypnosis, so you should experience hallucinations only going into or coming out of a trance state. After a few more sessions, I expect that your mind will adapt. The hallucinations will stop."

She nods quietly, almost imperceptibly. "I guess salvation doesn't come without a price," she mutters.

"What?"

"Nothing."

# 8
# *Visionary*

*T*he windshield wipers pulse as she waits at a red light two blocks from the clinic. All day she has been wary of things that could accidentally hypnotize her—the dripping kitchen faucet, ticking clocks, the humming air filter in her fish tank. She knows this fear is ridiculous, but she feels profoundly exhausted, as if her body recognizes for the first time how deprived it has been. It wants to make up for lost time, not celebrate small victories.

Once again, she thinks of Frank. Every time the phone rang this afternoon, she grabbed it hastily, hoping it would be him. She wanted to hear his voice, to think about him and the investigation instead of herself. But he never called, and everyone else—telemarketers, a friend from work, a wrong number—had to listen to the disappointment in her voice.

In junior high, she remembers now, she spent many afternoons like this waiting by the phone for Larry Boyle. Larry wasn't athletic, popular, or particularly smart, and he was picked on mercilessly for his Coke-bottle glasses and two enormously gapped front teeth.

She had a crush on Larry because of something he said to her by the tetherball courts at school.

"I hate my glasses."

"You can always get a new pair."

"No, I mean...Well, I just wish I could see you without them, that's all."

He smiled with those enormous teeth, and at that moment, she thought he was the next Simon Le Bon. They decided to go out on a date.

Waiting for the date was maddening and exciting. She couldn't believe that someone who wasn't in the room had the power to make her nervous, excited, and frustrated at the same time. Two days later, his mom drove them to the mall, and they played video games while eating greasy cheese pizza off thin white paper plates. Their romance only lasted a few months, but to thirteen-year-old Samantha, it was magical.

She felt some of that nervousness today, waiting for Frank to call, but these feelings only made her angry. He'd left for a career. He'd left because it was safer to fly across the country and start a new life than to wait for her love. His voice had sounded dry when he told her it was over, five months ago. He was already living in Washington, and the telephone connection punctuated his voice with static. She listened to him talk and didn't make a sound, because she knew how much he hated silence. He rambled through apologies and excuses that were really neither. *I'm sorry. We just don't know how long we'll be apart. What else can we do? I mean, you want to stay there for your job, to be near your father....*

The truth was that he didn't trust someone who was afraid to say "I love you." Maybe he was right not to trust her, she thinks. Maybe she couldn't say those words because something was missing in her. She wasn't sure then and still isn't. All she told him that afternoon was "At least I'll never lie to you." She meant it, and believed herself to be honorable for it. But silence can be more hurtful than a lie.

Frank sent her a letter a few days later with only five lines.

*Of all that you have done, and been; [...]*
*Of things ill done and done to others' harm*
*Which once you took for exercise of virtue.*

He'd always liked T. S. Eliot. He didn't want to use his own words to hurt her, so he borrowed them from someone else. After that, he didn't speak to her for six months.

Until two days ago, in front of the church.

Sitting at the edge of her bed in the clinic, she looks up at Dr. Clay. "Did Phebe have any hallucinations?"

"You know I can't discuss my other patients with you." Dr. Clay looks tired and worried.

For the first time she wonders if he has trouble sleeping. "I just didn't get to see her this morning. Is everything all right? Arty said she was upset."

"Did he?" Dr. Clay asks, surprised and somewhat irritated. Then he admits, "She didn't sleep well last night, but I'm sure she's fine, Sam. We should get started—"

"Do you think she'll show up?"

"Not tonight."

"Why?"

He pauses. "A lot of people are afraid to get clinical treatment."

"Why?"

"Because they're worried that it's their last chance. That if they don't get better this time, they never will."

He looks distracted as he flips through Samantha's chart. She lies down and waits quietly for him to place the electrodes on her temples. He hands her the goggles, and she notices a tremor in his left hand.

"Do *you* think this is our last chance?"

He pauses before answering. "No, I don't." He smiles weakly and adds, "Not by a long shot. Besides, it's working for you."

"I guess so." The hope she felt this morning fades with the thought of Phebe at home, sitting alone and staring into the darkness. For a moment, Samantha feels grateful—grateful that it is Phebe, not she, who has to face the helpless terror and frustration of knowing that she won't sleep through the night. But this relief makes her ashamed. Suffering does that to people, she thinks. It makes them selfish and shameful. It transforms them into something ugly.

She puts the goggles over her eyes and waits for the lights and sounds to begin.

A red light glows on the other side of a closed door. Shelves filled with books and loose papers are barely visible in the weak glow of candlelight. Wax has been spilled, drying in long streaks on the wooden floor. Curtains flap by the open window. The ledge is moist from rainwater.

A moan hangs in the air like a note from an oboe. It sputters and coughs, fading to silence. The door opens, and everything is bathed in red light. The moaning starts again. It comes from a shadowy figure pressed against the window. It jerks and twitches with such violence that it seems moments away from crashing into the room. Then a piercing scream as the door slams shut. Glass shatters. The rainwater becomes blood. The body writhes in terrible pain, climbing, towering into the sky—

Dr. Clay is holding her shoulders, and Samantha realizes that she is sitting upright. A male nurse stands on the other side of the bed with one hand resting gently on her back.

"Samantha? Hi, Samantha. You've woken up with quite a start, but everything is all right. You've been asleep for seven hours and forty-two minutes."

Samantha is breathing too heavily to speak, too shaken to congratulate herself for sleeping.

"It was awful."

"What was awful? Did you have another hallucination?"

"Yes." Her voice sounds hollow.

"Look at me, Samantha. What you saw was not real. It's—"

"No. Something terrible has happened." She looks into his eyes. "I know it."

# 9
# *Memento Mori*

*S*amantha steps out of the shower in her apartment to a ringing phone. Still preoccupied with the images that woke her less than an hour ago, she answers distractedly. Large drops of water fall from her body onto the bedroom carpet. She imagines the puddle at her feet turning hard, like wax.

"Hi, Sam."

She can barely hear Frank because of the sharp, urgent voices behind him. "What happened?"

"I got a call ten minutes ago. The police found another body—a woman hanging from a fire escape outside her apartment."

Silence. She twirls the phone cord between the second and third fingers of her right hand, certain that she already knows what he is going to say.

"Hello?" Frank asks. "Sam?"

She swallows hard before asking, "What's her name?"

"Phebe McCracken."

Samantha closes her eyes and sees the smiling frog from

Phebe's T-shirt. "Where are you?" The words leave her mouth reluctantly.

"At her apartment in Chinatown. What's wrong?"

She pauses again, looking at the water spreading out from her body.

"I know her."

Samantha hurries up four flights of stairs. The narrow hallway seems to turn sharply every few feet, obscuring the layout of the floor, and she follows it tentatively. Looking for the apartment number, Samantha wonders if Phebe found solace in the confusion of this labyrinth, if she saw it as a reflection of her own exhausting and elusive path to sleep. The air feels warm and still, as if it is trapped between the low ceilings and worn carpet. She tugs at her sweatshirt, pulling it away from the moisture on her stomach.

She doesn't want to think about Phebe as a victim to sleeplessness or a violent man. She doesn't want to see herself that way either. A sudden flash of anger makes her face burn. She wants answers. For Phebe. For herself.

The hall cuts around another corner and stops abruptly. There is one closed door to her right, and there everything glows inexplicably red. The walls, the carpet, even Officer Kincaid's face appears sunburn-pink. He hasn't noticed her yet. His head is slightly bowed toward the door as if waiting for someone to answer. He stands before a welcome mat that shows a cheerful frog saying "Hop on in!" Two wrapped newspapers are stacked in the corner.

"Hi."

He turns, startled. His smile seems strained, almost embarrassed, and Samantha realizes that he has been eavesdropping. He starts to explain that Detective Snair won't let him inside, but she interrupts.

"Why is that bulb red?" She looks toward the light fixture across from the door. A naked bulb juts out like the tongue of a bell.

"I don't know."

"Can you ask the landlord?"

"Well, I'm really not supposed to leave. I'm kind of on guard."

"I see." She stares until she obviously makes him uncomfortable.

"Well, I guess I could run downstairs real quick."

"Thanks."

He relaxes at the sight of her smile and goes.

She knocks, and the door opens quickly. Frank nods as she enters. The light in the room is filtered through a white plastic tent that has been set up around the window to protect forensic evidence, or so Samantha assumes. Neatly arranged music scores fill most of the bookshelves, but one is lined with porcelain frogs of all sizes and colors. Everything else in the apartment seems to lack order and organization. A single frog has been knocked to the floor, leaving several broken pieces and a smattering of white powder. Dozens of novels, magazines, and notebooks are stacked in haphazard piles on the floor. A framed poster leans against the left-hand wall, waiting to be hung, and well-used cat toys litter the floor. On a rolltop desk adjacent to the window, stacks of CDs and several candles surround a small stereo. One fat red candle has hollowed itself out around the wick and bled over much of the desktop. Another has fallen to the wood floor, spilling long lines of wax away from the desk like rays of sunlight. In the opposite corner, a cello case lies next to a chair and music stand.

A marble-faced man in a wrinkled linen jacket is taking pictures. A bright flash fills the room, then fades. Two uniformed officers look through desk drawers and a file cabinet.

Samantha turns toward the tent and feels Frank's hand on her right forearm. He looks drawn and somewhat sad.

"I don't know if you want to see this."

She looks at him briefly without speaking, then moves to the tent flap and steps inside. It's the windowsill from her vision. Dried blood spilling like a waterfall over the ledge and down the wall, forming a coagulated puddle on the floor. Most of the broken glass is scattered on the landing of the fire escape, where Phebe's body is suspended upside down, taut, from rope. Her feet have been tied to the landing above, and her arms are fastened to the railing on either side of her. Her blouse has slid down to her neck, exposing her white skin, black bra, and the circle carved into her chest and upper stomach.

Samantha covers her stomach with one hand and looks down at the grate beneath her feet. The circle takes her back to that night in the library over two years ago. Right before it happened, there was his smell—so out of place among the books and recycled air—and the muscles of his hairless arm wrapping around her neck. He pressed her against the cold floor and carved a half-circle into her body with a knife. She inhales rapidly, as if she can't get enough air, and wonders: *Did the same man—? Was this meant for me? How?* She tries to control her breathing and lets her hand fall to her side.

Samantha looks at Phebe again. Her face, stained with dried blood from the wound and the gash across her neck, looks agonized, tortured. The other cuts and scrapes on her body suggest a struggle. Her black slacks are ripped at the knee, and her right foot has torn through its stocking. She may have been pushed through the window—or at least thrown on top of the broken glass and splintered wood—before being hung.

Samantha turns around, not wanting to remember Phebe this way.

Someone else is on the landing now. Detective Snair. His body rigid. He has been watching her.

"Who found her?" she asks assertively, as if the right words will convince him, convince herself, that she belongs here.

"A woman who lives four floors below. At around six-thirty this morning, she stepped outside to feed her cats and noticed that the water bowl and food dish were bloody. Then she felt something drip down her cheek and looked up. It wasn't a raindrop."

"No one else saw anything? On an open-air fire escape in San Francisco?"

"I've already gone over this with Mr. Bennett."

"I was just about to fill her in, Detective." Frank, who has been standing behind her, steps forward.

She looks directly at Snair, her hands resting on her hips. "Humor me."

"All right." He moves closer to Samantha and speaks with strained reserve. His breath smells of stale coffee and a freshly smoked cigarette. "We're facing an alley behind several stores—none of which are usually open between one and four in the morning. This apartment is being earthquake-proofed, so the first three floors on this side are covered with scaffolding, tarp—all sorts of crap that makes it pretty hard to see. It rained all night, which means we don't have much in the way of forensic evidence. And—this is my favorite part—the neighbors directly below are away for the weekend. So our killer is either really smart or really fuckin' lucky."

"Sam, can I talk to you?" Frank interrupts before she can respond. He leads her back into the apartment. "What are you doing?"

"Trying to find out what happened." She looks over his shoulder and sees Snair's shadow against the tent.

"You said on the phone that you knew her."

"We met two days ago at a sleep clinic."

"A sleep clinic?"

"Frank, I saw this place in my dreams."

"What?"

One of the officers dusting for prints looks over, and she lowers her voice. "The windowsill, the wax on the floor, a red light, her body hanging outside ... all of it."

"I don't understand. Are you telling me that you *knew* this was going to happen?"

"Not exactly. I—" Thinking about how to explain it to Frank, to herself, she glances across the room and notices a red light glowing on the stereo.

"Was that on when the police arrived this morning?"

"What?"

Samantha walks over to the rolltop desk, ignoring the frustration on Frank's face.

"Does anyone know if this was playing this morning?" Neither officer in the room answers. "Who was the first person on the scene?"

Silence.

"Who was the first—"

"I was." A young woman in uniform walks out of the bedroom.

"Was any music playing?"

"Uh, yeah." At first she sounds surprised, then guilty. "I assumed the victim was listening to it last night. All I did was press the stop button."

Samantha takes a tissue out of her pocket and presses EJECT. The disc slides out.

"Someone needs to dust this for fingerprints."

"Sam, what's going on?" Frank steps over to the desk and looks down at the CD—the *Goldberg Variations*.

"It's the same piece of music you found in the tape deck of Catherine's car."

"*Pssst.* Ms. Ranvali?" Everyone turns to see Officer Kincaid sticking his head through the front door. He steps inside warily, scanning the room for Detective Snair.

"I talked to the landlord about the light fixture. The bulb burned out last week, and he only had a red one to replace it. It's temporary until he can get to the hardware store. He's had a lot of trouble getting around because of a bad back. Most likely, it's just the mattress on his bed, but mattresses are expensive, so he keeps putting off—"

"Why did he have a red bulb in the first place?"

"I asked that too. It's from his darkroom."

"Thanks." Samantha nods.

"Kincaid, what the hell are you doing in here!" Snair roars as he comes through the tent.

Officer Kincaid's face blanches.

"We might have a print here." Samantha steps into Snair's path.

He looks into her eyes, and she can't tell if he is surprised, furious, or amused. Maybe all three. He turns to the desk. "On a CD?"

"Yes. It's the same recording Frank found at the first crime scene."

"Detective Snair"—an officer steps through the tent—"I think you should see something."

"Jacobs, dust this for prints," Snair barks. Without looking at Samantha, he turns and follows the other officer through the tent and back onto the fire escape.

Frank steps toward the window, and Samantha touches his arm. "I'm going to leave, okay."

He pauses, then nods quietly. "Sure."

She can tell that he is looking for some sign of weakness in her. She realizes that she is covering her stomach with her hands again and drops them to her side, pressing her lips tightly together to keep them from shaking. "Go on," she says. "Let me know what you find out." She starts quickly for the front door.

"One more thing."

"Yeah?"

"What do you know about Phebe?"

"She was getting treatment for insomnia at the San Francisco Sleep Clinic. That's where I met her. She and I are—were—part of a new study with Dr. Clay. He calls it Endymion's Circle." She shifts her weight from one foot to the other.

"Endymion?"

"He was a figure from Greek mythology."

"Like the guy who slept with his mother and poked out his eyes?"

"No, that's Oedipus. You obviously weren't a classics major." She smiles faintly.

"Who in their right mind would be a classics major?" Frank's voice shifts in tone, becoming softer, more sincere. "Sam, when did you start having trouble sleeping?"

"A little over six months ago." Her head falls to the right.

"After I moved?"

"Before," she says quickly and looks up. "Anyway, the first treatment didn't work for Phebe, so she left."

"What kind of treatment was it?"

"Electrohypnosis."

"Why didn't you tell me?"

"I didn't think it was a big deal."

"You didn't think it was a big deal?" he responds incredulously, placing his hand on her right shoulder.

"Frank, it doesn't concern you. Just call me later and let me know what you find out, all right?"

"Okay." He lets go and walks to the tent.

* * *

Samantha rushes out of the building and drives away. At first, she doesn't know where she is going, but soon she is sitting in the back pew of the church. She doesn't want to see Phebe again, not as a piece of evidence. Phebe. Phebe. Phebe McCracken. Samantha says her name again and looks at the porcelain frog in her palm. She feels guilty about taking it from the apartment, but she needed something to think about other than that bloodred circle. Phebe loved frogs and the cello. Like Samantha, she wanted desperately to sleep again.

There are fewer people than usual at the nine o'clock service, and Samantha finds this comforting. As the choir starts singing William Byrd's *Ave Verum Corpus,* she notices an elderly Hispanic woman sitting at the end of her row, holding a rosary in her lace-gloved hands and rocking slightly back and forth.

One Sunday morning with her mother, Samantha remembers, a gray-haired woman walked on her knees from the back of the church to the altar. As she got closer to the front, the organist stopped playing, men and women looked up from their prayers, and the church became still. The priest watched in disbelief, subtly motioning her to stand, but she didn't. Not until she reached his feet did she stand up and take a seat in the front row.

Watching the Hispanic woman and thinking about the one who walked the length of the church on her knees, Samantha envies the power of their faith. She longs to feel the kind of comfort that must come with such devotion. She wraps her fingers gently around the frog, closes her eyes, and listens to the voices of the choir as if they're speaking her own silent prayer.

> *Truly you have suffered on the cross for mankind . . .*
> *May we have tasted of you at the hour of our death . . .*
> *O gentle, loving Jesus, Son of Mary, have mercy upon me . . .*
> *O gentle, loving Jesus, Son of Mary, have mercy upon me. . . .*

# Parasomnia

*A woman wrapped in a black leather jacket and scarf sits in a pew at the back of Saint Peter's Church. Her face appears to shift in the flickering candlelight, and her tired eyes seem to weep without tears. She stares down at the cover of the weekly bulletin. It's a black-and-white print of Caravaggio's* The Crucifixion of Saint Peter. *Peter's face cries out with fear and anguish as three shadowy men lift and push his cross. Humiliated and wretched, he waits for death.*

*Putting down the picture, she walks slowly to the confessional. A choir is rehearsing Pergolesi's* Stabat Mater. *Violins accompany the somber voices of two women as they sing about a weeping mother who stands beside the cross of her son. "Stabat Mater dolorosa iuxta crucem lacrimosa..." She understands the words without knowing what they mean.*

"Bless me, Father, for I am a sinner."

"We're all sinners."

"Not like me."

Father Murphy pauses. The music sounds muffled in the confessional. "What do you want to confess?"

"I think I've killed two people."

"Excuse me?"

"I'm not sure. I don't remember much, but I have visions of things I've done."

"I don't understand."

"I can see what I'm about to do and can't stop it, Father."

"You're wrong." He leans back, startled. "It can stop right here. If you've hurt someone, we'll get help. We'll go to the police. Together. You can ask God's forgiveness—"

"I need sleep more than forgiveness."

Father Murphy hears the curtains pulled apart on the other side of the grille, and he opens the confessional door. Quick footsteps. A figure in black darts into the vestibule. He hurries after her.

The small room is dark and smells of the pine trees outside. To his left, a circular stairway leads up to the balcony, and the shadow of a swaying tree appears through a stained-glass window halfway up the wall. A stack of bulletins has been spilled across the floor, leaving dozens of Saint Peters staring up at him.

Maybe it was some sort of prank, he thinks, looking around the empty room.

Suddenly, the music starts again: "Quando corpus morietur." Father Murphy translates the words as he stoops to pick up the bulletins. "When my body dies..."

There is a sound behind him. He turns quickly. Nothing. "... let my soul be granted the glory of Paradise."

Then a burning in his neck.

She flings herself at him, driving two knives into opposite sides of his neck. Father Murphy falls forward from the force of the attack—one hand clutching a wound, the other pressing against the floor. Before he can look away from the dark green marble beneath him, a blade pierces the back of his right hand. The pain is blinding. He turns his head to the figure crouching beside him, then hears a gust of air as her arm moves quickly, like a door closing.

She arcs her left arm toward the ceiling in one fluid motion, slicing the knife deeply across his throat. She removes the other knife from his impaled hand and rolls him over. She carves a circle into his upper chest.

Quando corpus morietur,
fac ut animae donetur
Paradisi gloria.

Father Murphy watches the moonlight pass faintly through the stained glass above his head. He doesn't feel the rope knotted around his ankles, nor is he fully aware that his body is being hoisted from the railing of the staircase until he hangs upside down. His hand bleeds onto the green marble and white bulletins, staining Peter's suffering red.

Amen. Amen.
Amen. Amen.

She must hurry now. Outside, the cool wind stings her cheeks as she runs to her car several blocks away. Her legs feel heavy. Sitting behind the steering wheel, she looks frantically for her keys, but it's too late. Darkness. She collapses into the passenger seat.

## NOVEMBER 16, 1986
### 10:43 A.M.

*Her mother is a notorious worrier. Since moving home six weeks ago, Christina has gone out several times and not returned until morning. She never remembers where she has been, and her mother never believes her. When Christina was in high school, her mother once called the police and said three rosaries when her only daughter missed curfew by an hour and thirteen minutes. So it is no surprise that she is waiting at the kitchen table, rosary in hand, when Christina walks through the door.*

*"Where have you been?" She doesn't wait for an answer. "I was so worried. How can you do this to me? You know I sit up all night, worrying, talking to Mrs. Lehntman on the phone—you remember Mrs. Lehntman—her daughter just got married—and wondering, Should I call the police? Should I look for her? Or should I just find a new daughter!"*

*"Mama—"*

*"You think you're not a child anymore. That you can take care of yourself. But you can't. You leave Washington to follow your father and me here, but you won't talk to either of us. You don't talk to any of your friends. You're tired all the time, Christina. I need to know what's wrong."*

*"I'm sorry, Mama. This is just something I need to figure out myself."*

*"Is it a man?"*

*"No."*

*"A young lady doesn't behave this way."*

*"It's not a man."*

*"I keep asking myself, What am I supposed to do, and just yesterday I thought of Father Murphy. I'll have her talk to Father Murphy. And then that terrible news—"*

"What news?" Looking at her mother's face, Christina realizes that something else is wrong. "What news, Mama?"

"It's been on the TV all morning." Her mother becomes visibly upset as she gets up and turns on the small black-and-white television in the kitchen. A reporter holding a notepad is speaking in front of a church.

"Father Patrick Murphy was found murdered in the vestibule of Saint Peter's Church in Durham, North Carolina, yesterday evening. Police believe that it happened sometime between seven and eight P.M., while Father Murphy was hearing confession. At this time, officials are not releasing any details about the crime, but sources say that the victim's throat was cut and his body bound with rope...."

"He was hung upside down." Christina speaks in a monotone voice, without being conscious of the words.

"What?"

"I need a shower."

"You still haven't told me where you were last night."

"I don't know."

"Christi—"

"I don't know," Christina snaps. "I just don't." She pauses and exhales slowly. "I'm going to take a shower now."

She goes to her room and opens her journal. She writes about the news report and waking up this morning in her car several blocks from the church. She glances through the earlier pages, comparing this record to other accounts she has pieced together recently. For several months, her amnesia and blackouts have coincided with reports of killings. Her nightmares have become more vivid.

She takes out a folded paper from her pocket. It's this week's bulletin from Saint Peter's Church, crumpled and discolored with brown stains. Christina quickly refolds it and places it in the journal.

*For the rest of the day, the image of Saint Peter stays with her. She sees him in the shower, on television, even in the dark when she listens to Bach—which has been less effective every year.*

*But what keeps her awake now is fear—fear of herself and a future she can't control. The* Goldberg Variations *hum softly in her ears. At most, she will sleep for two or three hours. She listens anyway, waiting and praying, as always, that at any moment she will somehow fall asleep.*

## 10

# Boxes to Fill

On the top shelf in her bedroom closet, Samantha keeps a shoe box filled with memories—love letters, Mother's reading glasses, euros from a backpacking trip to Europe, postcards, her first ribbon from a fencing tournament, several photographs. The box feels heavier now than she remembered, but maybe the past is always that way. She places it on the desk and removes the dusty lid, trying to decide whether to put Phebe's frog inside.

A second edition of F. Scott Fitzgerald's *The Great Gatsby* sits on top. It was the last gift Frank gave her before moving to Washington. Months before, she'd jokingly called him Gatsby after a fight in which he asked how many lovers she'd had before him, and she wouldn't answer. *Does it really matter? You only need to be with one person to know how to make someone else happy.*

Frank wanted to know about her past so he could stop feeling that her kisses were borrowed, learned from someone else for a love he and she didn't share. At least that's what he told her. But Samantha didn't think he really cared about numbers, names, and reasons that no longer mattered. Like Gatsby, he wanted to erase the past, to believe that true love happened only once—and with one person.

She picks up the novel and notices a faded piece of notebook paper sticking lightly to the back cover. She pulls it off and recognizes the handwriting immediately: *You look beautiful today. I love you.—Alex*

Yes, some things she couldn't tell Frank. Everyone has something—a secret place or name—that can open the pain of the past.

For her, it is Alexander.

Samantha was a sophomore in college when she met Alexander. He dazzled her with sophistication and intelligence—a graduate student of history, a connoisseur of wine, an insatiable traveler. Everything about him seemed magical to her. The unexpected touch of his fingertips on the back of her neck. The way he misplaced his glasses two or three times a day. The smell of sweat through his shirts.

Samantha wanted so much to have the love she'd seen in movies that she made excuses for his cruelty. At least, she accepted his excuses for hurting her. He didn't want to be in love, she realized later. He wanted the power of knowing someone loved him. She remembers the first of many nights that she drove to his apartment, a two-room unit attached to the back of a house, and saw the car belonging to his ex-girlfriend parked on the street. All the lights were off. They were inside.

She didn't pound on the door or yell like an infuriated lover. She just left. If she wasn't sure about his infidelities, she could go on believing in their love.

Samantha broke up with him every time it happened, but he was always indignant—claiming innocence, blaming her for jumping to the wrong conclusions, for being unreasonable. In truth, he wanted to see how far he could push her.

Eventually, he ended it, saying he'd never loved her.

That was something Samantha couldn't forgive, even though he had asked her back the next day. He moved away to take a job somewhere on the East Coast, and mostly she doesn't care where. She doesn't want to be with him again. They had only been together for a year. She just wants the ideal that he made her believe in.

When she met Frank, she realized that love could happen more than once. You're just not the same person when it finds you again. With Frank, she had silences and walls to hide behind.

She had Alexander.

Samantha decides to leave Phebe's frog on her desk. She replaces the book, balls up the note from Alexander, and closes the box. After seeing the apartment today, she is convinced that the only way to find Catherine and figure out what happened to Phebe is by opening up the past.

She drops Alexander's note into the wastebasket beside the desk and picks up the phone.

Frank paces absentmindedly as he tells her about two possible matches for the first victim. Only two recent missing-person reports from the Salt Lake area fit the height, sex, and estimated age of the man found under Catherine's car. J. P. Nelms was a used-car salesman with no family and a long list of creditors interested in finding him. Three weeks ago, he didn't show up for work. Nelms had a reputation for being a heavy drinker, so his boss waited a few days before calling the police. The second man, Gabriel Morgan, had been a Catholic priest for three years. Just over a month ago he had participated in a gay rights demonstration in downtown Salt Lake City. The church had subsequently ordered him to take a leave of absence.

"I'll know for sure tomorrow," Frank concludes. "The dental records will be here first thing in the morning."

"That may explain the dinner. If Catherine found out that Morgan was a priest, she may have confided in him, paid for dinner at the end of the evening, even offered to drive him to San Francisco."

"If that's true, it builds a case against her as the murderer, not the victim. Why drive halfway across the country, buy dinner for someone you've never met, give him a ride to San Francisco, then kill him? It doesn't make sense."

"Maybe the killer stalked both of them at the restaurant? Or came across them here in the city? We still haven't figured out why she drove to San Francisco."

Samantha wants Frank to sit, to stop moving. She remembers how he always seemed in motion to her, as if stillness would suffocate him. He's like a shark that can never know sleep. "There's something else."

"What?"

"Do you think the first victim was hanged upside down before being tied to the car?" Her voice sounds tentative.

Frank stops and looks at her. "Possibly. That could explain the two sets of rope burns on his ankles and wrists."

"Check this out." She spins around to the laptop on her desk and opens a color image of Caravaggio's *The Crucifixion of Saint Peter*. "I went to church this morning, Saint Peter's. That's where I made the connection."

"What connection?"

"After he was condemned to death, Peter asked to be crucified upside down. He didn't feel worthy of dying like Christ." She pauses, her face lit by the computer screen. "Typically, the condemned were tied to a cross, not nailed like Christ and Peter. And Peter even asked not to be nailed." She wonders about Frank's expression as he lifts one eyebrow slightly. He looks at her as if she's speaking in tongues. "The first victim was hung by his feet, then tied underneath the car—arms stretched out, feet bound together, and body upside down relative to the car. An inverted crucifixion. Like Peter. Like Phebe."

Frank considers the possibility. "But why?"

"Apparently Peter embraced his martyrdom. Crowds of people wanted to free him, but he begged them not to. He wanted to be martyred."

"Why would anyone—"

"Eternal life. To be assured a place in heaven for all time."

Frank lowers his eyes and begins pacing again. "But if these crimes are supposed to reenact the crucifixion of Saint Peter, why didn't the killer make the ritual more clear with the first victim? And why leave a recording of the *Goldberg Variations*?"

"I don't know. But you're right. We need to find out more about that piece." Samantha picks up a pencil on her desk and twirls it between her fingers. "That's why I called Don today—to ask if he could look into a few things for me."

"Don? Donald Tarnas?"

"Yeah."

"Don, the history professor, the guy we used to drink with in law school? What does he have to do with any of this?"

She smiles tentatively, switching the pencil from one hand to the other. "He now teaches at the University of North Carolina in Chapel Hill."

"So?"

"According to the file you showed me, both Catherine and her roommates went to Chapel Hill." She pauses nervously. "Maybe he could talk to them—"

"For Christ's sake, Sam, you shouldn't be telling anyone about this."

"Don isn't just anyone. He's our friend and an expert. Catherine's disappearance, Phebe's death, the man under the car are all linked to the *Goldberg Variations*. If we're going to solve this case, we need to know more about that piece."

Frank looks at the floor, shaking his head.

"Don is the best person to ask," she continues.

"Fine. Let him do some library research and see what he comes up with. But he doesn't have any legal jurisdiction to interview—"

"And I do? The only reason I have access to any of this is because I'm pretending to work for the Palici Corporation. He can do the same thing. Say he's a consultant for the group."

"Sure, why not? Maybe he can deputize some grad students while he's at it. You know, for extra credit."

"No one is going to find out."

He exhales audibly.

"Frank, we need answers sooner rather than later. Who knows how much time we have before the police find another body?"

"Let me know what Don finds out, and I'll think about the interviews. Okay?"

Samantha nods and places the pencil on the surface of the desk. Frank has been watching, and she can tell that he notices the porcelain frog. She desperately tries to think of ways to justify taking it, but she doesn't want to lie. His eyes have a piercing honesty to them, as if he wants to see the truth in others. She wonders incidentally what they will look like as an old man. Bright and cheerful? Absent and longing? Sad and watery? She sees hints of sadness already.

He doesn't mention the frog.

"So tell me more about your insomnia," he says.

## 11

## *Connections*

*F*rank drives Sam to the sleep clinic, grateful that she is talking of inconsequential paperwork and neglected e-mail. Of anything but her sleeplessness and the anxiety it's causing her, which only gets worse as she talks about it. He always knew her to be a champion sleeper. No car alarm or barking dog could wake her in the middle of the night. She slept through movies, books, classes, long phone conversations. She even dozed off once while kissing him. Once—after an eighteen-hour trip to Versailles without sleep. For Sam, sleep had been like oxygen, easy to come by. Eight to ten hours a day. What changed? Was the past that she had worked so hard to block out catching up with her? Was he to blame for moving?

No. She abandoned him. He might have moved, but she withdrew her heart. His moving just made it easier.

His first night in D.C. was spent on a cold hardwood floor wrapped in a sleeping bag with a broken zipper. His friend's studio apartment near Dupont Circle had a futon couch, an enormous television, and a broken floor lamp from Target. Three bottles of Rolling Rock and a half-empty container of Grey Poupon were in the fridge.

He listened to the sounds around him for a long time before falling asleep. Rain tapping lightly against the window. His friend snoring like a congested old man. Then a dream woke him.

A dream that his heart looked like the surface of the moon.

They arrive at the clinic, and Sam introduces him to Dr. Clay. They decided in the car that Frank would tell him about Phebe's murder, but he hesitates at the sight of Clay's tired, sagging eyes. The long white coat accentuates his bony frame, and his gray-brown hair, more gray than brown, is disheveled.

They stand, facing each other. A triangle of silence.

"I'm sorry to have to tell you this . . . ," Frank begins, but he isn't fully conscious of the words, just that Dr. Clay recoils as if slapped in the face. His mouth slightly open, his eyes blinking steadily.

Frank asks some questions, but can tell from his answers that Dr. Clay didn't really know Phebe. Does he know Sam any better? Probably not. Frank wonders if this detachment helps him do his job.

A nurse enters the room to prep Samantha. Dr. Clay nods.

"If we're going to keep on schedule," he says halfheartedly, "you need to get ready." He turns to Frank. "Can you give us a minute?"

"Actually, I'll just come back tomorrow. Thanks." He looks at Sam and adds, "Good night."

She smiles sadly, and Frank wonders if she is thinking of Phebe, the long night ahead, or him.

Frank drives away from the clinic, passing familiar streets and turning into the shadows of windy neighborhoods. He is just driving now. Not wanting to stop or slow down. The night air is cold, but he keeps the window down, listening to the rush of fast-moving air and the clamor of city noises.

He turns another corner quickly and sees Saint Peter's Church, where he found Samantha just a few days ago. He has not driven here consciously, but he is not entirely surprised either. He considers going inside. The car engine hums as he looks at the church's looming spires and Brobdingnagian oak doors. He hasn't been inside a church in almost fifteen years, he thinks.

After Susanna died, he had no need for churches.

Strangled by a necktie and old pants that had been fitted to a younger waistline, Frank's father looked as uncomfortable as he must have felt. It was already about eighty degrees at eleven-thirty in the morning, when the service began at the chapel of Holy Cross Cemetery.

The green, well-manicured hills of the cemetery rose up for miles, and in every direction Frank could see thousands of homes surrounded by high-rises and billboards and telephone wires. The sprawl of a city named for angels. The cloudless sky offered no relief from the heat. Only a slight breeze cooled the sweat on his forehead. Frank remembers smiling and greeting cousins he hardly knew, uncles and aunts he had forgotten, and some of Susanna's friends, most of whom he had never met. The organist played Gershwin's "Summertime," and the chords sounded flat as they drifted into the dry, dusty air.

When the chapel was finally ready, men and women from the mortuary orchestrated the service like ushers at a concert. They handed out programs and carnations, escorting each customer to a seat with steady arms and gentle voices. Men and women dressed in suits. Smiling. Reassuring. Death was their job.

The organ continued groaning wistfully about summertime as the pews filled.

Everyone had agreed on Gershwin. It was the easiest decision of the day.

\*   \*   \*

When Frank was eight, his father had taken him and Susanna to the tide pools just north of Malibu Beach. He drove with Susanna next to him in the front seat, Frank sitting beside her. As they got closer to the coast, Frank stuck his head out of the window like a puppy and let the stinging-cool air redden his cheeks. He tasted the salt in the wind. The last act of Gershwin's *Porgy and Bess* started playing on the radio as they pulled off the highway. Their father wanted them to listen carefully, so they were quiet for the rest of the drive, even Susanna.

Stepping on the slick, uneven rocks, they looked into the clear water of the tide pools. Susanna held Frank's hand as the waves rushed in. The white foam disappeared, and they watched the sea anemones, crabs, and purple starfish until the breaking white waters covered them again.

Father waited in the car until the opera ended.

The doctors had diagnosed Susanna's tumor as malignant almost five years ago. They removed her left breast, and for a while she lost most of her hair. The hair would grow back.

Unlike Samson, her boyfriend at the time, Frank didn't blame God. Samson took his name's biblical origins seriously and never cut his hair above shoulder length. But that didn't matter. According to Susanna, he once tried lifting weights in the gym where they met, but his grasshopper-thin arms could hardly raise the bar above his chest. When Susanna died, he felt that God had betrayed him, that he hadn't given Samson enough strength to protect her.

No one was that strong.

Samson sat next to Frank during the service. His hands rested heavily in his lap. Like Frank, he was weeping.

Now Frank places both hands on the steering wheel. Avoiding the stare of Saint Peter, whose white marble body stands in the courtyard, watching all those who enter, Frank looks one last time at the architecture, then notices a homeless man sitting in a dark corner of the entryway. He pulls something around his shoulders, a blanket or sleeping bag, Frank assumes, for warmth.

Empty churches are cold, lonely places, he thinks, and once again the night air rushes into the car and against his face.

## 12

# Dangerous Crossing

MONDAY

$S$he wakes abruptly, wondering if she has slept at all.

"Almost seven hours," Dr. Clay tells her. He seems pleased, but his manner has changed. He looks like someone burdened by a secret he can't tell. She wonders if he'll say something about Phebe. Will he lose sleep because of what happened? Perhaps there are nights when no one should sleep, she thinks. When one should think about loss in order not to forget it. Samantha feels guilty for sleeping soundly after Phebe's death.

She says good-bye quickly and leaves the building.

Samantha's cubicle in the Oakland Legal Clinic is not impressive. She hasn't decorated it with pictures of family and friends. She hasn't cut out cartoons from newspapers and taped them to the corners of her computer screen. As a staff attorney, she thinks she should have a private office—to interview clients, to concentrate on her casework. So she protests in silence by not getting too comfortable. It doesn't change anything, but it makes her feel better.

She is behind from taking Friday off but feels somewhat better after sleeping through the night without visions. Seventeen pending case files are stacked ominously in piles across the desk. She should start by reviewing and summarizing medical records for three clients in need of disability benefits. She also has several estate documents to prepare. But every time she opens a file, she sees Phebe.

The phone rings.

"Hey, babe, how y' doin'?"

"Don!" She is relieved it's not a client. "How are things?"

"Good. Just giving my grad students hell. You know, the usual."

"I'm sure they love you."

"Well, I wouldn't say that, but I'm perfectly happy living in denial. Anyway, I found some interesting material on that piece you asked me about—the *Goldberg Variations*."

"Yeah?"

"Supposedly, a man named Count Keyserlingk commissioned it from Bach in the early 1740s. He was an insomniac who wanted a musical soporific. So Bach wrote this piece—a theme and variations—and the count had his musician-in-service, Johann Goldberg, play it for him at all hours of the night." He pauses for a moment, then adds: "And I thought getting tenure sucked."

"Insomnia," she echoes.

"Yep."

"Did it work?"

"Did it work?" he says, surprised by the question. "I don't know. It's a pretty long piece; maybe it bored him to sleep." He laughs.

"I mean, is there any record of the count's response to it?"

"Not that I know of, but I only did a preliminary search."

"Can you find out if there is more to the story?"

"Sure, I can talk to a few people, check a few sources—"

"That would be great, Don. I'd really appreciate it."

He pauses, then asks, "So when are you going to let me in on the secret? You said this has to do with a case you're working on. How so?"

She sighs. "Where to start . . ."

"How about 'Once upon a time'?"

"All right. . . ."

For the next two hours, Samantha works halfheartedly on three cases and watches the phone, once again waiting for Frank to call. She begins a will for one of her HIV clients, but now Catherine's face looks back at her from the computer screen. Samantha's head starts to pound. She turns away from the screen, closing her eyes for a moment, then decides to step outside.

A mist has settled over the parking lot, and a cold wind pinches her cheeks. Samantha won't be able to stay long without her jacket, which she left dangling on the kitchen chair in a rush to leave for work. She lingers, hoping the cool air will ease her headache. *Is this a side effect of the treatment?* she wonders.

A sudden pain pierces her ears and temples, as if she were descending too fast in a plane with poor cabin pressure. Everything becomes white.

*Two red eyes glow in the darkness. No, they are not eyes, she thinks, but doors. Crimson doors. She walks toward them slowly, then climbs a few steps leading to an enclosed porch. Something is waiting in the corner. She can hear it breathing.*

*The figure steps toward her.*

*She lifts her arm instinctively, as if a gesture might stop him, and she sees a knife in her own hand.*

*He takes another step.*

*She doesn't wait for him to get any closer before lunging at him with the blade.*

"Sam? Samantha!" The legal clinic's director crouches above her with one knee on the ground. She places her right hand on Samantha's cheek. "What happened?"

"I must have fainted. . . ." She blinks several times.

Julie looks doubtful as she helps Samantha stand. Julie's usual composure and professionalism have been replaced by fear. Helplessness. Thick and powerful, Julie can usually handle board meetings, conference calls, belligerent clients, and disgruntled lawyers. But seeing a friend lying unconscious on the ground rattles her.

"Maybe you should see a doctor. Let me drive you."

"No, really. I'm all right."

"Your cases can wait. I'm taking you to a doctor, for Christ's sake." The assertiveness returns. She takes hold of Samantha's left arm.

"Let me come inside and sit down for a bit. Okay?"

"All right." She nods and opens the door. "Thanks, Julie."

Samantha isn't sure if she is dizzy from the fainting spell or just furious with Dr. Clay for putting her in such danger. She could have been driving, she thinks. Or crossing the street. Skydiving. Taking a shower. There are always stories in the news about people who die from slipping in the shower.

She sits in her cubicle and rubs the back of her neck with both hands. Julie walks by a second time. The phone rings. It takes Samantha a few moments to realize that it's Olivia from the San Francisco AIDS Foundation.

"I'm sorry. What were you saying?"

"Jeez, you're out of it today. Did you hit your head or something?" Olivia laughs.

"In a manner of speaking. What's up?"

"I checked with the volunteer office like you asked. The foundation trained eight new people two weeks ago."

A pause. "How many women?"

"Um . . ." She rustles through some papers audibly. "One—Isabella Harris." She pauses. "Huh, this is strange."

"What?"

"There's a lot of information missing from her application. She hasn't listed any previous employment or experience. Nothing about her educational background. No one to contact in case of an emergency—"

"What about an address?"

"Yeah, but no phone number."

"Can I get that from you?"

"Her address? You know I can't—"

"Olivia, I *really* need it."

She is silent, and Samantha can hear her desk chair squeak from leaning back.

"I'm asking for a favor."

"How about dinner and drinks one night next week?"

Olivia has been asking her out since the day they met two years ago.

"Sure, anything. Just give me the address."

"Be careful now. I just might take you at your word."

Samantha knocks on Julie's office door, then turns the knob and steps inside. The desk is immaculate, compulsively organized with color-coded stacks of papers and lethally sharpened pencils.

"I'm not feeling so great after all."

"I'll take you to the hospital, then." Julie pushes back from the desk and starts to get up.

"No, that's okay. I already have someone coming to pick me up."

"Who?"

Samantha hesitates. "Frank."

"Frank?" Julie grimaces.

Samantha hadn't told her that she was talking to Frank again, and she can see the shock in Julie's face. Julie had watched them steal kisses in darkened movie theaters and hold hands under restaurant tables. She had also watched Sam walk around like a ghost after he left. So she'd done what any friend would do. She'd learned to hate him.

"Are you sure?" Julie says with surprising calm and restraint. "I really don't mind taking you."

"Yeah, I'm fine. Thanks, though." She drops her eyes, staring at nothing in particular, then smiles uncomfortably. "I'll call you later today."

"Okay," Julie says with a smirk. "Just don't fuck him."

"*Julie!*"

Samantha is waiting in the parking lot when Frank pulls up.

"So what's this emergency you couldn't tell me about over the phone?" he asks as she gets into the passenger seat.

"What took you so long?"

"I was waiting for those dental records when you called." He reaches for a manila envelope in the backseat and hands it to her. "We have a match—Father Morgan."

She thinks about the tooth she found at the crime scene and shudders. Holding the clear plastic X-ray up in her right hand, she's not sure what she is supposed to see. The black-and-white outline of teeth, some bright with fillings. It crackles with each bend, like twigs in a fireplace. "What happens now?" she asks quickly.

"I'm catching a flight later to Salt Lake. I'll talk to some of Morgan's friends, then stop at the restaurant where Catherine had dinner. Maybe one of the waiters will remember seeing them there. So what's going on with you?"

"I talked with Don today, and you're not going to believe this. The Bach piece we found at both crime scenes was written as a kind of soporific."

Frank is silent, and she adds, "To cause sleep."

"I know what *soporific* means."

"Phebe was an insomniac. What if Father Morgan was too?"

"I don't think it really matters."

"Why not?"

"We found Catherine's fingerprint on that CD."

"That doesn't make her a killer." She hears an almost defensive quality in her voice and realizes that Frank doesn't understand the frustration, the anger that comes with not being able to sleep.

"It puts her at two crime scenes." Frank adjusts his seat, uncomfortable with the steering wheel pressed so close to him. "Has it occurred to you that she may be guilty? That she may have killed Father Morgan and Phebe?"

"A fingerprint isn't a hell of a lot of evidence, and it sure doesn't explain how a thin, five-foot-six girl from North Carolina managed to string up two people."

"She may not be acting alone," Frank says evenly.

She considers his words but thinks, *No, she* is *alone—tired, scared, haunted by nightmares, and desperate for help. Like me. Like me.* She hands Frank a piece of torn paper.

"Who's 'Isabella Harris'?"

"I think she might be Catherine."

"*What?*" he asks.

"Olivia just called and told me about this woman who started volunteering at the San Francisco AIDS Foundation two weeks ago. Her application is filled with gaps—no information about her background, no family or friends mentioned, only an address."

"That doesn't make her Catherine."

"No. It just makes her our best lead."

In the thick fog, the flashing red lights of Coit Tower look like muted stars. The chill seems to seep through the windshield as they drive slowly up Aquavista Way. Samantha strains to see each number: 1534, 1536, 1536½, 1538, 1540. A gray cat, its fur matted from the moist air, darts across the street and scurries alongside a duplex with peeling beige paint.

"That's it."

Frank pulls into the driveway and turns off the engine. The windshield wipers stop diagonally across the glass, and Samantha can see her reflection cut in half by the blade. He reaches into the backseat for his satchel and pulls it into his lap. He takes out a holstered gun.

"What the hell are you doing?"

"I'm licensed to carry a firearm." He doesn't look at her as he closes the bag and removes the keys from the ignition.

"Don't give me that crap. I'm not going up there if you're bringing a gun."

"Fine. Stay in the car." He gets out and shuts the door quickly.

Samantha watches him pull back part of his thin black leather jacket and fasten the holster to his belt.

She is behind him now, stepping cautiously on the stone path that leads to the front door. It is lined with cracks that look like creases on an open palm. The prolonged rain and lack of sun have made several stones slippery with moss, and the thick bushes appear stiff and lifeless. A black mailbox underneath the doorbell reads "1542."

"It must be around back," he says.

She follows Frank along the side of the house. Olive trees line the dirt path, and the saturated leaves brush against her face and hair as she pushes past the branches. They walk the length of the house before reaching a small patio with dirty white plastic chairs, a rusty barbecue, and a small bowl filled with cat food. Everything appears old and unused: carelessly scattered garden tools, a bicycle with no seat and two flat tires leaning precariously against the fence, an orange road sign lying on top of three black plastic garbage bags. Samantha reads it aloud as they climb the steps to the back door—"Dangerous Crossing."

Frank takes out his gun and signals her to be quiet. Samantha worries that her pounding heart will give them away until Frank knocks with the back of his fist. The number 1542½ has been painted carelessly on a brass slot in the door, and the uncollected mail sticks out through an opening at the base of the jamb.

"Hello? Is anyone home?" He tries the handle, and the door swings open quickly and easily. "Isabella?"

A sudden hiss. Samantha freezes. Frank pivots toward the sound.

Nothing at first, as their eyes adjust to the darkness. Then, movement in the corner behind them. The gray cat with matted hair and yellow eyes cowers, then darts away.

"Damn." Frank chuckles. "What a cliché."

They step inside, and Frank pulls open a large curtain. A gray-white haze fills the room. Crumpled sheets cover a mattress in the center; several containers of Chinese takeout lie next to it, and a black book is open on the pillow. There is nothing else in the room. No chairs or posters or shelves. Just empty space. Their footsteps reverberate against the wood floor.

Walking to the far corner, Samantha slowly opens the bathroom door and stops, frozen. The room is illuminated by a sky-light. Dried blood stains the white tiled floor, and the shattered mirror above the sink reveals a piece of black tar paper. Shards of glass are visible on the basin and floor. A worn, dark yellow shower curtain hangs around the bathtub.

Samantha stands in front of the curtain, searching for the courage to pull it back.

"Sam," Frank calls out as he walks into the bathroom, "it was open to the Book of Job. She has several passages earmarked and underlined."

His voice sounds distant. She recognizes the black mirror and tiles from her first vision and is afraid—afraid of finding Catherine or another victim in the tub, afraid of visions that lead her places too late to change the past. Taking a deep breath, she flings the curtain open in one motion.

Nothing but a rust-stained tub.

"I'm calling the police," Frank says, looking at the bloody floor, the shards of glass, then her.

As he dials Detective Snair, she carefully takes the book from his hands.

> When I say, *My bed shall comfort me, my couch shall ease*
> *my complaint;*
> Then thou scarest me with dreams, and terrifiest me
> *through visions:*
> So that my soul chooseth strangling, and death rather than
> *my life.*

She walks back into the main room, reading the underlined passage aloud. God allows Job to suffer as a test of his faith. Does Catherine see herself as suffering unjustly? She turns the page and for the first time notices the smell of rotting Chinese food.

The front door suddenly swings open, and Samantha sees the outline of a tall figure holding a baseball bat. He steps inside, blocking the light from the window. Her legs feel like sandbags. She tries calling out to Frank but can only gasp for breath. The Bible falls from her hands, spilling onto the floor with a thud, and the figure takes another step. She can't see his face because of the light behind him.

Suddenly, the thunder of Frank's voice explodes behind her. "*Drop it!*"

The bat launches into the air, and the figure yelps wildly as he retreats through the door. He must have seen the gun. Frank rushes past her, and she follows, leaping down the steps and ducking past the olive trees. She can see a skintight, neon-orange shirt bouncing up and down with each stride. His arms flail like a bird with an injured wing, and at any moment she expects the windshield on Frank's car to shatter from the high-pitched screech. He turns onto the sidewalk, still screeching, and Frank tackles him as he turns toward the house next door.

Crouching above him, Frank turns him over violently: "Who are you?"

Standing behind Frank, she can see the man in orange more clearly now. His rail-thin body looks fragile in the shadow of Frank's expansive shoulders. His fingers twitch as he talks, and his sweat-drenched neck expands with each breath.

"Get your hands off me!"

"Who are you?" Frank asks, his voice thin from being winded.

"B. J. Manassas."

Frank blinks. "That's . . . quite a name."

"Who the hell are you!"

"I'm with the police."

"A cop? In that outfit? *You've* got to be kidding."

"Well, actually I work with—"

"I ought to sue your ass!"

Frank stands quickly and pulls B.J. to his feet. "What were you doing back there?"

"Feeding that ingrate of a cat. Little pussy peed on my shoes last week."

"You normally carry a baseball bat to feed the cat?"

"When I hear two cop impersonators rustling through my olive trees, yes, I grab a bat to check on my neighbor's house."

"So you live next door to Cath—I mean, Isabella?" Samantha asks.

"Isabella?"

"You said you were taking care of her cat?"

"Bob owns that house. I take care of Bob's cat. He just started renting out the back room to some woman."

"Have you met her?"

"Once, out here. She was smoking. Bob doesn't let anyone smoke in the house."

"When did you meet her?"

"About a week ago. She was sitting on the curb over there. We talked a bit."

"What did she say?" Frank's voice sounds edgy and impatient.

"That's none of your business, Chuck Norris!"

"B.J.," Samantha says earnestly, "we actually do work with the police. We're investigating a disappearance, and anything you could tell us would really help. I'm Samantha Ranvali. This is Frank Bennett."

"She's missing?" He squints slightly.

"Yes, and a lot of concerned people are looking for her. What did she tell you?"

"I don't remember much actually." His voice is softer, more genuine. "I had just gotten back from a club and was pretty toasted." He chuckles uncomfortably. "Anyway, we didn't talk for long—a couple of minutes, max." He pauses, then adds, "Oh yeah, when she finished her cigarette, I asked if she was going to bed, and she said no. She said that she didn't sleep anymore. That was it."

Samantha glances at Frank, then says to B. J., "I want to show you something." She steps over to the car and grabs Catherine's picture from the file in Frank's satchel.

"Is this the woman you met that night?"

"Yeah, that's her," B. J. says.

"Thanks."

A car quickly pulls up alongside them, and Detective Snair steps out. A squad car soon follows. Frank leads all of them around back as Snair grumbles about contaminating the crime scene.

Samantha stops listening to his voice as they enter Catherine's apartment. She looks around, trying to imagine her there. When Snair disappears into the bathroom, she picks up the Bible one more time and opens to the first underlined passage in Job:

> *For the thing which I greatly feared is come upon me, and*
> *that which I was afraid of is come unto me.*
> *I was not in safety, neither had I rest, neither was I quiet;*
> *yet trouble came.*

# *Parasomnia*

*Christina works the closing shift at Luna, a small coffeehouse hidden in the remnants of a forest. The tall, full trees block any hint of the surrounding town. When it's too cold to sit on the patio or under the mustard-yellow awning of the front porch, people cram inside for seats. The small tables are too close for work, the lighting too faint for reading. It is a place to socialize, to wax philosophic, to flirt. Like its eclectic decor, Luna attracts a diverse crowd—regulars with pierced tongues and tattooed arms, forlorn lovers, people who talk about themselves without reserve and look into your eyes when they speak.*

*That's why Christina likes working there. The customers make her feel normal, as if everything will be all right.*

*Two dirt roads leading to the entrance serve as parking lots, and they were almost full when she arrived, forcing her to park near the life-size statue of a red buffalo. But now, after closing time, they are empty. She can see only a few feet in front of her. Strong winds whip the trees like sheets on a clothesline and kick dust into her eyes. She hurries with her head down.*

*A hoarse voice calls out like a whisper in her ear: "Christina."*

*Spinning around, heart pounding, she strains to see something in the darkness. Then, several feet away, a figure emerges from the swaying branches.*

*She has seen him before. He is a regular customer. Always alone. He watches her sometimes but never speaks. He must have overheard her name. His eyes, which usually dart nervously, seem invisible now.*

*"What do you want?"*

*"To talk."*

*"No, thanks."*

*Before she can move, he leaps forward. A hollow thud explodes around her, and she feels the coldness of the car door against her back. A long, icy blade touches her right cheekbone. She breathes in quickly but can't exhale. He presses his left forearm against her throat and removes the blade. Her vision blurs. She becomes faint from the pressure, the lack of air.*

*She hears him panting. His breath smells of garlic and onions. He lets go of her throat and pauses, looking into her eyes. He smiles awkwardly.*

*Suddenly, she drives her forehead into the bridge of his nose, grabs each wrist, and lifts a knee into his groin. She holds on as he staggers, pulling his right wrist forward and down. She twists her upper body, crashing her right elbow into his jaw. His head and shoulder collide into the car. She turns clockwise, scoops up the knife, and spins back, slicing across his chest.*

He falls backward, yelping, his eyes bulging and white with fear.

She takes a step forward and notices a shooting star. It fizzles on the horizon. She feels distant from her body and thinks about making a wish. Crouching above him, she lifts the blade again but doesn't notice the butterfly knife that he has pulled from a strap around his ankle. As she slices his chest, he jabs her abdomen.

Holding on to the knife with one hand, he grabs the back of her neck with the other. She struggles to break free and falls on top of him, sinking her teeth into his collar bone. With a yell, he tries to push her away, but she holds on.

They both lie in the dirt, breathing heavily. He tries to raise himself by his elbows, but collapses. For a moment, he sees Orion, the timeless warrior, posing fearlessly overhead. Then he closes his eyes.

The next time he opens them Christina is lying perfectly still. He doesn't know how much time has passed before he gets to his feet. An icy wind stings his face as he drags her body to the edge of the forest.

He didn't want to kill her.

He walks home, and as he turns up the street to his apartment, it starts to rain. The water falls heavily, and he thinks of a story his mother told him when he was a child.

Hundreds of exotic animals marched into a great boat as the rains started falling. The ark creaked as if it was going to snap apart, then began floating away in the torrential floods. All the people who had mocked Noah stood on a rock, crowded together, pleading to get on board. But it was too late. The waters washed over them and all the earth. Only Noah, his wife and children, and the animals were spared.

*Thinking about this story, he imagines himself on that rock. It is only a matter of time, he thinks, before the waters rush over him.*

APRIL 10, 1987
10:17 A.M.

*"Butner Creedmoor, you lazy piece of pony shit, hurry up!"*

*Jake, the driver, slams on the horn. Perhaps the only benefit of working at UPS for twenty-five years is tormenting new runners during a delivery schedule, and Jake capitalizes on this every day. He knows most of the residents on his route and enjoys withholding certain details from Butner—like the fact that Ms. Jackson, who goes "just wild" for men in uniform, is clearly a he, and that the dog at 123 Sycamore is never on a chain. Jake watches from the truck, laughing until his stomach hurts and tears well up in his eyes. He is particularly impatient today, and that can only mean one thing—the joke will be on Butner, again.*

*"For Christ's sake, B.C., you're droopin' like my granny's ass. Let's move."*

*Jake accelerates hard, and Butner leans back, closing his eyes.*

He hasn't slept much since killing that girl. She was going to kill me, *he thinks*. Hell, I wasn't planning to hurt her. I just wanted to talk.

*But the words wouldn't come. They never come, and somewhere inside he wanted to scream. He grabbed her. She smelled so good, like flowers and cinnamon. He remembers wanting to taste that smell. Then he felt the fire of a blade slicing into his skin. Why did he bring those damn knives in the first place? To scare her. Yes, to scare her. He had lived his entire life around*

*people who didn't feel anything for him. At least fear was some-
thing. But like everything else he tried to do, he failed. She
became angry. She tried to kill him. He was defending himself,
but the police would never believe him. He brought the knives.*

The next morning, when the marks on his chest looked more
like cat scratches than a knife wound, he wasn't sure what had
happened—not until the television news reports. The pictures
of her on-screen were radiant. More beautiful than any movie
star or princess, too perfect for words. He thought of turning
himself in, convinced that the police would find him in a matter
of days. He kept going to work, enduring Jake's pranks, and
wondering when the cops would come.

But no one came.

The nightmares became unbearable, and sometimes he felt
relieved not to sleep. Bodies suspended upside down, bleeding
into a red, flowing river. A circle carved into each chest. He
never recognizes their faces, but he can see them clearly. Gradually each face starts to change, one anguished expression fus-
ing into the next. Before waking, he always sees the same face
on every body—Christina's. Her eyes open and her mouth
moves soundlessly, saying words that he can't hear. Then his
shirt becomes damp and sticky from an invisible wound.

"Nap time is over, big guy. We got a package for 1310 Wil-
low Drive." Jake points to a one-story yellow house with large
bay windows. Much of the front room is visible from the
street—the back of a couch, a china cabinet and matching dining room table, a simple but elegant chandelier. Butner grabs
the clipboard and a small box from the back of the truck.

Before ringing the doorbell, he looks back at Jake, who stifles
a laugh. The front door swings open, and an enormously over-
weight man without any clothes on steps onto the porch.

"Hello?"

*"Uh . . ." Butner turns away, trying to figure out what to say.*

*"You have a package for me?" The voice is deep and jolly.*

*"Yes . . . uh . . ." Butner looks intently at the clipboard, then at the man's marshmallow feet and hairy legs. "Mr. Lawrence Cassuto?"*

*"Yep." He takes the package, signs for it, and bellows, "Hey, Jake. How's it hanging?" His flesh ripples with each word, and Butner can feel his own face and neck turn red.*

*"Low and lively, Larry. How about you?"*

*"See for yourself."*

*They both laugh, and Butner smiles awkwardly. Jake had probably been waiting for weeks to deliver a package to Larry, the naked man.*

*Butner turns to him as he climbs back into the truck, muttering, "No job is worth this."*

<br>

APRIL 11, 1987
3:57 A.M.

<br>

*From the rooftop of his nine-story apartment building, the city looks peaceful and dark. Another nightmare had driven Butner out of bed—his T-shirt soaked with sweat and cheeks moist from tears. He doesn't remember getting dressed and walking to the roof. He's not sure why he's standing at the ledge, looking out at the quiet with envy and loathing. His bare feet sting, and the cold drizzle makes his face numb.*

*Like the people who mocked Noah, Butner watches the blackness for some sign of forgiveness. The tide rises, and there is only one thing left to do—one thing to stop the visions, the sleepless nights, the constant fear of discovery.*

*He leaps.*

*With arms outstretched, his body arcs over the ledge. For a* moment, just the briefest instant, he seems to float, not like a bird but like something lighter... high above the night, free from himself, the past, and a terrible future....

### 6:23 A.M.

*Lying beneath the bumpers of two parked cars, Butner wakes up with a headache. He tries to push himself up, but his body tingles as if he is thawing from a deep cold. He looks at his hand, which is smeared with red, and rubs his fingers together—transmission fluid. The strong stench of motor oil makes him nauseous, and the puddles on the moist ground glisten with rainbow colors. Rolling onto his back, he sees a long grassy incline leading from his apartment building to the parking lot. The grass is ripped and matted down in a path toward his body. A deep impression marks the spot where he first hit the ground and started rolling downhill.*

*He gets up slowly—his body aching as if he's pulled muscles all over—and takes an elevator to his room. Nothing feels broken. Only scrapes and bruises. Falling into bed, he looks at the ceiling and, as if in answer to his prayers, falls asleep.*

## 13
## *Other Voices*

Most of the passengers are wearing business suits and reading newspapers. They probably take one of these commuter flights to Los Angeles several times a week, Samantha thinks. They have grown accustomed to roasted peanuts, strained conversation, and the smell of recycled air. She can't pass as a regular because she doesn't like sitting so close to strangers and being served by people who are paid to smile.

Ten months ago, she flew to L.A. to see her father. He had been rushed to a burn unit at UCLA after firefighters pulled him from the house. Decayed wiring had started an electrical fire in the living room just after midnight. Within minutes the entire place was ablaze. Father was asleep until a flaming beam from the bedroom ceiling crashed onto his back, causing second- and third-degree burns. The doctors said he was lucky to be alive.

When she and Frank arrived at the hospital, Father was lying facedown in a hammock, his face sweating and lined with pain, drool streaming from his mouth onto the floor. His arms were stretched out to his sides. In one hand he clutched a morphine button that released a dose as needed, but only up to once every five minutes. He pushed it incessantly. Blood seeped through the gauze on his back so quickly that it seemed to turn yellowish-brown almost immediately. Every time a nurse came in to change it, gently lifting each strip off his moist, blistering skin, Samantha had to leave the room.

His back healed, leaving only scars and discoloration, but Samantha's father said nothing could heal the memory of those long, agonizing moments underneath the flames, waiting for the end. Since then, he hasn't slept well. He tells her that the fear of another fire keeps him awake. Every night he walks around his new apartment three or four times before going to bed, checking each electrical socket. He still wakes up terrified by nightmares, sweating from the heat of imaginary flames and sniffing the air for smoke. Every time she looks at him, she can see the imprint of that fire, as if black ash were permanently etched onto parts of his face.

While driving to the campus, she thinks about calling him, but she didn't even take time to pack. After leaving Catherine's place, she considered returning to work, but as soon as she got home, Don called. Apparently Goldberg kept a list of monthly expenditures, travel records, letters. And all of these documents were currently housed at the Schoenberg Music Library at UCLA; a musicologist on campus was studying and translating them. Don had already contacted him about getting her access, and she left for the airport immediately. Flights ran every hour.

"You're here for the Goldberg papers," the librarian says as Samantha approaches the front desk. The woman's dark brown hair is pulled back, and she has a pale, round face.

"Yes."

"Wait here."

Samantha looks around the room anxiously. It has been a long time since she was in a library. Other than a few computer terminals, everything looks the same as in her undergraduate years—the metallic gray bookshelves, the scratched tabletops, even the same unimaginative posters. She took music history classes as a senior and spent a lot of time listening to CDs in the library. She also had a crush on the conductor of the university symphony, making excuses to hang around the department. She secretly admired his commanding stage presence at concerts, which made most girls in the orchestra, and even some of the boys, fawn over him. She is fairly sure that he never knew her name, but that just made the fantasy more bittersweet.

Other parts of campus have been transformed by years of endless construction, to the point where she doesn't recognize things—new bookstores, coffee shops, athletic fields, dorms—but the music building is stuck in the past. This sameness comforts her, as if she were still part of this place.

The librarian returns and places the registry book on the counter. "Sign this and come with me."

Samantha follows her down the hall to a door marked Special Collections. Closed cabinets line each wall in the small, windowless room. There is a circular conference table in the middle with five long rectangular boxes on top. She hands Samantha a pair of white gloves and a list of the boxes' contents.

"Wear these gloves at all times while working with the materials. Nothing may be removed from this room or photocopied without permission. This box has both original and translated documents. The others have not been translated—so they're still in German."

"That won't be a problem, thanks."

Samantha can't read or speak German. She studied Spanish in high school and can't speak that either, but she wants to surprise this woman with the answer, to break through her stoic professionalism. Instead, the librarian smiles at her indifferently and leaves the room.

According to the catalog, there are a hundred and twenty-five letters. Only fifty-seven have been translated and grouped according to date and addressee. Notated index cards have been paper-clipped to the top left-hand corner of each, and Samantha assumes that they belong to the musicologist Don contacted.

Goldberg started working for Count Keyserlingk in 1739 and wrote dozens of letters to his brother Carl during the next few years. Several detail a romance with a woman referred to as G—, but most describe the living conditions at Keyserlingk Castle.

*17 November 1740*

*Carl,*
*It has been almost three months since the count has slept through the night. He calls on us at all hours—demanding meals, companionship, and music, so much music. Sometimes I play until sunrise.*

*He wears all black, like one who mourns for himself, a red scarf, and a strange circular pendant around his neck. Even on the hottest summer day, he wears these clothes and walks about like a madman, mumbling to himself. No guests come to the castle, nor does he leave at night.*

*His chamber is filled with potions, dried herbs, and exotic plants. I caught a glimpse through the open door and am reluctant to pass by again. Most of the servants walk around like ghosts, trying not to make noise and incur his anger. This is a strange place.*

*I have little time to work on my music and am often too*

*tired to concentrate. I pray things will get better, as I pray*
*for you and Father.*

*Your brother,*
*Johann*

Several letters describe the restrictions imposed on Goldberg and the other servants. None of them was permitted
to leave after sundown, nor could they enter the count's
private chamber under any circumstance. They were also
forbidden to leave the castle on Sunday.

*3 January 1741*

*Dear Brother,*
*The count is furious again. He has taken down all of the*
*crosses in the castle. Remember the one Father gave me*
*before I moved to Dresden? The count tore it off the wall*
*above my bed and threw it in the fire!*

*He blames God for his inability to sleep. "God has pun-*
*ished me enough," he keeps saying, but for what, I do not*
*know.*

*I played a new keyboard piece for him last night, and he*
*was very pleased. Sometime before dawn, he interrupted to*
*tell me about the Seven Sleepers of Ephesus—a group of*
*Christians who were persecuted for refusing to worship*
*idols. On the eve of suffering the emperor's wrath, God*
*willed them to sleep for three hundred and seventy-two*
*years to protect them. He woke them to restore the city's faith*
*in resurrection.*

*"What kind of Lord would be so cruel—to deprive some*
*of sleep and will it to others for centuries?" He clenched his*

*fist and shook with rage as he spoke. "Imagine being one of those seven, waking up to find a world that had left you behind. Empires fallen. Friends, family, wives, and children buried. To find yourself forgotten. Yet for me it is worse, Goldberg. I am forced to watch this every hour, every day. Like this circle"—he lifted the pendant from his chest—"I am trapped in a never-ending band without sleep or joy."*

*He turned away, and I left the room as quickly as possible. I have been afraid ever since. Each day I think of leaving, running far from this city, but he watches like a hawk. I must go—*

*Yours,*
*Johann*

The warm, poorly ventilated room is stifling, and for the first time, Samantha feels uneasy in the quiet. She takes off her jacket, hanging it over the back of a nearby chair. Fluorescent lights buzz steadily overhead, and a low clicking starts to echo in the far distance. It gets louder, and she realizes that someone is walking down the hallway. The footsteps mark time steadily.

*Tap, tap, tap, tap.*

Her heart is thudding, and she grabs the edge of the table with both hands. Her neck is damp with sweat.

*Tap, tap, tap, tap.*

*She couldn't see where the sounds were coming from. They seemed to echo in every direction with the steady rhythm of a clock ticking. She had been studying for hours, not aware of the exact time, not aware that the other students around her had left for the night. In her cubicle, notes from her constitutional law class looked as if they had been scattered by a gust of wind. An empty bottle of* water and half-eaten bag of almond M&Ms were barely visible above the debris of books and papers.

The sounds stopped. She looked over her shoulder, scanning a row of uniform stacks.

Nothing. Just tall shelves casting short shadows.

She turned back to her work.

Samantha smelled him just before he grabbed her from behind. Sweat and grease, like the men where she got her car repaired and oil changed. His thick, smooth arm wrapped around her neck like a boa constrictor. She grabbed his wrist and forearm, struggling to breathe.

In one motion, he seemed to throw her out of the chair and onto the floor. Her head smacked hard against the tile.

A flash of white. The room drained of color until she saw the sliver blade slice through her yellow cotton shirt.

His open hand pressed forcefully against her throat. Her stomach felt warm and sticky, and she imagined sinking into the floor as if it were quicksand. A thick heaviness covered her.

"I've marked you." His voice was deep and steady. "You're mine now."

She remembers his pitted face close to hers. Yellow-green eyes and thick purplish lips. Hot breath. The smell of grease.

Then darkness.

A young man and woman were kneeling beside her when she woke. Another had run off to call the police and paramedics. Samantha found out later that they were law students too. The woman had accidentally left her reading glasses in one of the cubicles and returned with two friends on their way to a bar.

The man attacking Samantha must have run at the sound of their approaching voices. None of them had seen him, just Samantha's body lying on the floor. Her shirt black with blood. Pools of red on the white tiles.

* * *

*Tap, tap, tap, tap.*

The footsteps come together and stop outside the door. Everything is still. Her face flushed and warm.

"Hello?" Samantha's voice is deadened in the soundproof room.

The footsteps start again, moving in the opposite direction. They aren't hurried, but steady and deliberate. Samantha exhales slowly and tells herself not to be afraid. She breathes again. The sounds in the hall fade to silence.

She turns back to the letters and the next index card.

Goldberg's terror seems to lessen somewhat when Bach visits the castle several months later. His fear is replaced by fascination, a newfound curiosity about the count's alchemical practices.

*5 October 1741*

*Dearest Brother,*

*The great J. S. Bach was <u>here</u> at the castle a few days ago! I introduced myself before G— showed him to the waiting room. My hand is still shaking with excitement.*

*The count has commissioned a piece to help him sleep. It sounds absurd, I know, but the count is earnest. And Bach has agreed to try. In the meantime, the count summons me daily to assist with his work. He has become too ill to manage on his own.*

*Yesterday he pointed out several potions in his chamber and said: "This is how it began, Goldberg. With a search."*

*"For what?"*

*"Everlasting life. It is what God promises the righteous, those who can wait a lifetime for judgment."*

"I don't understand."

"I was impatient. Afraid of oblivion, of not knowing. Let me live forever, I prayed. I will suffer whatever pains and torments, just leave me here—where I know what to expect."

He was quiet after that, and we continued to work.

At first I thought of the miserable Struldbruggs, in Swift's book, who live forever but never stop aging. Watching their bodies and minds decay, they become dejected and melancholic, lamenting at every funeral—envious of those who die. But the count is not like this. He is a victim not of fate but of his own deeds.

I'm learning of a world I never knew, Brother. There are powers here that you can't imagine. Be well and write soon,

Your brother,
J

Before returning to Leipzig in early November, Bach delivers the *Variations*. This is the last letter Goldberg writes for the next six months.

16 November 1741

Carl,
Bach composed a set of miraculous variations for the count. His performance was sublime. So much so that I began to feel spiteful—as if its beauty ridiculed me, laughing at the excuses I have made for my own failures. Why am I chained in servitude to this embittered man? If only I had the time and freedom to compose. I am capable of so much more, of a kind of greatness, yet I have grown comfortable with my own failings.

The count's manner has only gotten worse, and the ser-

*vants become more frightened every day. As my animosity toward him grows, so does my sympathy for him. We are bound together now, like brothers. For the first time I understand his need for something more, something beyond this life.*

*Stay well,*
*Johann*

Samantha searches for the next letters, the ones from six months later, but can't find them. They are still with the untranslated documents in Box C. According to the catalog, three more were written in the last week of May, but after that, nothing. As far as documented history is concerned, Goldberg disappears after May 30, 1742. She sets these letters aside, hoping that Don's German is as good as he says it is, and walks to the door. She leans close, listening for any noise on the other side, then opens it quickly.

She is relieved to feel the cooler air as she returns to the front desk. She asks the librarian to copy the letters left out in the Collections room and walks upstairs to the stacks, searching for a score of the *Goldberg Variations*. It's on a dusty shelf in the far corner of the building. A thin shaft of light from a streetlamp pours through the porthole-shaped window facing the parking lot. The pages are yellow and fragile with age.

Samantha takes it to the listening library, checks out a copy of the 1981 Glenn Gould recording, and sits at one of the listening stations. As the music starts, she lets herself feel tired from the morning, the flight, the loose ends of this case. Folding her arms, she leans back and closes her eyes.

*. . . The white porcelain tub feels colder than the water covering her face. Strong hands press her down as she struggles for air.*

*Blood suddenly appears in the water like a cloud. She breaks above the surface and breathes furiously. He pushes down again. She wants to scream, but her voice sounds distant, as if she were falling....*

"Miss? Miss?"

She jumps back with a start and looks up at the librarian, who is tapping her on the shoulder, then at the CD player in front of her which reads "Stop. 32 tr. 0:00."

"Sorry. We're closing the listening library for the night. The main library will be open for another three hours."

"What time is it?"

"Seven o' clock."

"*What?*" Samantha checks her watch.

"Seven o'clock. You've had a bit of a nap." She smiles faintly, then hands Samantha a folder. "Here are the photocopies you requested. Do you need anything else?"

"No, thanks."

As the librarian walks around the room turning off all the electronic equipment, Samantha wonders about the strange origins of this piece and its promise to make people sleep. Did the haunting melodies of the *Variations* finally lull the count to sleep, as they did her? Or was it another source of pain and disappointment? She touches her stomach where the scar lies hidden beneath her shirt. She knows about pain and disappointment that won't go away.

The librarian coughs softly. It is time for Samantha to leave. She glances down at the score.

She hadn't even turned past the first page.

# 14
# *The Small Crucifixion*

After the flight lands at 10:55, Samantha decides to stop by her office and fax Don the letters. She has already missed her time at the clinic and wonders if she will sleep at all tonight. A yellow streetlight glows at the edge of the empty parking lot, and in the shadows the dirty brick building looks as if it has been abandoned for years. She locks the front door behind her and turns on the lights. One fluorescent bulb flickers like a horror-movie chandelier as she picks up a phone.

"Did I wake you?"

"No, just reading." But Frank's voice sounds groggy and full of sleep.

"What did you find out about Father Morgan?"

"Well, the bartender at Lucci's recognized pictures of him and Catherine. He said they ate dinner at the bar and stayed until the restaurant closed—that's why he remembered them."

"Did they come in together?"

"No, but they left at the same time."

Samantha pauses. "Well, that's a start."

"Barely. We still don't know if Father Morgan left Salt Lake voluntarily. His superior, Monsignor Pollard—the one who suspended him for participating in that gay rights parade—doesn't think so. He said that Morgan was upset, but not the kind of man to shirk his other responsibilities with the parish."

"So Pollard thinks he was abducted?"

Frank can hear the disbelief in her voice. "Look, Sam. He filed a missing persons report for a reason. He says Father Morgan wouldn't just leave, and I believe him."

"Morgan's murder doesn't prove that he was taken to San Francisco against his will. We're missing something, Frank." She adds, almost to herself: "What could make him leave so suddenly?"

"Another gay rights parade?"

"He was already angry with the Church. Maybe Catherine convinced him somehow. Maybe they both came here looking for the same thing?"

"I don't know." Frank sighs. "I might be able to find out more tomorrow. Father Morgan's mother lives in Salt Lake, and I'm going to see her in the morning before flying back. According to Pollard, Morgan and his mother were very close. Perhaps she knows something."

"I hope so."

Samantha hangs up and imagines Frank in that hotel room by himself—sitting with his back against the headboard, reading some paperback from an airport bookshop. He never watches television or takes snacks from the minibar. He brings his own soap, shampoo, and towel. If it weren't for the unmade bed in the morning, no one would know that he had been there.

When they took trips together, she never asked why he didn't feel comfortable in these places. In part, she was too busy shoving hotel lotions into her suitcase, opening desk drawers, glancing at the Bible, and flipping through cable channels.

She walks over to the fax machine and enters Don's number. She feels guilty for not telling Frank about scheduling an interview with Catherine's roommate for tomorrow. In truth, she is afraid of what he'd say. Afraid that he is already convinced of Catherine's guilt. But she needs to find out why Catherine really came to San Francisco, and Don has agreed to help. Catherine's former roommate is still an undergraduate at UNC and even took Don's nineteenth-century American history course last year. Through the camera attached to Don's desktop computer and the conference equipment in her office staff room, Sam will be able to see and talk with her online at three o'clock.

It beats a six-hour flight and a bag of unsalted peanuts.

She opens the file from UCLA and begins faxing her copies of Goldberg's last three letters. On a cover sheet, she scribbles: *Don, can you translate as soon as possible? Thanks! S.* She watches the machine devour, then regurgitate each one. Underneath the last letter, she is surprised to find an additional sheet of paper. It is a reprint of a painting. An emaciated Christ hangs from the cross, his feet twisted and flattened by an iron spike, each finger writhing in frozen agony from his impaled hands. Three women—their eyes, like the landscape, too dry for tears—stand below him in mourning. The bottom right-hand corner reads: "Matthias Grünewald's *The Small Crucifixion.*"

The librarian must have included it by mistake.

Samantha wonders if this, the last gasp and agony before death, is what the count feared. He wanted everlasting life without sacrifice. . . . She looks again at Christ's feet and thinks of Peter's request not to have his own impaled. It seems to her that most people try to live with the least amount of sacrifice. She looks down at her shoes, still stiff and shiny from the department store, and picks up the letters.

She then flips off the lights and leaves the office—thinking about what she might have to sacrifice for a night of sleep.

# 15
# *Dead Ends*

**TUESDAY**

*D*on waits anxiously for Sam's call.

They started UCLA together as freshmen but didn't meet until the fall of senior year—fourteen months after the car accident that permanently damaged his right leg. They sat next to each other in a seminar on *Paradise Lost* and passed notes like sixth-graders in the back of the classroom. Sometimes he let his hand linger for a moment, briefly touching her long, silky fingers when she handed him a folded paper. The feeling was electric. Sometimes her hands seemed charged, alive, like a conductor's in front of an orchestra; but instead of music, he heard only the rhythmic sounds of a longing heart.

He fell in love with her that semester.

She was dating someone at the time. Alexander or Andrew. Something with an A. It didn't matter. She rarely talked about him, and Don liked it better that way. He told himself that she couldn't love him.

Besides, he could wait.

A few months later, they were both accepted to graduate schools up north. He would start a doctoral program in history at Berkeley while she studied law in Palo Alto. He imagined possible futures with her. Romantic dinners, trips to the beach, a first kiss. He wondered what her coffee-brown eyes would look like a handbreadth from his face. But after graduation, she spent the summer in Sri Lanka visiting her grandparents.

He was used to waiting.

Graduate school began, and for the first few months, the distance between Berkeley and Stanford seemed far greater than any space on a map. They were both busy, overwhelmed by new places and countless hours of studying. Finally, they met for dinner. He was nervous. His palms sweated steadily. The pain in his leg surged.

That night, she told him about Frank. They had met in an ethics class. On their first date, he did nothing more than hold her hand as they strolled from the restaurant back to his car.

Don's heart threatened to stop with each word. . . .

The phone rings.

On the computer screen, the visible part of Don's office is just as she imagined it—a complete disaster. The bookshelves defy gravity, with stacks of journals, student papers, and books on the verge of spilling onto the floor. Several picture frames hang on the wall directly behind him, but the images are blurry. Four ornately painted wooden elephants—a gift from her after one of her trips to Sri Lanka—appear to march across his cluttered desk in a perfect line. An oasis of order.

Don wears a neatly pressed shirt and tie. His rectangular glasses accentuate the sharp angles of his jaw and cheekbones.

She remembers their long weekends together. The three of them, Frank, Don, and herself, wine tasting in Napa Valley, getting drunk and stuffing themselves at overpriced restaurants.

The white sun, high above the fields of green and red grapes, warming their faces.

The tilt of Don's head suddenly reminds her of a trip to the Gilroy Garlic Festival several months before graduation. Frank was out of town, but he didn't mind missing it. (He wasn't passionate about garlic, and she promised not to smell too bad by the time he got back.) So Don and she drank beer and ate garlic bread, garlic pizza, and dozens of foods that shouldn't have had garlic in them. She is certain that they smelled awful, but no one around them could tell the difference. The sun was setting on the festival, on their lives in school. They decided to leave. After unlocking the passenger door, Don kissed her.

Well, they kissed each other.

They didn't talk on the drive back to Palo Alto, and they never did speak about the kiss. Don said thank you when he dropped her off, and that was it. She thinks it was something they both wanted to do, just to know. Frank and she graduated in June, and two years later, Don was hired as an assistant professor of history at the University of North Carolina at Chapel Hill.

"Can you hear me all right?" Don smiles brightly into the camera. Some of his movements are choppy from the connection.

"Yeah, everything sounds and looks good—even the elephants."

"Great." He nods, then turns to the young girl sitting next to him. "This is Sage Olsen. I've told her that you're investigating Catherine's disappearance with the San Francisco Police Department and need to ask her a few questions."

Don is in full professorial mode—the seriousness of his tone and stern expression almost make her laugh. He's very convincing, no doubt a dynamo in the classroom, but she is more used to his flippant remarks and sexual innuendos.

Sage squirms a bit in the uncomfortable chair, smiling nervously as Samantha introduces herself.

"Sage, do you have any idea why Catherine would take a trip to San Francisco?"

"No, ma'am, I don't."

Samantha grimaces at the word *ma'am*, realizing for the first time how much older she is than Sage, how much older she must seem.

Sage's voice is surprisingly deep and sonorous. Her dazzling blond hair and perfectly straight teeth seem more fitting for the cover of a magazine than the confines of a professor's office.

"Like I told the police before, she didn't know anyone out there. She'd never even been to California."

"How long have you known her?"

"Since we were kids. We grew up in the same neighborhood in Raleigh. She was like my big sister."

"Catherine was older than you?"

"Yep. Three years."

"Did you notice anything different about her in the last few months?"

"No, ma'am."

"No detail is too small, Sage."

She shrugs, looking down at the floor. Samantha can't read her body language through the monitor. Is she upset about Catherine? Afraid of something else? Samantha wants to reach out, to feel something other than the coldness of the conference room.

"Did she get along with her parents?"

"Yes."

"Did she ever talk with you about traveling or taking a vacation from work?"

"No."

"Sage, was she happy?"

For the first time, the girl hesitates. "Happy?"

"Yes, was she happy?"

". . . Yeah, I guess."

"You realize," Don interjects, "that Catherine is in danger?"

"She was my best friend—"

"And you want us to believe that she didn't talk to you about any of this stuff? That you didn't notice any changes in your *best* friend before she ran away?"

"Yeah. I mean no. I—"

Don leans forward in his chair. "She could die, Sage. She may already be dead. But who cares? She's just your best friend. It's a hell of a lot easier not getting involved, right?"

"That's not true!"

"Then what is the truth? What happened to Catherine before she left?"

She looks down again, her body perfectly still.

"Is this how you show your friendship? With secrets and lies?"

"I never lied!"

"Silence is the worst kind of lie, Sage. If you'd read any of the books for my class, you'd know that." Don turns to the screen. "Well, Miss Ranvali, I thought we could be of some help today. I'm sorry we wasted your time." He leans forward to turn off the monitor.

"She fell in love!" Sage blurts out with a cry that sounds as if she's yelling and weeping at the same time.

Don backs away from the monitor. They're all silent for a moment, and Samantha lifts her hand to the monitor, touching Sage's face on the screen.

Sage says in a small voice, "Catherine didn't want anyone to know."

"Where is he, Sage? We need to find him." Don's tone is much softer, almost paternal.

"He's dead." Then she starts weeping—grief and guilt shaking her body like a tremor. "I'm sorry, Cath. I'm so sorry—"

*Eleven months ago, love crashed into Maxwell Harris at a Wendy's drive-through window. A medium Coke, extra-large fries, and a double cheeseburger catapulted out of his hands on impact. The bag fell to the ground with a splat, and most of the Coke spilled on his white long-sleeved shirt. She ran to his window and started to apologize.*

*"I'm sorry. My foot slipped off the brake and—" Her eyes began to water, not from anxiety or frustration, but from laughter. And the harder she tried to stop, the worse it got.*

*"This isn't funny," he protested.*

*It was Max's first day in the development office for the Durham Police Department. He had been recruited to direct fund-raising because of his success as a grant writer for the Raleigh Arts Center. Naturally, he wanted to make a good impression. Wearing a Wendy's meal wouldn't help, but her laughter was too infectious to let him stay angry. He smiled in spite of himself.*

*"Here." She grabbed her order from the startled girl at the window. "You can have everything but the fries." A car honked behind them, and she handed him her card. "I don't see any damage, but here's my number if you need to get in touch with me. I'm Catherine Weber."*

*He looked at her card, then back up to her. "You work for the Durham Police Department?"*

*"Yep."*

*"Me too."*

"They loved telling me that story," Sage explained during the interview—in part because Sage was the only one who knew about them. They kept their romance a secret from coworkers for political reasons, and Catherine, though she wanted to tell, knew that her parents weren't ready for their only daughter to be dating a black man. So Catherine and Max decided to keep a low profile. She often compared their love to a ballroom dance—floating across the floor without being conscious of each step, confident it would last as long as neither one let go. At least, that was how she felt for a few months. Then Max started to change. He became introverted, complained about migraines, and stopped sleeping through the night. Catherine asked him to see a doctor, but he refused. She started feeling alone, even when they held each other. She tried everything she could to fix things—staying up with him, maintaining appearances at work. She hated watching their love fall out of step.

Three months ago, he killed himself, jumping off a bridge onto the tracks of an oncoming train. Catherine was with him that night but never spoke about it. His death squeezed something out of her. Other than Sage, no one knew about them. No one understood her pain, her need to mourn. She had spent so much time keeping their love a secret that she wasn't sure it had been real after he was gone. She had nothing left but the memories she shared with Sage.

After that, Catherine shut herself off from friends. She came and went at erratic hours. She lost weight, smoked more heavily, and started taking sick days off from work. Late one night, Sage woke up to the clamoring of pots and pans and the sound of running water. She found Catherine hand-washing dishes in the kitchen.

"It's four o'clock in the morning, Cath. What's going on?"

"I'm doing the dishes. This place is a sty."

"It's four o'clock in the morning."

"I heard you the first time." She didn't look up from the plate she was drying vigorously.

"Are you all right?"

"It's happening to me too," Catherine replied after a moment. "What is?"

"I'm getting sick, like Max." Still looking at the plate in her hands.

"What are you talking about?"

"I'm not sure."

"Cath? Talk to me."

"It's nothing, really. I'm just tired." She looked up, having regained her composure. "I'll be all right once I get some sleep."

Sage walked over to her and put a hand on her shoulder. "I'm sorry about Max."

They hugged for a long time before Catherine let go and said good night.

After Max's death, life was like this for Catherine—keeping to herself, doing the dishes, and listening to classical music. Max used to take her to concerts at Meymandi Concert Hall in Raleigh. Their last one was a performance of Stravinsky's *Symphony of Psalms*. Catherine bought a recording the next day and listened to the second movement for weeks—the wind instruments crying out one at a time in anguish, asking for help and waiting for voices to reassure them:

> *I waited patiently for the Lord; and he inclined unto me,*
> *and heard my cry.*
> *He brought me up out of an horrible pit....*

Catherine listened, waiting herself.

Before leaving the office, Samantha tries calling Dr. Clay one more time to apologize for missing last night's session, but no one answers the phone at the clinic. He needs a new receptionist, she thinks.

Her phone rings as soon as she places it on the receiver. It's Frank calling from the airport.

"Hi, Sam. I'm on my way to the hotel. Can you meet me there?"

"Sure . . . ," she replies, and Frank hangs up before she can say anything else.

"What!"

"You were in Salt Lake. Don had already set up the meeting."

"Because you told him to."

"I thought it would save time. Besides," she adds flippantly, "we found out that Catherine had a boyfriend."

"Good for her." He turns to the window. "You lied to me, Sam. I asked you not to involve Don until I said it was okay."

"I don't see what the big deal is. We're wasting time arguing about—"

"You lied to me." Frank spins around, his face glowing red with anger.

"No, I just didn't listen to you." She smiles slightly, hoping to deflect his anger.

"You should have told me about the interview last night. Not telling me was a lie."

They stand in a silence that Frank doesn't rush to fill, and Samantha understands how Sage must have felt under Don's didactic scrutiny.

"You're right." Her voice is soft. "I should have been honest with you about the interview. I'm sorry." She looks down, not wanting to see the hurt in his eyes.

He turns to face the window again. "All right."

It isn't quite enough, but it will have to do for the time being, she thinks. She tells him about Max, tentatively at first. The suicide. Catherine's erratic behavior. He sits on the edge of the bed with both hands in his lap. He looks tired. Whether it's from his trip to Salt Lake, the fact that they haven't found Catherine yet, or her, she can't tell. Behind him, from the twentieth floor, the city appears silent and safe.

"Do you buy it?"

"The suicide? Not really."

"Neither do I. I'll call the Durham police first thing in the morning and review the autopsy reports."

"I also have these." She hands Frank copies of the letters she sent to Don.

"German."

"They're letters written by Johann Goldberg."

"Where did you get—"

"I went to L.A."

"*What?*" He almost drops them.

"I flew down to look at the Goldberg archives at UCLA. I read through his other letters and asked Don to translate these. Now get this." She continues breathlessly, talking through his surprise. "The count who commissioned Bach to write this piece was obsessed with immortality. He believed God was punishing him for his attempts to create everlasting life on earth."

"Punishing him?"

"Yes, by taking away his ability to sleep."

"What does that have to do with anything?"

"This piece was playing at two different crime scenes. Both Catherine and Phebe had trouble sleeping—"

"So did Father Morgan." Frank turns suddenly. "I talked to his mother today. She said that he had been complaining about insomnia for almost a year."

Samantha looks at him, nodding. "I think the killer is an insomniac as well."

Frank pauses. "Do you think he's getting treatment here in the city?"

"No. Though my guess is that he's tried treatment, but it didn't work."

"And this is some kind of payback?" Frank tilts his head slightly.

"I don't know, but it could explain why he identifies with the count's anger. The frustration, the rage of not being able to sleep." Her words have become more impassioned, and she wonders if she is talking about the count or herself.

Frank's cell phone rings. She takes the letters from his hands, studying them instead of his face. Frank jots something down on a notepad. He hangs up.

"We've gotta go."

"What?"

"That was Detective Snair. They've found Catherine."

# *Parasomnia*

*Sitting on a small incline of uneven rocks, Butner gazes at the muddy waters of the Mississippi. Behind him the French Market is quiet. No one clamors to buy herbs and spices. No jazz ensemble plays for tips. Only a few late-night lovers and intoxicated college students pass along the nearby walkway.*

*He fidgets uncomfortably in the thick, humid air, sweat covering his skin with a sticky film. He tosses a pebble at the river, waits for the sound—plunk—then picks up another. It disappears high in the fog before falling.*

Plunk.

*He wishes it were clear enough to see the stars. He knows only one constellation, Orion, which he learned about for a sixth-grade field trip to the city observatory. His teacher, Sister Mary Virginia, assigned each student a constellation, and one at a time, they stood in front of the class at the observatory and read notes from index cards prepared at home. Butner still remembers every-one listening to him as they looked into the sky, sipping hot choco-late with marshmallows and shifting restlessly on their blankets. The grass was wet. The night air cool. He pointed out the red shoulder of Betelgeuse, three belt stars, and a mighty sword hang-ing from his side. Orion, the ruthless hunter. Club poised, ready to strike the prey already dangling from his outstretched arm.*

*As Butner pulls back his arm to fling another pebble, he hears a crunching noise behind him. Rocks shifting and scrap-ing together. Someone is walking toward him.*

*He has been running from the police and himself for two months. It all started with Christina. He only meant to scare her, to make her feel something for him. Over and over, he has replayed that night—the way his fear became anger when he touched her, the vengeful fury in her eyes, and Orion snickering in the dark sky overhead. Something changed that night. Some-thing took control of him.*

*At least, that's what he tells himself.*

*He's afraid to believe the alternative—that it was always in him. Unlike Orion, he never wanted to hurt anyone.*

*The heavy footsteps suddenly stop, and a deep, hoarse voice with a Creole accent whispers: "I need somethin'."*

*Butner tosses the pebble and sits silently.*

*Plunk.*

*"I said I need somethin'. For the pain."*

*"Pain is all I have."*

*He steps closer. "Gimme your wallet, man."*

*"I don't have anything."*

*In a slow, hypnotic voice, the stranger says: "Either you hand it to me, or I take it from you."*

*For the first time, Butner turns his head. A bulky dark figure stands a few feet away. "You can't hurt me. No one can."*

*A switchblade snaps in front of him, and the man grabs But-*

ner's arm and shoulder, pulling him to his feet. The edge of the blade points at his throat.

The robber is about to speak when something slices the side of his neck. He gasps, pressing the wound with his left hand and staring in disbelief at the small knife in Butner's fist.

Butner moves to strike again, but the man is faster, stronger. He stabs Butner in the chest with a forceful thud, knocking him onto his back. Stones slice his skin, and his head splashes into the water. Before Butner can move, the man falls on top of him, squeezing his throat and holding him underwater. Butner's mouth fills with the muddy sludge of the Mississippi.

He stabs the man again and releases the knife. It juts out of his body like the lever on a slot machine. Butner pushes him to the side, and the man rolls onto his back. Butner flings himself on top of him, but the man catches his wrist with one hand and clutches his throat with the other. Butner, suspended above him, sees his own blood spilling onto the man's face and throat. A knee suddenly smashes into his ribs—propelling him onto the rocks a few feet away.

On his back, Butner looks into the cloudy sky and gasps for breath. Everything feels still, and he realizes that something is different. Strength drains from his body like fluid out of a syringe. A blackness is coming, darker than the river and the night sky. Too dark for any constellation to appear. But he looks up anyway. For a light, for something to give the darkness meaning. . . .

6:41 A.M.

John Pouliot thought he was either dead or seriously shit-faced. Lifting his left arm out of the cold, foul-smelling water, he suddenly remembers that he didn't pass out from another bender *but from a fight with some wacko. Yet when he touches his sore neck, the wound feels small. The bleeding has stopped. He sits up slowly and sees a body next to him. It's lying motionless on its back, its head mostly submerged in the river.*

*Pouliot reaches around to touch his own rib cage. Pulling up the damp, sticky shirt, he sees a gash several inches below his armpit. Red and black from coagulated blood. It must not have been as deep as he thought.*

*Crawling over to the body, he lifts the head out of the water and shakes him. "Hey!"*

*There is no response.*

*"I don't believe this." Pouliot stands up and looks around at the empty shoreline. "White people always make things so fucking difficult."*

*Most of them get scared off by his deep voice and size. White tourists usually stay clear of blacks, and once you fake a Creole accent, they'll hand over whatever it takes to make you go away—cash, watches, trolley tokens, underwear. New Orleans already spooks them with its cemeteries and all that voodoo stuff. Add a few French-sounding words, throw on a necklace with chicken bones (his are from Kentucky Fried Chicken), and voilà—easy money. But this crazy guy didn't even flinch. He just sat there as if he were waiting for Pouliot to do something.*

*Pouliot checks the man's pockets quickly. A money clip with almost three hundred dollars.* Maybe my luck is starting to change after all, *he thinks. He kicks the body a few times and shoves it the rest of the way into the river.*

*"Take that, you dumb bastard."*

*Pouliot is a reasonable man. He's never wanted to hurt anyone, but the fool stabbed him first. He stumbles up to the road, listening to the voices and drunken laughter of the Quarter. He doesn't see anyone along Decatur and hurries through the nar-*

row streets, away from the straggling tourists and shopkeepers. He moves in the shadows, making his way home. He just wants to sleep, to rest for the game tomorrow night. It might be his last chance.

MARCH 1, 1990
8:34 P.M.

Pouliot wakes up suddenly and looks at the clock—less than an hour till game time. Surprised that he slept so long, he jumps out of bed and hurries to the bathroom. In the mirror, he studies the red marks on his neck and the cut above his rib cage. Both look smaller than he remembered. No open wounds, only dried blood on his clothes. Staring at his reflection, he remembers dreaming of a woman in a bathtub. Upside down, one hand impaled against a tiled wall, the other against Plexiglas. She opens her eyes and screams.

That sound stays with him as he takes a shower, grabs a cold piece of pizza from the fridge, and leaves for Thomson's place.

"My wife wouldn't let me go. So it's either here or we don't play at all!"

"No need to get pissy, Thomson. Sure you don't want me to run over to the market and pick up some tampons first?"

"Fuck off, Baxter."

"Hey, let's get started."

"Keep your panties on, J. P. I've never known anyone in such a hurry to lose." Baxter cackles.

Pouliot fidgets impatiently. He needs to win big tonight and watches carefully as Thomson deals the cards.

"I can feel it, boys. My luck's changing."

"Twelve hundred in the hole with Toomer, another two grand with me. I'd say you're just about shit out of luck, J. P."

Thomson and Toomer haven't cashed in or broken any of his fingers, because they want more than money from Pouliot.

"Suicide kings wild, aces high."

They are low-time, high-impact crooks. Their newest scam involves causing accidents, faking injuries, and collecting on the other drivers' insurance. At first, they used their own piece-of-shit cars. Now, they "borrow" from neighborhood guys who owe them money. After stuffing the trunk or hatchback with Styrofoam, pillows, cardboard, and comforters for padding, they pile people in the backseat and head out to Highway 10. As soon as they see an expensive car, they pull in front of it— usually in the fast lane—and slam on the brakes. The other driver is always deemed at fault, and the insurance company cuts checks to Thomson or Toomer (depending on the day) and the other injured parties in the car. T and T, as the neighborhood guys call them, always take a percentage of the backseat money as well.

If Pouliot doesn't win big tonight, he'll be their next crash-test dummy. They'll take him out tomorrow night, smash up his car, and collect the entire settlement check. Depending on the accident, they could make five times what he owes them. A good day's work.

Pouliot starts with a full house, two queens and three sevens, but loses to Baxter's four tens. The next two rounds go the same way. He's getting decent cards but not good enough to win.

When he was eleven, Pouliot and the other boys in his neighborhood were climbing an oak tree, trying to see who could go highest. Pouliot rose above the others, and for a moment, he won, looking down at the boys who clung to branches below him. Then he fell and broke his arm.

When his father took him to the hospital, he said, "Some

people are born risk-takers"—he looked at his son, who was wincing and tearing in the passenger seat—"even if they're losers."

From that day on, bad luck followed Pouliot like a shadow. Mostly small things, but small things add up. Gambling never made him feel like a winner because he couldn't stop long enough to celebrate. He always wanted more—to play one more game, to have one more drink, to love one more woman. His father was wrong that day. Pouliot wasn't destined to be a foolhardy risk-taker. He was destined never to be satisfied with life. And with Thomson's straight flush, he knows that he'll be crammed in the back of his hatchback tomorrow, praying the collision won't kill him.

He asks to lie down on the couch before leaving. He can hear Baxter's and Toomer's voices but isn't listening to the words. The hallway walls are covered with family pictures. A child's crayoned drawing of a bright sun with dark glasses, a large purple tree, and two people holding hands is taped alongside one of the frames.

"Who drew that?" Pouliot asks.

"My nephew. He's seven." Thomson is surprised by the question. "Why?"

"I don't know. It just looks familiar."

"Yeah," Baxter interjects, "like every other kid's picture. Get a grip, J. P. Not even you can lose forever. Later." Baxter leaves, and T and T take a seat by the couch.

"So, J. P., about the money you owe us . . ."

# 16
# Quicksand

*F*rank drives her to a neighborhood near the Castro district, hurrying past houses and shops that blur together. He is uncharacteristically quiet. Everyone on the street seems in a hurry to be somewhere else—bundled in thick coats and walking quickly with their heads down. It is a clear night, and the only people loitering are those without places to go.

The flashing blue lights of police cars make the crime scene easy to find. Light bounces rhythmically off the faces of curious onlookers and nearby buildings. Frank and Samantha get out of the car, and a uniformed officer leads them through a gate between two duplexes. Their feet squish and slide in the soft, muddy alleyway. At the far end, a group of detectives with flashlights crowd around several garbage cans. Flashbulbs explode with a *pop*. Detective Snair nods a greeting to Frank and steps aside.

"We got a call about forty minutes ago. The owner found her while taking out the trash." He shifts his weight from one foot to the other.

Catherine sits upright with her back against the fence and her legs out in front of her like the number 4—her right leg bent toward the left, touching the knee. She is dressed entirely in black, wearing Doc Martens, slacks, and a tight-fitting shirt, but no jacket. Her head droops against her chest, and her face and hands, which rest in her lap, are bluish white. In the shadows of this unlit alley, Samantha can't tell how she died until Detective Snair, as if answering an unspoken question, lifts up her shirt. There is a deep laceration in her abdomen.

Another flashbulb fires. *Pop.*

"We found a small gym bag in her lap. It had some rope in it, a book, and two knives—both stained with blood." Detective Snair looks at Frank only.

"What book?" Samantha asks.

"I'm pretty sure we'll find someone else's blood on them," Snair continues, and Samantha can't tell if her voice was too soft or if he is just ignoring her.

"Another victim's?" Frank asks.

"That's my guess—"

"What book, Detective?" she repeats, louder.

"A Bible," he says flatly.

"So what do you think happened?" Frank inquires as two men walk toward them with a stretcher. The yellow print on the breast of each jacket reads CORONER

Detective Snair starts walking to the front of the house with Frank, clearing the way for the stretcher. Samantha follows.

"I'm not sure. We'll have to see what forensics turns up with the bag. It's possible that she was fatally wounded while offing her last victim. Made a run for it and only got this far."

"And this 'victim' fatally wounds her but doesn't have the strength to dial 911?" Samantha blurts out, angry both from finding Catherine murdered and from being shut out.

"Maybe he's bleeding to death somewhere or hanging upside down!" Snair says sarcastically.

"Well, that would explain it."

Snair turns around completely, facing her for the first time. "Her prints are going to turn up on those knives. And I'll bet money they're the same knives that killed Phebe McCracken and Gabriel Morgan."

"What makes you so sure that Catherine's blood isn't on those knives?"

"Experience." He spits out the word with disdain. "We've got the murder weapons. We can place her at two crime scenes." He steps closer to her, lowering his voice. She can feel mud seeping through the toe of her right shoe. "You've done nothing but waste my time since the day you got here, Miss—whatever your name is. I'm not here to teach you how to work a crime scene."

"'Experience'?" she asks angrily. "Is that what you call it? It sounds more like expedience to me."

"What?" Snair sounds confused, then annoyed. "As far as you're concerned"—he points his right index finger at her face—"this investigation is over! You were here to find a missing person. Now you've found her."

"This investigation is just beginning." She wants her words to strike him like a closed fist. "None of your evidence proves that Catherine killed anyone. The only thing we know for sure is that a killer is still out there."

He snorts dismissively.

"Someone is responsible for her death. That person put her here so that we would find her. Why? And what's the relationship between her killer and the other crimes? We need to be asking the right questions, not building a case against a dead woman."

"If it was the same killer, *this* woman would be hanging upside down from some fire escape right now."

Samantha looks away from his face for the first time and mutters, "We're missing something."

"I don't have time for this crap. The only reason you're not in jail for impeding a police investigation is because of the Palici Corporation. And I'll make sure any further access to this case is off-limits to you and your group." Snair walks to his car and opens the door.

"These murders aren't over," she yells after him. "You're going to find more bodies. Then what are you going to do?"

"Maybe I'll arrest you." He slams the door and starts the engine.

"What the hell was that?" Frank demands.

"What?"

"You can't be pissing off the San Francisco Police Department in the name of the Palici Corporation. You're here at my request. Now they'll hear an earful from Snair, and I'm going to have to take the heat for lying about your involvement."

"Give me a break. This is more important than whether you're going to get in trouble."

She stops and watches Catherine's body being carried to the hearse.

"To die like this...," Sam continues, her voice flat, "thousands of miles from home. I wanted to talk to her, Frank. To let her know that someone was looking for her."

"Come on, let me take you home." Gently, he places his hand on her shoulder.

"What are you going to tell her parents?"

"I don't know."

"No one should die like this." She stands perfectly still as the men pass her with Catherine's body wrapped in a black bag.

"No, they shouldn't."

"No one should die alone."

*　*　*

After Frank drops her off, Samantha drives to the sleep clinic. The silence in the car makes her somewhat edgy. At a stoplight, she watches crowds of people crossing the street. Some laughing. Others somber and serious. Most just cold. Then a woman with a scarf around her neck looks at Sam. She is far behind the others, content to be at a distance.

It's Catherine—the delicate white skin and deep-blue eyes.

Samantha looks again, leaning forward against the steering wheel. The woman's face is different now. Older, more stern.

The light turns green.

The clinic feels unnaturally still tonight, as Samantha walks past her empty room to the drinking fountain at the end of the hall. The dry tightness in her throat makes it difficult to swallow, so she lets the cool water press against her closed lips. Placing her hands on each side of the fountain, she bows her head. The water spirals clockwise down the drain, and she imagines herself moving with it, away from this place, away from so much suffering and death.

She tries humming the theme from the *Goldberg Variations* but can't recall the melody. Instead, she hears her mother's voice. Samantha remembers falling asleep, her head pressed against the rise and fall of Mother's chest. Her favorite lullaby was a folk song, but she never mentioned its name or sang the words.

Sometimes, when Samantha can't remember her face clearly or hear the cadence of her speaking voice, she hums every note of that song. It keeps them together.

She backs away from the fountain and notices the sound of rustling paper behind her. It is coming from Arty's room. She steps into the doorway and sees him sitting on the edge of the bed, a newspaper spread out on the mattress next to him. She knocks on the doorjamb, and Arty looks up, smiling weakly. His loose T-shirt and sweatpants mask the contours of his body, but Samantha can tell that he is much more muscular than she first realized.

"Hi." Samantha's voice sounds hollow and rough. "Anything interesting?" She glances at the paper.

"Oh, not really. This is just what I do."

"What do you mean?"

"When I can't sleep, I read newspapers. They make me feel more relaxed, I guess." He slowly brings together the two halves of paper, closing it.

Samantha is surprised by the gentle timbre of his voice. "I find the news depressing," she says, trying to sound lighthearted.

"For me, it's not really about the news. It's about . . . preserving the events of people's lives. Making the things we do last."

"Does that help you feel less lonely?" As soon as she asks, Samantha worries that the question is too personal, so she adds, "I mean, that's the worst part for me. Not being able to sleep makes me feel isolated. Desperate for—"

"Everyone is desperate."

Arty's words cut her off, but before she can respond, Samantha hears a woman's voice call her name. She looks down the hall and sees two women standing outside the door of her room.

"I better go," she says to Arty, still thinking about his last words. She walks down the hall and wonders how she would have finished her sentence. Desperate for what exactly? Help? Answers? Love? What did she mean to say? What would she say if Frank had asked her the same question? She isn't sure.

At her room, the taller of the two women introduces herself. "My name is Dr. Cooper. I'll be assisting with your therapy this evening." She is a striking woman with gapped front teeth and an elegant accent. "Dr. Clay is ill, but he'll be back tomorrow."

"Australian?" Sam asks, trying to place her accent.

"No, South African." She seems irritated by the guess. "This is my assistant, Nurse Bogart. She'll get you prepped. I'll be back in just a moment."

"Did you speak to Dr. Clay?"

"No, a message was left at my office. Don't worry. I won't bite." She smiles.

"I just want to talk to him, that's all."

"He'll be back tomorrow. It's time to get started."

Samantha wakes up restless, remembering fragments of a dream—not a dream with a story, but an image.

A hooded figure wrapped in a body-length coat stands before her. His mouth moves, forming words too softly to hear. His lined face makes no expression. She leans closer and closer until her ear almost touches his mouth. She inhales, and his breath smells of hay and animal dung.

The face changes. Skin twisting, tightening. It is younger now, but no less tortured. The changes start happening more quickly—different skin colors, ages, genders. Dozens of faces. Pained. Sad. Suddenly, she is staring into Catherine's face. There is no hint of vitality, like the smile from her picture. Just emptiness. One more change, and a new face forms, somehow familiar—

Nurse Bogart enters the room, congratulating her on a successful night of sleep. Samantha nods without really hearing the words. She is thinking about that last face, certain that she has seen it before.

# 17
## Simon Falls

Samantha can't concentrate on her work, especially after Don's e-mail with the translated letters, so she escapes to the rooftop patio of the office building. When it's warmer, most of the staff take coffee and lunch breaks here. The seven-story building rises above everything else in the business district, and her colleagues enjoy the view. She has never gotten close enough to the edge to see for herself.

Samantha has always been afraid of heights. As a child, she never wanted to go on roller coasters or stand at the top of monuments and tall buildings. She preferred being on the ground, where everything was certain and secure. Even driving across the Bay Bridge makes her knees weaken and her stomach knot. Frank used to laugh at her for being afraid. He is fearless when it comes to gravity and always wanted to take her to high places. She refused. Whether recreation or romance, she likes to keep her feet on the ground.

The patio is empty this early in the morning, and she stands near a circular wooden table, damp from rainwater. Unfolding the printed e-mails, she begins reading the letters. The air is surprisingly still, and clouds stretch across the sky like gauze covering a wound. Car horns honk on the street below.

*25 May 1742*

*Carl,*

*I am sorry it has been so long since I have written. The count is in a rage—screaming at us, tearing apart every room. A fortnight ago, we were almost consumed by fire, and I fear it was not an accident.*

*I have been making preparations to return to Berlin, and shall leave with G— in a week's time. Not a moment too soon, I think. The other servants have been disappearing, and the castle feels haunted without them. At first, I assumed they ran, exhausted from the strain of being here, but during the fire, I saw something that shook me with doubt.*

*I ran to the count's chamber, carrying a bucket of water from the well. I forced the door with my shoulder. Inside, nothing stirred. My eyes burned from the smoke. Then something moved in the corner. It twisted and gurgled in the shadows. Stepping closer, I caught the outline of a body. Its arms were stretched out like wings. Before I could get any closer, something struck the side of my head, throwing me back into the hall. The bucket fell from my hands, spilling water onto the floor, and I looked up. The count towered above me, screaming through clenched, bloody teeth— "OUT!" He slammed the door.*

*We put out the fire soon after, but the count never left his chamber. The next day, while he took a walk in the garden, I went to his room, terrified at what I might find. But there was nothing.*

*He calls for me at present. I must go. God willing, I will
be with you before too long.*

*Your brother,*
*Johann*

The door opens behind her, and Julie steps outside.

"Oh, hi, Sam. I was just going to, uh . . ." She holds up a pack
of cigarettes and shakes it. "I don't imagine you want one?"

"No, thanks."

"No one in this city does. It's like having the plague."

"I thought you quit."

"It's a process." She smiles.

Samantha looks down at the next letter.

"Oh, I forgot to tell you. A man came by the office looking for
you yesterday."

"Who?"

"I don't know. He didn't leave a name. I just happened
to be at the front desk when he came in. He said he'd get ahold
of you eventually." She lights a cigarette and takes a quick
drag. "I assumed he was a new client. I'd never seen him
before."

"What did he look like?"

"Tall, thin, short brown hair. Nothing very distinctive, sorry."

"That's all right. I'm sure he'll come back." Samantha feels
slightly uneasy at the idea.

Julie takes another puff and walks to the ledge.

*27 May 1742*

*Carl,*
*Oh, Brother, G— is dead! The count killed her! Because he
learned of our love, because the happiness of others was like*

*a hot coal pressed into his flesh, he destroyed her. And now he has destroyed me as well.*

*Last night, I came upon them in the stable. The early evening was cool and crisp, and I heard the horses whinnying restlessly. Inside, the smell of dung was overwhelming, and I covered my nose until I saw him on top of her. Her clothes were blood-soaked and torn. I charged him, but with one arm, he tossed me aside like a loose garment. He did not move from her. His hands were stained and dripping with blood. He looked at me, his eyes wild with fury, and tossed me a knife.*

*I threw myself at him. I wanted nothing more than his death at that moment, no matter what the consequences. I dove. The knife sank into his chest. Air exploded from his mouth. Then, I felt a sudden fire in my belly and looked down. He had stabbed me as well.*

*He held on to me, though I tried to push away. Only when he gasped his last breath could I free myself. I immediately crawled to G——, holding her, certain that these were my last moments on earth. She felt so heavy and cold.*

*I fell asleep with her in my arms. I don't know when I woke, but it was raining steadily. Thunder echoed in the distant hills as I carried her to the edge of the forest and buried her.*

*My wound seems to be healing quickly, though I wish otherwise. I must hide now. One thing is for certain. I've killed the count. They will be after me soon.*

*I don't know when I will see you, Brother, or if I will again. All has been taken from me. I am nothing.*

*Yours,*
*Johann*

"Well, I should get back to work," Julie drops the remnant of her cigarette, extinguishing it slowly with her toe.

"I'll be down in a sec."

Julie lingers another moment, then asks: "Are you sure you're feeling better?"

"Yeah, I'm fine. Thanks." For the first time since starting to work for Julie, Samantha notices a small silver cross around her neck. "I didn't know you were religious." She points to the dangling chain.

"Oh, not in the conventional sense. My mother gave this to me. It was a gift for my sixth-grade confirmation." She holds it between her thumb and index finger. "She was so hurt when I stopped going to church in college. I think my lack of faith was one of the biggest disappointments in her life." Julie pauses, her face more somber now. "When she died six months ago, I started wearing it again, sporadically."

"What made you stop going?"

"Lots of things. A rebellious streak, sleeping in, reading the Sunday paper. Mostly, I just couldn't accept the idea that God was petty."

"Petty?"

"Yeah. The church says that you have to believe in Christ to get into heaven—that God denies everlasting life to those who don't believe. How can that be? Some of the most generous, selfless people I know aren't Christian. They're better Christians than most Christians I know. So how can they be less worthy of God's love? I just feel that love, like faith, shouldn't be conditional. Don't get me wrong—I believe in God. I just can't accept that God would be so petty, so unjust."

Her cell phone rings suddenly, and they both jump.

"Hello? . . . Yeah, hold on a second." She looks up apologetically. "I've gotta take this. See you downstairs." She steps inside and the door closes after her.

Samantha feels a chill from the cold air as she turns to the last letter.

*30 May 1742*

*Carl,*
*I watched it from the hillside. Other than a few servants and a city official, no one came to his funeral at Saint Peter's Church. No one shed a tear as they lowered the count's coffin into the ground. I wept from far away, for G— and myself, not him.*

    *I have stayed in the cemetery for several days, waiting for him to return, for I believe he will. I've seen his magic and know it is only a matter of time. When he does, I will stab him as soon as he rises, putting him back into the ground. Over and over again. For as long as it takes.*

    *I have been unable to sleep. At night I lie close to the count, staring up at a statue of Peter being nailed to his upside-down cross. Tonight, the moon casts his shadow over the count's grave.*

    *I dream of Berlin, as I do of G—. I am lost without her. I am nothing. I feel only anger, hatred. It grows inside of me. It keeps me from sleep.*

    *Pray for me. I am*

*your brother,*
*Johann*

The letter slips from her hand and somersaults toward the ledge. Samantha lunges for it instinctively. She misses and gets a sudden glimpse of the street below. Her stomach turns.

She crouches, feeling safer near the ground, and tries again. She reaches for it quickly.

"Ouch!" She pulls back her hand, dropping the now-crumpled letter at her feet. The deep cut on her index finger bleeds purple red, and she scans the ground for the cause—a triangular shard of blue glass. It must be from a broken bottle of some kind, she thinks.

She picks up the letter more carefully now. Her blood has smeared across several words, including Goldberg's name.

She studies the red mark on the paper, then leafs through the letters one more time.

"The blood . . . ," she says aloud. "Blood."

She hurries down to her cubicle and calls Frank. As the phone rings, she starts putting sheets of Kleenex around the wound. The blood seeps through each one almost immediately, as if it might never stop flowing.

# 18
# Transmutations

**P**ractice hasn't started yet. Samantha walks out of the locker room, carrying her fencing mask in one hand and a foil in the other. Several members of the Olympic team, who train at this gym before local tournaments, are stretching. One practices defensive parries. His body moves with the quickness of a fox, his arm light and agile. Two others engage in a practice bout. Her muscles ache as she watches. It's been about a week, and her body feels sluggish from being away for so long.

"Sam?"

She turns around quickly, surprised to see Frank.

"What are you doing here?"

"I was on my way to the airport and thought I'd stop by." He looks at her sleek white uniform and the mask gripped in her hand.

"Where are you going?"

"Raleigh, North Carolina. To see Catherine's parents." He grabs a folder out of his satchel and hands it to her. "I want to show you something."

She places her mask and foil on the floor and takes the folder.

"This is a copy of the autopsy report on Catherine," Frank says. "She died from a knife wound to the stomach—*almost a week ago*. The night before we found Father Morgan."

"*What?*" Samantha opens the file.

"She couldn't have killed Phebe or Father Morgan." He pauses, expecting Samantha to appear relieved, but her eyes stay focused on the report. "Forensics also found two types of blood in Catherine's apartment—hers and, presumably, the killer's."

Samantha still doesn't speak.

"I also talked with the sleep clinics in the area," Frank continues. "There are four: two in San Francisco, one in Berkeley, and the Oakland Institute. They can't release any information, so Detective Snair is getting a court order."

"He's going along with this?"

"For the time being. He agrees with your idea that we should check out anyone who has abandoned treatment in the last year."

Samantha closes the folder but doesn't look up.

"What's wrong?" Frank asks.

"I have something you should see."

She picks up her gear, and Frank follows her to the locker room. Three pairs of fencers begin bouts as Samantha leads him around the edge of the piste. The fencers' feet slide back and forth on each strip with rhythmic precision. Their foils clash and part like embers springing from a hot fire. The opponents closest to Samantha are fencing a short bout to five touches. Green and red lights flash on the score box above the piste, registering each hit. Frank lingers to watch as she goes to her locker.

She returns and hands him the translated letters.

Frank skims through the first. "What are these?"

"Goldberg's last letters."

"The musician?"

"Yes."

"What am I looking for?"

"The count was an alchemist."

"My mother was Irish Catholic. So what?"

"From the Middle Ages to the nineteenth century, alchemy wasn't simply the prototype of chemistry. It involved transmuting one thing into another."

"What are you talking about?"

"I was doing some research today, and . . ." Her voice trails off. She turns her face to the side, away from Frank's. "What if the count, in his attempts to find immortality, really did lose the ability to sleep?"

"You mean through some kind of drug or something?" Frank shrugs his shoulders.

"Maybe. I don't know." She faces him. "Alchemists believed that their scientific practices would ultimately create a universal remedy for all disease. What if the count did the opposite? What if he manufactured a disease by mistake, a kind of curse that could be passed on by blood."

Frank stares, mouth open slightly. "A curse?"

"Passed on by blood," she adds.

Frank's expression doesn't change.

"Read Goldberg's description of the count's death in the last letter." She continues hurriedly. "After they cut each other, the count holds on to him. Only then does he die."

"What the hell are you talking about?" He notices an almost imperceptible line on the skin near her eyes. It is new since he left. Since her troubles with sleep.

"I'm not sure." She stops and lowers her eyes, staring at nothing. "I was thinking about the ritual today, and . . . maybe we're dealing with something more powerful than we realize."

He touches her shoulder gently and says, "Sam, I think you're getting carried away with this story."

She can see the look of concern on his face—the raised eyebrows, the half smile. "You're right. I'm sorry," she says to escape his caretaker gaze. She remembers how quickly it can turn to pity. "I'm just tired."

"Sam," he begins again.

"Really, it's nothing."

"I know you've always wanted an explanation for what happened to you. But this curse isn't the answer—"

She steps back angrily. "Don't patronize me, Frank. I'm not suggesting that the bastard who cut me is the killer."

"I know. I didn't say that—" Frank starts.

"You don't know me as well as you think," she says defensively. "But even if I am still looking for an explanation, what's wrong with that? The police never came up with anything. No one else saw him. Don't you think I deserve an answer?"

Frank bows his head slightly.

"I do. And I hate the fact that I'll never get one." She taps the tip of the foil against her right foot.

"I'm sorry," Frank says, his eyes still lowered. He hears the sounds of clashing foils and sliding feet.

The silence between them makes him uncomfortable.

"So what's going to happen in Raleigh?" Samantha asks, her voice still strained and uneasy.

Frank looks up. "Well, when I first get there, I'm going to get ahold of the autopsy on Catherine's boyfriend, Max. Then I'll meet with Catherine's parents."

"What are you going tell them?"

The muscles in his face tense with the thought. "That their daughter was murdered and that the corporation can assist with the police investigation if they wish."

"And if they don't?"

"Then it's over."

"Over? What do you mean, 'over'?"

"If they don't want us involved, we can't do anything."

"You mean if they don't want to pay extra."

"The corporation was hired to find her, that's all. We don't have jurisdiction over this case."

"That's a load of crap and you know it."

"It's not a load of crap. We're *not* the police." He stops, frustrated. "Look, I have a flight to catch." He hands her the letters. "I'll call you from Durham, okay?"

Samantha nods, then watches as he turns and leaves the gym without looking back.

Putting on her mask, she steps onto the piste, ready for battle.

She doesn't expect to hear the choir singing when she walks into the vestibule of Saint Peter's. It's only Wednesday, but as soon as she picks up a copy of Sunday's bulletin, two soloists start singing an aria from Bach's cantata *Aus der Tiefe rufe ich, Herr, zu dir*. They must be rehearsing early this week, she thinks.

The soprano's voice hovers above the bass's like the faint cry of a frightened child.

> *Have mercy on me, for my load is great;*
> *Lift it from my heart—*
> *Because you have atoned for it*
> *On wood, in mortal agony,*
> *So that I do not suffer now by*
> *Allowing my sins to overcome me,*
> *Nor evermore despair.*

Samantha's feet and body ache from practice, and after sitting in the back pew, she considers taking off her shoes. On the bulletin's cover, several men, mostly hidden in black shadows and a ghostly haze, strain to raise an inverted cross. One seems to be yelling at the others to pull their ropes harder, while Roman officials oversee the execution. A skin-colored light peers through the charcoal sky, and two angels watch Peter's body through the clouds; his feet and hands are tied to the cross. The text underneath reads: *Crucifixion of St. Peter* by Luca Giordano.

She tries to imagine the room where Frank has to tell Catherine's parents about her death. Will they sit on a couch together, clinging to each other in the hope that the thing they feared most won't destroy them? Are family pictures staring down from the mantel, mocking them with memories of a past now dead to them? Or will the television blare in the background as her father sits in an easy chair and her mother struggles to hold back a small, yapping dog?

Samantha was sitting next to Rachel, watching afternoon cartoons, when the police knocked. She got up amid a sea of potato chips on the couch, the floor, their clothes—as if the bag had exploded. Father told them never to open the door for strangers, but something about the three strong knocks didn't sound like a request. As soon as the officer stepped inside, she heard Father behind her. She doesn't remember his words, just the dish towel falling from his hands and the sounds of her sister sobbing and gasping for breath. Rachel always cried easily, at almost anything, in fact. But Samantha is her father's daughter, she thinks.

Neither of them cried at the funeral. She walked close behind him to the casket, looking at the hard, straight angles of Father's shoulders. She kept thinking, *If I only look at his shoulders I won't cry.*

Without tears, the rest of the world might not know how deeply she had been wounded.

At the wake, people whispered of the tragedy and the injustice of it. They compared notes like students preparing for a test.

"No, the driver was coming from the other direction. He lost control of the car and crossed the median. They hit head on."

"She couldn't have seen him coming."

"She died immediately."

Empty words to fill the awkward silence, to mask the fear of mortality and the guilty relief that it was someone else.

Friends and family hugged as they left. They told her that mourning was the first step to healing. But some scars on the body never heal. Why should the heart be any different?

Samantha looks at her watch and gets up to leave for the clinic. The voices of the choir float into the rafters, echoing off the buttresses and stained-glass windows.

*I wait for the Lord, my soul waits, and in his word I hope.*

She steps outside, and a sudden wave of cold air stings her face, almost making her eyes water.

Almost.

She too is waiting. She has been waiting her entire life. Not so much for hope, but for tears—tears to release her from the pain of the past.

# Parasomnia

John Pouliot's head pounds like waves against the boardwalk. He grips the rail, trying to stare at an anchored boat across the river, but his vision blurs. Everything moves in and out of focus. He closes his eyes.

"Come on, Biggins," he mutters, then turns around slowly. Several children run past, dragging balloons in their wake; a jazz band on the promenade starts playing Duke Ellington's "East St. Louis Toodle-Oo," and lovers kiss to the rhythm of the music.

Feeling light-headed, Pouliot eases himself to the ground. He needs something to focus on, so he grabs the well-worn deck from his back pocket and starts dealing a hand. The cards feel smooth, like his father's baseball glove, and he is calmed by the sliding whisper and quick snap of each one between his fingers. He's not playing a game, just watching them spill into uneven piles. *The Suicide King and his Queen fall next to each other, and for the first time Pouliot notices their faces. The King of Hearts thrusts a sword through his own head in an act of passion, while his Queen smirks, thinking,* Only a fool would kill himself for love.

*Each pair tells a similar story of how lonely togetherness can be. The King of Spades heads off to battle, anguished that he may never see his Queen again, while she wears a stern, resolute expression. For her, kingdoms and power come before love. The Clubs look aged and tired. They have grown apart. Their faces register sadness at this unspoken truth. The Diamonds live separate lives. Perhaps it was money, infidelity, or fate that pushed them apart. No matter what, love has fallen short of their hopes, leaving the King with a gambler's face— indifferent, confident, desperate. Pouliot puts this card in his breast pocket and gathers up the rest.*

*It has taken him almost a year to figure out that he had killed Thomson and his wife. At first, he thought the visions were only nightmares. A long blade slicing someone's throat. Blood spraying against the crayon drawing of a tree and the picture frames filled with smiling faces. A circle carved into the chest of a woman's body. For months, these visions ended the same way— with a dark figure lumbering toward the front door, breathing heavily. Grabbing the doorknob, he turns to the mirror on his left. The face is too dark to see. It's swallowed by shadows.*

*Eventually, it became clear. The face was his.*

*Since then, he has seen several deaths this way. Last week, it was a woman hanging upside down in a public shower at the YMCA. The room was silent. No running water or blood swirling down the drains. No steam filling the room. Just silence, and white walls splattered in red. He decided to leave, to run away from New Orleans, from himself if he could.*

Walter Biggins was the only friend he knew who lived farther away than Shreveport. Several years ago, he and his brother moved to Wilmington to start a business, to start a new life, and no one heard from them again. The old neighborhood complained bitterly, talking of them as if they were wartime deserters, but Pouliot understood the need to make a clean break. Sometimes the past can take over, making you feel as if nothing is ever going to change.

That's also why he gambles. Each game promises something new—every win a surprise, every loss a reminder that there is always more to lose.

"J. P., I'd recognize that fat head anywhere. What the hell are you doing down there?" The cheerful voice startles him, and Pouliot looks up.

"Resting. It's about time you got here." He strains a smile and stands up. Biggins seems more athletic, even younger than he remembered. His gray suit and shiny shoes look out of place on the boardwalk.

"I was surprised to hear from you. It's been a long time." Biggins glances at Pouliot's worn, tired body. "What are you doing here?"

"Things aren't the same back home. I needed to get away."

"And you just happened to end up in Wilmington?"

"Well, I remembered that you came here and looked you up in the phone book. I just got in this afternoon."

"Remind me to get an unlisted number." Biggins laughs at his own joke, and they start walking along the riverfront.

Biggins asks about home, old friends, favorite hangouts, and past lovers. He's been away long enough to be nostalgic, and his manner becomes more relaxed as he reminisces. It's always easy to love something when you know you're never going back to it, Pouliot thinks.

"I need a place to stay for a few days. Maybe a week."
Pouliot wrings his hands as he talks. The last few years have
sapped his instinctive charm. His voice sounds unsteady, thin.
"I just have to get back on my feet. I haven't slept much since
Thomson died a few years ago, and I've ... I've been down on
my luck—"

"You never had any luck."

"You know what I mean."

"No, I don't, J. P. I don't know you anymore. We've changed.
I've changed." Biggins looks at him, then adds: "You in trouble
with the cops?"

"No. It's not like that. . . . I'm just tired of losing, that's all."

Biggins doesn't answer at first, then stops. "A week tops. I
have a new life here. I left the past behind for a reason."

"I'm just trying to do the same."

The outside of his apartment building looks worn and eroded
by years of rain, high winds, and an unforgiving sun. The peeling paint reveals colors from decades past, white-red brick and
part of a 1950s Coca-Cola advertisement painted onto the
wall. The past is pushing its way to the surface, and something
about this makes Pouliot afraid of the future.

Inside, the small apartment smells like a tuna fish sandwich
on toast. A yellowing couch with frayed pillows and no shape
fills most of the living room. Across from it, a cardboard box sup-
ports a small TV and VCR. The clock flashes 12:00 repeatedly,
and Pouliot wonders if Biggins has ever bothered to set it. Several
unmarked videotapes are scattered on the floor, and dozens more
line the shelves of a lopsided bookcase. Only a few books and
magazines have been stacked on top. Pouliot follows Biggins to
the kitchen, where Biggins opens the fridge and tosses him a beer.
They sit at a poker table with chairs that don't match. A poster of
North Carolina lighthouses is tacked to the wall behind it.

"I just moved in last week." Biggins concentrates on his drink as he says this, and Pouliot can tell that he doesn't want to talk about the apartment.

Not knowing what to say next, Pouliot asks, "How about a game?"

"Sure."

They play poker for hours, taking turns as dealer and adding new rules and variations every round. Pouliot can't remember the last time he played just for the game, not money. Maybe never, but it doesn't matter. He drinks a six-pack like water, smokes three cigarettes, and talks about old neighborhood games that lasted till sunrise. Maybe his luck is starting to change after all.

After losing four in a row, Biggins pounds the rest of his beer and says: "I need to get to bed, J. P. I've got to get up early. There's an extra room."

"Thanks." Pouliot follows him to a room filled mostly with unpacked cardboard boxes and a mattress next to a wrought-iron heater.

"I'll get you a blanket and pillow."

When Biggins leaves, Pouliot strips down to an undershirt and boxers, opens his knapsack, and pulls out a pair of hand-cuffs, laying them on the bed. The room is stuffy and thick with dust. He tries to open the window, but it's painted shut. Sitting on the mattress, he locks one side of the cuffs to his right wrist and waits.

"Here you go." Biggins walks into the room with a comforter and pillow. "I only have a—what the hell?"

"I need you to keep this for me till morning." Pouliot holds out a tiny key in the palm of his left hand.

"Jesus Christ." Biggins chuckles nervously. "This isn't some kinky sex thing, is it?"

"You wish." Pouliot smiles. "I sleepwalk, and sometimes . . . it's dangerous."

"I've never heard of anyone chaining himself to a heater before."

"How many people do you know who sleepwalk?"

"Well, none, but this seems a little fucked up. I mean, what if you have to go to the bathroom?"

"I have a strong bladder. Can you put this somewhere till morning?"

"Sure." He takes the key tentatively. "Just don't break the heater while playing with yourself."

"I'll try to keep that in mind."


### JUNE 11, 1994
### 5:33 A.M.


It's still dark outside when Biggins walks into the room and sees J. P.'s contorted body. His right shoulder and arm look as if they're trying to pull away from the rest of him, and his face seems lined with pain. Biggins steps closer and places the key on the floor. Everything is quiet except for the muffled sound of his footsteps against the carpet. He doesn't hear J. P. snoring or breathing, and the stillness makes him edgy. He hurries out of the apartment to catch the bus. The cool air feels invigorating against his face.

For the rest of the day, he wonders about sleepwalking. What did Pouliot mean about it being dangerous? What happened to make him run away? He wants some answers but doesn't know how to ask. By the time the last shift ends, his head is spinning with questions, and it's as dark outside as it was when he left this morning.

J. P. isn't there when he gets home. His bag is still on the floor in the guest room, and a card has been placed on the kitchen table—the King of Diamonds. Biggins takes this as a

*sign that he'll be back. He waits up until 1:15 A.M., watching
television and eating tortilla chips, then goes to bed. Not wanting to lock Pouliot out, he leaves the front door unbolted.*

JUNE 13, 1994
9:41 A.M.

*After reading the Sunday comics and slurping through another
bowl of Froot Loops, Biggins glances at the front page: "College
Student Killed at Wrightsville Beach." A junior at UNC Wilmington had been found on the beach early yesterday morning.
Her body was buried under the sand—arms stretched out to
her sides and feet bound together. A local resident noticed a
card protruding from the ground. The killer apparently placed
the Queen of Diamonds in her mouth.*

*Biggins puts down the paper. He can feel the already hot sun
warming the apartment, but his body is cold. Folding the paper,
he looks at the card still sitting on the table where J. P. left it.
The King's icy face stares at him, thinking not about his Queen
but about his inability to remember a time before her.*

*Biggins isn't so sure that J. P. will come back now, but just in
case, he gets up and locks the door.*

# 19
# *Scars*

Through the opening elevator doors, the sleep floor of the clinic seems abandoned. The empty hall and dim lights make everything feel hushed, and Samantha hurries quietly to her room like a latecomer to Sunday services.

Inside, Dr. Cooper is studying several charts attached to a clipboard. She checks her watch before looking up.

Samantha is twenty minutes late.

"Are you going to get ready?" Dr. Cooper asks sharply, then calls for the nurse.

"Sorry." Samantha expects Dr. Cooper to leave so she can undress, but apparently her tardiness makes such a courtesy unnecessary. She removes her bra without taking off her shirt, feeling uneasy as Dr. Cooper watches her body with clinical detachment.

"Where's Dr. Clay?"

"Still sick."

"Did you speak to him?"

"I'm not a secretary, Samantha. He left a message with my office saying he'd be out again."

Samantha slides her jeans to the floor and steps out of them awkwardly. "I'm surprised he's missing another day. I mean, the study just started, and—"

"Hi!" Nurse Bogart bounces cheerfully into the room. Samantha is glad to see her.

When she smiles, Nurse Bogart's face glows like a blushing schoolgirl's. Some of the freckles and a small scar above her lip disappear. Without them, her other features look disproportionately small, as if she's tasting something sour.

"You don't think it's serious, do you?" Samantha continues to Dr. Cooper, while smiling back at Nurse Bogart.

Dr. Cooper glances up from her clipboard. "Look, I'm not his doctor. He'll be back when he feels better, okay?" She leaves the room without waiting for a response.

"Sorry about that," Nurse Bogart whispers. "She's really anal about punctuality."

"I noticed."

The nurse laughs. After helping Samantha into bed, she starts placing the electrodes on her temples.

Looking up at her, Samantha can see the vertical scar above Nurse Bogart's lip more clearly.

"How did you get that?"

"Oh, a few years ago I was on a vacation in Brazil with some girlfriends, and one morning I woke up with this bump on my lip. I thought it was a pimple or something, but every day it got bigger and bigger until it split open."

"What happened?"

"I don't know. I went to several dermatologists, but none of them had ever seen anything like it. One thought it was an allergic reaction to a bug bite, but he wasn't sure. That's the strangest part."

"What?"

"Like you, everybody notices. They want me to explain it, but

I can't. I'll never know." She pauses, looking at the wires attached to Samantha's body. "I just think it's weird that something like that can happen in your sleep. Without your knowing it, something can change you forever. All right, you're set."

"Thanks, Nurse Bogart."

"Call me Meredith."

"See you in the morning, Meredith."

## 20

# Master of Escape

THURSDAY

*H*arry Houdini could escape almost anything—chains, strait-jackets, prison cells, coffins, sunken chests, milk jugs. He made a career out of tempting fate and cheating death—jumping into icy rivers with his hands bound, hanging upside down from tall buildings, being buried alive.

One morning, while resting on a couch in his dressing room, Houdini had a visitor. A young man wearing a black overcoat entered the small room, which smelled of sweat and rotting flowers. He pulled up a chair, looking at Houdini's sallow skin and the dark circles under his eyes.

The visitor didn't introduce himself. He simply started talking, about sleeplessness and death, but Houdini was too exhausted to concentrate. He had another show in a few hours, and all of this listening made him tired. He usually did the talking.

"Some people yearn for the peace that death offers, but you treat death like a game. It isn't a game, Mr. Houdini." The young man paused, then abruptly changed the subject. "I hear that you *can withstand any blow to the stomach. Would you mind if I tried?"*

*When Houdini was younger and healthier, facing this type of challenge had helped his career, but even when he had nothing to prove, he couldn't resist a challenge. He accepted with a smile and started lifting himself off the couch to get ready. Before he could stand, the man struck his abdomen repeatedly. The blows caused a crippling pain, and Houdini motioned him to stop, muttering breathlessly: "That will do."*

*Several days later, on October 31, 1926, Houdini died from an infection following a ruptured appendix.*

As Don tells Samantha this story over the phone, her head pounds. She searches her desk for aspirin and takes two with a sip of coffee. She's been unconsciously drawing circles on a pad of paper, linking them together like a chain. She adds one more, and something about the doodle recalls the dream that woke her this morning. A closed fist, partially buried in mud, opens slowly. Blood seeps from a circle carved into the skin.

"Don't take this the wrong way, Don, but why are you telling me this?"

"It's the next part you'll be interested in."

"Then why didn't you start there?"

"It's a better story this way."

"Don—"

"Okay, fine. When the stranger left, Houdini tried to follow him. He wanted to ask why he had come, why he talked so much about sleeplessness and death. But the pain in his abdomen was too great. That night, he was admitted to the hospital."

"I'm not in one of your classes—"

"The next morning, Houdini saw the man's picture in the paper. His name was Ezekiel Armus. He had been stabbed to death in an alley only hours after leaving Houdini's room. The police found another man by his side, unconscious, who later claimed that he had been assaulted by Armus, then stabbed. But his injuries were minor."

"Then what happened?" she asks eagerly.

"According to a newspaper article, the man was charged with murder, but after that, there is no record of him."

"So you think Armus was a victim of the curse I told you about?" Her voice is soft and tentative.

"No."

"Then why did you call?"

"I'm worried about you, Sam. After reading your e-mail the other day, I thought you were crazy." He pauses, then adds sarcastically, "Even more so than usual."

"So all of this is just a coincidence? Armus's insomnia. The fact that both men were *bleeding* when the police found them. There are probably dozens of documents that link these crimes back to the count—"

"You're probably right," he interrupts. "But even if I found similar stories dating back to the eighteenth century, it wouldn't prove anything. You're only seeing a connection here because you're looking for one."

"So it's not possible that it's really there?" she adds with notable irritation.

"Well, I think there *is* a connection. You said it yourself. Catherine listened to this piece. Phebe was a professional musician, so she must have known it. Both of them had trouble sleeping. Maybe that's how the killer chooses his victims."

Silence.

"Have you considered that these clues might be for someone like you? A person who knows something about music. A person who hasn't slept in such a long time that. . . . that she's desperate for answers?"

"Is that what you think?" Her voice wavers.

"What if you're next on the list, Sam? Have you thought about that?"

Silence.

"Are you still there? Did you hear me?"

"Yeah, I heard you. I just realized something."

"What?"

"I've gotta go."

She hangs up before Don can protest, and she dials the clinic. *Come on, come on. Answer....*

## 21

## *The Face*

Meredith is reluctant to help. Through the receiver, Samantha can hear her tapping a pencil against the desk.

"I can't give out his address, Sam. If anyone finds out, I'll lose my job. Besides, he hasn't called in yet, so he's probably coming back tonight."

"It can't wait. He might be in danger."

"Danger?"

"I'll explain later."

"I really can't—"

"How about this. I'll read out all the addresses for Robert Clays in the phone book, and you just say yes to the right one. That way, you don't have to do anything wrong, and I don't have to call a dozen people."

"Is this the kind of stuff they teach you in law school?"

"Yes, we have an entire course on deception."

After two names, Meredith just gives her the address, and Samantha drives to Dr. Clay's house in the Berkeley hills. Her car cuts through the thick rain, and her windows fog from the cold. The defroster, which has been broken for months, clears only a small circle on the passenger side, so Samantha rubs the windshield with her sleeve and leans forward to see. The oncoming headlights are blinding, and she squints like Janet Leigh before stopping at the Bates Motel.

The small, unlit road dead-ends in a stony cliff. On the other side of the street, Dr. Clay's shingled house is built on the downslope. No lights glow from the inside. No flowers bloom in the rose garden beside it. A long hill leads away from the side of the house, and at the bottom, construction equipment surrounds a large rectangular hole.

Samantha runs from her car to the front porch. It is piled with rotting firewood and covered in a thin layer of moss. She steps deliberately to the doorbell. A strong gust of wind sprays her with rainwater.

"Hello?"

To herself, her voice sounds faint, even vulnerable, in the darkness. She waits a few moments, listening to the rain strike the rooftop and rush forcefully through the gutters. She knocks, her knuckles numb from the cold, and tries the knob. It opens.

The entryway feels colder than the air outside, and after she steps over the threshold, she stands perfectly still, unsure if she should go any farther.

"Dr. Clay? It's me, Samantha. From the clinic."

Nothing but the drumroll of rain.

Two walls of glass face the hillside. A few lights glow in the distance, but everything nearby is dark. Samantha tries the light switch, then a floor lamp by the couch. No power. Her footsteps echo loudly against the hardwood floor as she walks to the middle of the room. A bolt of lightning cracks the sky.

"Dr. Clay?"

Her voice is swallowed by thunder rumbling through the

floor. She steps into the dining room tentatively. A wilted salad has been left on the table, and an overturned glass of red wine is pooling like oil on a damp city street. Cold wet winds rush through an open door leading to the deck. The floor is glazed with rainwater.

Passing through the dining room, Samantha enters the kitchen. Even in the dark, everything seems white: cabinets, tiled floor and countertop, toaster oven, microwave. Two windows look out onto the street where her car is parked. The sink is empty except for a wooden cutting board resting against one side. Walking past the knife rack, she spins it, listening to its gravelly rotation.

Something slams and rumbles beneath her.

She jumps at the noise. There must be a lower level or basement, she thinks. She waits for another sound—something other than rain and thunder—but the pounding of her heart fills each ear like water. She takes a few steps and realizes that she has almost come full circle. The entryway of the house is directly in front of her.

Then she notices a door to her left in the connecting passageway. She stares at it for a few moments before deciding to follow every horror-movie cliché.

The latch slides open loosely and easily. Inside, a narrow spiral staircase descends sharply, but it's too dark to see beyond a few steps. Samantha reaches for a light switch, feeling along the wall. She finds it, sliding it up, but nothing happens. She turns back to the kitchen and starts looking through drawers for a flashlight: utensils, matches, rubber bands, plastic bags, tinfoil, a deck of cards. She finds one. With batteries.

Another crash.

It sounds much louder through the open door, and she almost drops the light. She imagines hearing heavy footsteps behind her and the background music from *Halloween*. Before losing her courage altogether, she starts down the steps.

The crimson walls seem thick with moisture but are dry to the touch. The light bounces off them at angles, and the glow makes her hands look red. Her shoes squeak on the small steps, and she almost loses her balance at the first turn. Bracing herself against the wall, she continues more slowly. The space seems tighter and warmer with each step. She considers taking off her jacket, but then something drips on her head. She leans back against the wall, thinking about the woman who found Phebe. Another drop falls from the ceiling. She exhales and shines the flashlight overhead. Water. A leak from the rain.

The basement at the bottom of the stairs is small and cluttered. With her first step, Samantha accidentally kicks an open toolbox. The scraping clash of metal tools against the cement makes her cringe. So much for the element of surprise, she thinks. A clothesline draped with towels and shirts divides the room. A washer and dryer stick out from beneath the staircase, and several cardboard boxes, labeled with a black felt-tip pen, have been stacked against the west wall—Books, Ugly Clothes, College Notes, Trains.

Another crash. The walls shudder.

It's coming from somewhere behind the closed door at the other end of the room. Samantha walks to it slowly and grabs the brass handle. It turns easily, but the door won't open. She tries again, wrestling with the warped plywood. Pushing with her shoulder, she opens it abruptly. She stumbles into a studio with a grand piano, a cello, shelves of music, an old couch, and a covered easel. It's cold and damp from another open door leading to the backyard.

Samantha moves through the room toward the easel and lifts the cover. A face glued together from other images, a collage. Different-colored eyes, asymmetrical ears, cheeks that droop under the weight of so many angular parts. It doesn't look like one face but like hundreds, staring out both individually and together. Each one taking shape for a moment before getting lost in the others.

But the face isn't complete. There is an empty space where the mouth should be and a partial chin. Samantha wonders how many more pieces will be needed to finish it. Looking more closely, she imagines seeing Dr. Clay's face lost somewhere inside.

The door swings open from a gust of wind and slams into the piano bench. Moving to the door frame, she looks outside. The rain falls thick as party streamers in the white beam of her flashlight, and the muddy ground slides steadily toward that rectangular hole at the bottom of the slope. She pulls her jacket tighter and steps outside, almost slipping several times as she makes her way to the pit. From the construction equipment, she assumes that a patio and small swimming pool are being built.

A ladder leans against one side of the pit and descends about six feet into the ground. The uneven bottom is covered with a thin layer of water, and the walls seem to vibrate with oozing mud. The light reflects off something silver, and Samantha levels the beam. She is too far away to see the shape clearly, but it has an oddly lustrous surface. She leans closer. It shines like a distant star on a still, black night.

The wind-blown rain stings her face as she steadies the ladder. It sinks slightly into the ground with each step, shifting under the weight of her body. She steps off the last rung, grimacing as mud spills over her ankles. She smells the fresh soil as she walks to the center of the pit. Her right foot disappears into a deep puddle, and she pulls up too quickly. The shoe slips off with a slurping sound.

"Damn it!"

She stoops down and sticks her hand into the mud, feeling for the shoe. It is icy cold and thick. Her nose wrinkles as she reaches deeper. Nothing. She lifts up her hand. Dark slime drips from it slowly.

She is about to try again when she notices the silvery object near her feet. She picks it up—a watch, partially buried in the mud. She wonders if it is Dr. Clay's but can't remember him wearing one.

The beam of light catches another object. Something protruding from the ground a few feet from her, near the opposite wall. She moves closer, feeling the slime seep through her sock with every step. It looks like a pronged garden tool. She reaches for it. It's smoother than she expects—

*Fingers . . . a hand . . . an arm stretching to the wall.*

She drops the flashlight, loses balance, and falls sideways onto her knees. In a crawl, she lunges forward, seeing the outline of a body upside down against the wall. She starts wiping, frantic. She can see part of a shirt. Moving her hands closer to the ground, she feels a face taking shape underneath her fingers and palms. A body suspended from above. She searches for her flashlight. Thick handfuls of slime ooze between her fingers. She feels the metal rod in her hand. The light flickers, visible again above the murky water.

*Dr. Clay.*

Samantha stands up. With the light, she can trace his body, doused in mud, hanging against the wall of the pit. His ankles bound with rope and fastened to something over the ledge. His arms loose, lying on the ground beneath him. She shines the light on his face again. His mouth is slightly open.

She thinks of the black space on the canvas.

Stumbling toward the ladder, she wants to scream and weep at the same time. She steps onto the first rung, and a light shines from above her. She can see the outline of a figure standing on the ledge. The light blinds her. A voice calls out, but she can't discern any words. At that moment, she imagines suffocating, the mud closing in around her. With each step, the ladder only seems to sink farther into the ground, and she wonders if she'll ever find a way out.

She wonders if Houdini could.

Dripping with mud, handcuffed, soaking wet, and missing a shoe, Samantha sits in the backseat of a squad car. The police officer patrolling the neighborhood that night saw a flashlight beam bouncing up and down in the yard. He decided to take a closer look and found someone crouching in front of Dr. Clay's body. Samantha didn't try to explain herself as he helped her out of the pit. She merely said, "Call Detective Snair."

"Who the hell is that?" He put her in the car and called for backup.

Over a dozen officers are searching the house and backyard when Snair shows up with Officer Kincaid and the forensics team from Phebe's apartment. Snair speaks with several men from the Berkeley Police Department before walking over to Samantha and opening the door.

"Officer Kincaid is going to take you to the station for questioning."

Kincaid stands a few feet behind him, smiling sheepishly.

"What do you want to know?" Sam asks as she holds the blanket around her shoulders for warmth.

"Not here," Snair says.

"Why not?" Samantha snaps. "I'm tired and dirty, and I want to go home as soon as possible."

"That's not going to happen. You're under arrest for the murder of Dr. Robert Clay."

"What!"

"Officer Kincaid will—"

"Are you out of your mind?" She leans forward.

"Don't move," Snair says forcefully. His expression doesn't

change. "You were found positioning the victim's body in his backyard."

*"Positioning the body?"*

"What are you doing here?" Globs of rainwater drip from his hard, angled face.

"I was worried. He missed several days at the clinic, and with what happened to Phebe, I thought—"

"You're full of shit," he says, glowering at her. "You've had access to every crime scene. You knew both Phebe and Dr. Clay. Your prints were found at Catherine's place, and they'll turn up here."

"Of course they will. I told the other officer that I looked inside first. And if it weren't for me, you never would've found Catherine's apartment. Frank and I called *you!*"

He turns and signals Kincaid.

"You can't arrest me."

"I already have." He starts to walk away.

"Snair . . . Snair!"

He turns around.

"What aren't you telling me?"

He steps back to the open door, leaning close enough to be inside. "You don't work for the Palici Corporation. I checked. They've never even heard of you." He stops, turning to Kincaid. "Get her out of here."

"Come on, Snair. That doesn't make me a killer. Frank asked for my help with Catherine's disappearance." His expression remains stony. "You can't possibly think I committed these crimes."

"I'll tell you what I think. I think you're a liar who's going to spend the night in jail. Kincaid"—his face in profile to her—"she talks to no one but me."

"Someone else is in danger. Go to the clinic. Ask about Endymion's Circle. Find a patient named Arty." Her voice gets louder with each command as he walks to the house. "There's not much time!"

"Come on, Ms. Ranvali. We need to go." Kincaid looks at her nervously, then pulls out his inhaler.

*Hssst.*

# Parasomnia

*Pouliot doesn't know exactly where he is, and he doesn't care. The dark, noisy bar seems to crowd around him, and the smoke clings to his body like a wool sweater. He looks up from the empty glass in front of him and signals the bartender for another. His bloodshot eyes burn relentlessly, and the muscles in his legs ache. He has lived somewhere between sleeping and waking for so long that he thinks about only one thing— dying. He can't remember a time when he ever wanted anything else.*

*"Six-fifty." The bartender's hoarse voice cuts through the thick air.*

*Pouliot hands him the money, then pulls out the deck from his back pocket. The worn cards feel soft between his fingers as he shuffles.*

"*Do you know any tricks?*" Next to him, a petite woman with curly brown hair and green eyes watches his hands. She takes a sip from her martini and smiles.

"No, I'm not good with tricks." Pouliot looks at her body. A tight black skirt clings to her tan thighs, and several thin silver bracelets cover each wrist.

"I see. You're one of those honest men." She laughs delicately.

"I wouldn't say that."

"A gambler, then?"

"Not anymore. I used to play back home."

"Where's that?"

"New Orleans."

"I've always wanted to go there. Any city with drive-through daiquiri stands has to be a good place to live."

"It's a definite plus. So what about you?"

"I'm a local girl. I work at a library."

"Doing what?"

"Enforcing nuclear disarmament treaties. What do you think? I stack books. I check them out. I stack them again."

"So you're a librarian."

"That's generally what we're called."

"I've never met a librarian before."

"Is it everything you hoped it would be?"

"What?"

"Meeting a librarian."

He looks over her body again. "You're not what I expected."

"I don't wear this to work." She takes another sip and holds out her hand. "I'm Veronica, by the way."

"J. P." Their hands touch briefly.

"So, J. P., do you mind if we go somewhere else? I hate the VD scene."

"VD scene?"

"Valentine's Day. Haven't you noticed all the disgusting displays of affection?"

"Not really."

"Ass grabbing, clinging, slobbering. I feel like I'm back in kindergarten . . . well, except for the ass-grabbing part. Though I remember a boy in fourth grade who used to pinch my—"

"Look, you . . . you don't want to know me."

She finishes the last sip of her drink and smiles. "Who said anything about getting to know you? I was just planning to talk about myself." She stands up and walks to the door. Pouliot follows.

After all, he is a gambler.

Across the street, the Lucky Stars Motel is open for business. It's a place where most clients pay by the hour, and the management doesn't ask questions. Behind the front desk, a dark-skinned man with jet-black hair watches porn on a small black-and-white TV. He has no bottom front teeth, and his mustard-colored shirt is stained and frayed. Without looking away from the screen, he puts the key on the countertop. Veronica grabs it—Room 304—and puts down several folded bills. She leads the way without pausing to figure out which staircase to use.

Inside, the room smells like smoke and sweat. The only floor lamp gives off a faint yellow light that makes everything look sickly. The varnish is peeling off the wooden desk and matching chair, and like the rest of the furniture in the room, they're ready to collapse. The comforter on the king-size bed is dark green with circular stains, and one of the drapes has been torn. Most of it lies on the floor like a discarded nightgown. A thin white veil still covers the window, which looks out onto a brick wall.

*Veronica walks to the nightstand and opens the top drawer. Without saying a word, she pulls out the green, hard-covered Bible and a pen. She looks up at him. "What does J. P. stand for?"*

*"John Pouliot."*

*"That's a nice name." She writes something on the inside jacket and closes the book.*

*"What's that for?"*

*"To remember."*

*She puts the Bible on the desk and leads him to bed. The floor creaks as they step forward, and Pouliot suddenly becomes afraid—of lying down, of falling asleep. She pushes him back onto the mattress and climbs above him. Her hair falls down the sides of her face like a waterfall. The yellow light behind her flickers. She leans forward to kiss him and feels his stubble scratch her cheeks. Unbuttoning his shirt with increasing urgency, she touches his chest with her fingertips. His head and neck feel as if they're burning. The heat of his body seems almost unbearable. Then her foot bumps his ankle as she moves down to unbuckle his pants.*

*"Ouch," she mutters and looks at his legs. "What's this?" She tries to grab the metal object taped around his ankle, but he tears it from his body first. She yells at the sight of the knife and stumbles back toward the desk. He lunges at her. Before he can get to his feet, she smashes a glass ashtray into his temple, knocking him to a sitting position on the bed. He swings the knife blindly, slicing across her abdomen. He grabs her throat with his left hand.*

*She dives for the knife, breaking his grip, and bites his wrist with such force that she feels the bone. He moans, shoving her onto the floor with both hands. She gets up and runs to the door so quickly that he doesn't catch her until she's turning the knob.*

*He wraps his bleeding arm around her waist and starts pulling. Suddenly, she pushes against the door with her right leg, sending them both tumbling to the floor.*

*She tries to get away, but his grip is too tight. She throws her head back and hits his cheekbone. As she rolls off him and gets to her knees, he stabs her below the rib cage.*

*The pain is paralyzing.*

*It burns like fire racing along a windy trail of gasoline. She wants to scream, but can't find the breath. She gasps for air as he gets up slowly and unsteadily. In desperation, she flings herself at him. The knife flies from his hand. She dives for it and rolls on her back. He crawls above her in a moment but doesn't see the blade as she thrusts it into his upper abdomen. Then the strength leaves her body, and the room begins to spin. She tries to see over his bulky frame, which lies on top of her.*

*Both of their bodies are sticky with blood.*

*Everything goes out of focus. The hazy yellow light fades into blackness. . . .*

FEBRUARY 15, 1997
8:27 P.M.

*Somehow she's made it as far as home and her blue-and-white striped couch. She wipes the drool from her mouth and looks at her watch.* Crap. *Her face feels numb from the pillow, and her side aches as if she has been kicked by a soccer player. In the bathroom, the fluorescent light buzzes. Brown stains cover the front of her torn blouse. Last night starts coming back to her in flashes: J. P. at the bar; a fight in the motel room; his body on the floor this morning; the cab ride back to her apartment.*

*She lifts up her blouse and inspects the cuts across her stom-*

ach and rib cage. *The bleeding has stopped. She touches them tenderly.*

*Walking back into the living room, she turns on a lamp and sees the green Bible on the glass table. She doesn't remember taking it but must have done so out of habit. It looks new and even crackles when she opens the cover. In the top left-hand corner, the name John Pouliot is written in her handwriting. She throws it away and walks to the bedroom.*

*The sliding glass door to the closet is open, and a box peeks out from underneath her jackets and coats. It's too heavy to put on one of the higher shelves, so she keeps it on the floor. Sliding it over to the bed, she sits with it between her feet. Her side aches as she leans down. Inside, there are twenty-three bibles. She takes several out of the box and starts opening them. Each one is inscribed with a name and the hope that her doctors are wrong.*

*Doug Williams, Dave Sollors, Alan Bergman, James Larsen . . .*

It all started in college—the day Veronica skipped sociology class and met Marcus at the gym. Sweat was the one thing they had in common. They ran together, played racquetball competitively, and never missed an intramural basketball match. For someone so athletic, Marcus didn't move much during sex. He always stayed on his back, quietly concentrating on his own pleasure. He mostly kept his hands behind his head, scratching his scalp audibly while sweat dripped from every pore. The bed in her dorm room was small, so she always made him go back to his room to sleep. She needed space. And some time to dry off.

Since Marcus closed his eyes as soon as they undressed, Veronica figured that he didn't really care who was there. He tried to reassure her with talk of love and passion. But whatever fire may have burned for her was extinguished in a sea of sweat when he found out she was pregnant. The next day he *offered to pay for half the abortion and said nothing more. He just sat across the room with his hands in his lap.*

*He didn't look at her.*

*She cried after he left.*

*The day before her appointment, she stood at the top of a staircase in the gym. Trying to decide between life and death amid three floors of smelly bodies, Veronica listened to a cacophony of sounds: basketballs pounding on the court, referees with piccolo-whistles, the hum of rowing machines. She had been nauseated and light-headed in the mornings for over a week and shouldn't have been there. She started swaying from the smells and sounds until she fell. She didn't faint—she remembers seeing herself tumble down the cement steps. But she didn't try to stop the fall either.*

*The ambulance came. She bled.*

*The pain didn't scare her as much as the blood. Her shorts were sticking to her thighs with black-red blood, and she saw her body as something separate. Afterward, the doctors told her she would never be able to conceive again.*

*Joshua Trachtenberg, Keith Perkins, Albert Constantini, Jonathan Lears . . .*

*The memories of those evenings flash in front of her like scenes in a movie, but tonight she fast-forwards through the details. These stories all end the same way. She is still waiting for the miracle that will change everything. She puts the Bibles back into the box.*

I need to call the police about last night, *she thinks, but her body seems paralyzed. Lying back on the mattress, she looks at the ceiling. Several white stickers of stars, moons, and comets are clustered directly above the bed—probably put there by some child years ago. At one time they must have glowed yellow-green; now, only their outline is visible. The child is long since gone, and the apartment is perfectly still. There is nothing here but Veronica, looking up at the faded stickers and thinking about a box of Bibles.*

"I'll just rest a bit longer," she mutters.

## 22

# No Returns

Samantha slept soundly on the hard cot and woke up wondering if Dr. Clay had given her the gift of sleep after all. Fluorescent lights buzz like mosquitoes above her ears, and the circular yellow stain on the ceiling moves in and out of focus as her eyes adjust. It suddenly turns red, like the mark carved into Phebe's chest. *No.* She shuts her eyes and opens them again. The yellow stain returns. Is this the price for sleep? Terrible visions and nightmares that foreshadow devastating truths?

*After Frank moved in with her, Father said, "Samantha, for everything there is a price. Don't take what you're not ready to pay for."*

*"But this is about love," she said defensively.*

*"Especially with love." His voice wasn't sad, just matter-of-fact, like a librarian's.*

*Samantha didn't understand him at the time. She was in love with Frank. Confident. Arrogant, believing that what they had couldn't be lost or stolen. But eventually, things changed. Frank left because he couldn't keep giving to someone who only knew how to take. At least, that's how he saw it. And Samantha finally understood her father. For everything there is a price, and she discovered the cost too late.*

*Perhaps, she thinks, the only true gifts come from strangers. Like giving loose change to someone on a street corner. It might be a meaningless gesture, one that has more to do with guilt than caring, but at least you'll never ask for it back. Love shouldn't be something you can return like a present after Christmas, hoping to exchange it for something better or cheaper.*

*It just shouldn't.*

The metallic clash of a gate startles her, and she stands up. Footsteps click and echo against the linoleum as she waits. Louder and louder. They're not lumbering like Snair's, but even and fluid.

"Frank?"

"I always knew you'd end up behind bars." He smiles.

"Snair put me in here." She stands. "He found out that I don't work for the Palici Corporation."

"I know."

"You have to get to the clinic. Arty is in danger—Dr. Clay was killed, like the others. I went to his house—"

"I know." Frank nods.

Samantha stands quietly now, both hands gripping the bars. She turns her head to the side. "Snair thinks I did it, but he only asked me a few questions last night."

Another set of footsteps gets closer.

"The guard is coming to let you out," Frank says. "The charges have been dropped."

"Why?"

"Well, you're innocent, aren't you?"

"Funny." She forces a smile.

"I think Snair was just looking for an excuse to arrest you."

"Bastard," she mutters.

"I'm not sure I blame him."

The guard steps between them and opens the gate. Frank thanks him, and Samantha heads down the hall without waiting.

Frank hurries to fall in step beside her. "You shouldn't have gone to Dr. Clay's by yourself. It was dangerous. The killer could have been there."

"I didn't know he was murdered."

"You thought it was a possibility, Sam. You should have waited."

Samantha doesn't respond. Their footsteps echo loudly in the corridor. She looks straight ahead.

"So how did you find him, anyway?"

"The phone book."

"He's not listed."

She glances at him without breaking her stride. "Did I mention I lost a shoe?"


The blue sky smiles overhead with no memory of yesterday's storm. Samantha lingers a moment in the crisp clean air before getting into the car.

"We need to go to the clinic."

"The police checked—no Arty or Dr. Cooper. But they're keeping an eye on the clinic and both of their apartments throughout the day. If they show up, I'll get a call."

"No Dr. Cooper?"

"Well, let's not jump—"

"*What about Meredith?*" The question pops out of her mouth as if the wind were just knocked out of her.

"Who?"

"Nurse Bogart. She works at the clinic."

"She must have been the nurse that Snair spoke with last night. What about her?"

"She's being protected, right? Snair took her into custody?"

"I doubt it. He was looking for Arty."

"If Dr. Cooper is missing, the killer is after everyone involved with the study, not just the participants and Dr. Clay. We've got to find her, Frank!"

He opens his cell phone and makes a call. "Detective Snair, please. It's urgent."

Samantha takes a quick shower and changes while Frank waits in the living room. He doesn't hear her enter, and she watches silently for a moment. Standing by her desk, he holds Phebe's porcelain frog in his left palm. His body seems too big for the room, like a piece of furniture that doesn't quite fit, and she wonders if something more than the last six months makes him look so out of place.

"Thanks for coming to get me this morning." She is drying her hair with a white towel.

Frank turns, surprised to find her looking at him. "No problem." He puts the frog back on the desk carefully. "I checked up on Maxwell Harris, Catherine's boyfriend."

"And?"

"His body was too damaged by the train to provide any useful evidence, but the Durham Police don't think he killed himself."

"What changed?"

"An eyewitness account. A homeless man living under the bridge saw it. A few days later, the cops brought him in for public drunkenness, and he started talking about a guy being pushed off the bridge."

"Did he see him? The killer, I mean?"

"Not clearly, but"—Frank pauses—"he thinks he was a she."

"Catherine?" Samantha whispers.

"Well, she didn't have an alibi, but without any evidence, the police couldn't even suggest it, not the daughter of one of the wealthiest families in North Carolina. Even if this guy were sober enough to identify her, it would never stand up in court."

Frank's cell phone rings, and he pulls it out of his jacket.

"Yeah." He leans over to the desk and starts writing. "Thanks." He turns to her. "I've got Meredith's address. A patrol car is on the way there now. You ready?"

"Almost." Samantha puts down the towel and grabs the jacket draped over the back of the kitchen chair. "So I guess Catherine's parents hired you to find her killer this time."

"Yes. And on my behalf, the corporation asked the San Francisco Police Department to give you access to any other crime scenes. If it weren't for them, you'd still be in jail while Detective Snair took his time processing the paperwork."

"You don't need to get defensive, Frank. I wasn't implying anything."

"Yes you were." He looks at her briefly, then holds open the front door. "Come on, let's go."

# 23
# *Tiresias*

In front of Meredith's apartment, someone sifts through a shopping cart filled with plastic bags and aluminum cans. Samantha notices the shoulder-length black hair, leathery skin, and hands cracked and blistered from years in the sun. As she gets out of the car, the figure smiles at her, then goes back to work. He has oddly feminine features. A small nose, tight lips. His left eye is cloudy and unnervingly still. Hanging from his neck, he wears a silver pendant of two snakes joined together. She smells smoke and urine on his clothes.

Frank hurries up the front steps.

She starts to follow when a voice seems to whisper suddenly in her ear.

"She's not in danger."

She turns, but the man is already pushing his cart in the other direction. The wheels grind and squeak, as if reluctant to move.

"Meredith?" Frank calls out, ringing the bell a second time. He knocks impatiently, then tries the door. It slides open.

Samantha is afraid of what the unlocked door might mean.

The living room is sparsely furnished with a black leather couch, two matching chairs, and a television. A bouquet of sunflowers fills an indigo vase on the coffee table, and a framed print of a woman standing alone in the wings of a theater hangs on the far wall. Samantha steps closer. Edward Hopper's *New York Movie.* The hardwood floors shine from a pungent cleaner that still lingers in the warm air. An ironing board blocks the entryway to the kitchen.

Frank calls out again, but no one answers.

An oversized table and an exercise bike make the living room feel crammed. The *Chronicle* is open to the section with movie listings, and an unfinished cup of coffee has been placed carefully in the center of a coaster. The mug is still warm. On the other side of the room, a narrow staircase leads to the lower level, and Samantha walks downstairs without waiting for Frank. The space gets darker with each step. At the bottom of the steps, a bookshelf crowds the wall to her right. At the end of the hall, there are two closed doors across from each other, and having to choose between them makes her feel like a game-show contestant. She opens the one to her left, calling out Meredith's name. Her voice cracks.

The small bedroom smells like potpourri and vanilla-scented candles. A sliding glass door leads only onto a sunless porch, yet it still manages to brighten the room. A few clothes are scattered on the floor by the closet, and the bed is made. Samantha sees Meredith's smile and scarred lip in various pictures on the nightstand and dresser. She stands on a long sandy beach with friends, beneath the Eiffel Tower, and at the Hard Rock Café in London. One man appears frequently, and in a separate frame engraved with *I love you, Pete*, she kisses his cheek. They look happy.

In the corner, several papers clutter the writing table, and Samantha walks over to it. The loose sheet on top is handwritten.

*Dearest,*

*We've been apart for so long that I've gotten used to the pain of missing you, although it makes my throat dry and my body numb.*

*All my life, I thought love would fill me like water fills an empty glass, but loving you has only left me thirsty. It's not you. It's loving you now, loving you from so far away, that dries me up. Love isn't about finding the right person. It's about finding the right moment. And I'm afraid that I'll miss this if we stay with each other. I need to keep searching for a love that will fill me. We both do.*

*I'm going to miss knowing that you're there, even when you're thousands of miles away. But this is the best way. We have moments to be waiting for.*

*I still love you.*
*M.*


"What the hell are you doing!" Meredith stands at the door with Frank by her side.

"Uh, looking for you. We were—I was—"

"Reading my letter." She steps toward Samantha, taking the sheet from her hand.

"I'm sorry. . . . It's beautiful." Samantha stands still, arms at her sides.

"It's private," Meredith says softly.

"Meredith," Frank interrupts, "as I was saying upstairs, we think you might be in danger."

She faces him and stands quietly.

"Almost everyone connected with Dr. Clay's study has either disappeared or been killed in the last week," Frank continues. "We want to put you into protective custody. A patrol car will be here any minute."

"You're a cop?" She turns to Samantha, obviously shocked at what she thinks is another betrayal.

"No, I'm . . . I'm kind of like a consultant."

"A consultant? Were you lying to Dr. Clay about your sleep disorders? Did you know we were in danger?"

"No! I haven't been able to sleep for months—" Samantha looks at Frank, pleadingly at first, then back to Meredith. She pauses.

"Sam?" Frank asks.

"Neither could Dr. Clay, could he?"

"What?" Meredith looks confused.

"Did Dr. Clay have sleeping problems?"

"Yeah, I think so. Every once in a while he complained about not getting enough sleep."

"What about you?"

"No. Never."

"Then why do you work at a sleep clinic?"

"It's an internship for one of my electives. I'm getting my master's in nursing at UCSF. Why—"

"What do you know about Dr. Cooper? What kind of doctor is she?"

"Actually, she's a psychiatrist. What does—"

"Why would a psychiatrist be asked to fill in for Dr. Clay?" Samantha interrupts.

"Well, they're friends."

"That doesn't make her qualified to conduct the study."

"You don't need to specialize in sleep disorders to administer the treatment. Anyone could do it."

Someone knocks loudly on the door upstairs. "Hello? Ms. Bogart? San Francisco Police Department."

"We're down here. Hold on!" Frank yells, then hurries upstairs.

"I've got to go too. The police are going to keep an eye on you for a few days." Samantha moves closer to Meredith, who looks down at the letter in her hand.

"It's going to be all right," Samantha continues, trying to sound reassuring, but she can't tell if the words are for Meredith or herself.

"You shouldn't have read my letter." Meredith's voice is quiet, and something about it recalls the way Father used to express his disappointment in her, calmly, succinctly.

"I'm sorry," Samantha says.

"Me too."

Samantha watches Meredith turn and walk up the stairs.

Outside, Frank leans against the car with his arms crossed in front of his chest. He watches the police car as it pulls away with Meredith in the backseat.

Samantha waves, but Meredith doesn't turn around to see. "At least she let me help her pack." The words sound as if Samantha were asking a question.

"She'll be all right," he says.

Samantha turns, nodding and lowering her eyes.

"So why all the questions about Dr. Cooper?"

She raises her face eagerly to his. "I don't think the killings are about this study or Dr. Clay. They're about people with severe sleep disorders."

"What's the difference?"

"Other clinics may be targeted." She stands, clasping her hands in front of her nervously.

"You mean now that you and Meredith are being protected."

"I don't think Meredith is in any danger. She's not an insomniac. She doesn't suffer like the killer does, so she can't be martyred for it."

"Martyred?"

"After the count lost his ability to sleep, he tried to take sleep away from those around him. He wanted others to suffer in the same way. He kept his servants up till all hours. He—"

"None of that explains why the killer started with Dr. Clay's study," Frank says abruptly. He doesn't want to hear any more about Goldberg or the count's curse. "There has to be a reason."

"'*She's not in danger.*'" Samantha mutters, then looks up the street. The homeless man is bent over a garbage can at the end of the block. "How did he know?"

"What?"

"Hold on."

She jogs toward the homeless man, watching him as he finishes searching through the garbage can and starts pushing his cart around the corner. When Samantha reaches the side street, she half expects to see no one, but he is standing there, perfectly still, as if he has been waiting for her.

"Hi." She stops. "Uh...did you say something to me back there?" Now that she stands in front of him, waiting, she feels foolish.

Silence.

"I think you said, 'She's not in danger.'" Samantha continues. "What did you mean by that?"

His cloudy eye focuses directly on her, and the snakes around his neck glisten in the sunlight.

"Does the name Goldberg mean anything to you?"

He grabs her hands suddenly, almost violently. She wants to pull away, but his grip is too strong. He wrenches her palms upward, looking at them intently.

"You've been marked."

"What!" She yelps, twisting her arms and shoulders. She tries to inhale but feels a heaviness on her chest, as if something is wrapped around her, squeezing.

He stares at her stomach, and she looks down. The bottom

two buttons of her shirt have come undone, exposing part of her scar.

"It's destined to find you."

"No," she whispers. She pulls back hard, unsure about what is more terrifying—his words or his icy grip.

Samantha hears footsteps behind her, then Frank's voice. "Sam?"

She finally yanks her hands free, but the man continues to look down, as if they were still there. She is breathing heavily now.

"I don't understand," she says.

"Buses go everywhere." With those words, his eyes become sorrowful, not penetrating. The man turns around and starts pushing his cart again. The wheels grind and squeak. Cans and bottles rattle against each other.

# 24
# Love Letters

W hat are you thinking?" Frank looks straight ahead as he talks, fidgeting slightly.

"This music on the radio. I heard a story about it once in a music history class. It's kind of a sad love letter."

*Mozart's Mass in C Minor was a piece written not for God but for two women, her instructor said. At twenty-one, Mozart fell in love with Aloysia Weber, a soprano with an angelic voice and shapely legs. Though his passion for her was bigger than the Munich Opera House, his purse was small. She ended their courtship, saying that he needed to make his mark, to become a success. Only then would she marry him. In the meantime, she promised to wait.* "I'll always love you, Wolfgang," *she told him. But a short time later, she announced her engagement to an actor. With a battered heart, Mozart turned to Constanze, Aloysia's younger sister. In her arms, he found solace and eventually love— not the kind that ignites fires and starts wars, but the kind that offers shelter from a storm. He wrote the Mass for their wedding day, and Constanze sang soprano. Filling the church with her voice, she must have suspected that the lilting, mournful melodies were more a testament to what her husband had lost in Aloysia than to her or Christ.*

*Aloysia could have sung it better.*

*Mozart could have loved Constanze better.*

"Like Meredith's?" Frank looks straight ahead as he speaks.

"What?"

"Her letter."

Samantha lowers her eyes guiltily. "She said that love isn't about the right person, it's about the right moment. Do you think that's true?"

"It depends on the night," he says glibly, then laughs.

The sound of it makes Samantha smile. She watches him, waiting for an answer as he looks in the rearview mirror and changes lanes.

"For me"—his voice is cheerful but cautious—"love is cleaning the apartment . . . brushing your teeth, dressing nicely, that kind of stuff."

"Personal hygiene?"

"It's about being a better person. Or at least trying to be." He pauses. "The tricky part is finding someone who makes you want to keep trying."

"Did I make you feel that way?" Samantha is surprised by her own question.

Frank hesitates before answering. "Yes, you did." The truthfulness of the words makes them hard to say, and he wonders how she feels about hearing them.

Samantha wants to tell him that he did the same for her and that she doesn't deserve such a beautiful compliment. She has let him—let both of them—down. But as always, when it comes to her heart, she struggles with words.

They turn onto the street with the clinic, and Samantha is

relieved. The building glows orange-red in the light of the setting sun, and a police car is parked at the curb in front of the entryway. Frank pulls into a space across the street, and they both get out of the car quietly. He follows her across the street.

Unimaginative furniture fills Dr. Clay's office: brown leather chairs, oak bookcases, a brass lamp with a green shade. The black stapler and tape dispenser were clearly purchased at the same office supply store. Framed nautical prints hang on the walls. The desk is uncluttered. A few folders have been left in discreet piles, and a Post-it note sticks to a pyramid-shaped clock encased in glass: Lunch with Mike at 12:45. Today's date is scribbled across the top.

The officer who took them upstairs stands in the doorway. He watches as Frank goes through the file cabinet and Samantha studies the papers on Dr. Clay's desk.

They work in silence for a long time.

"Take a look at this," Frank says and hands her a manila folder. The label reads "Samantha Ranvali." "You said before that someone else was supposed to be in this study but never showed up. Did Dr. Clay ever mention a name?"

"No," Samantha says distractedly. She stares at her name, seeing it, for the first time, as evidence in the case. She feels uneasy opening the file and suddenly recalls Don's words from the other day: *What if you're next on the list, Sam?*

"Well, there has to be a record somewhere." Frank walks over to the desk and starts checking the drawers.

"It feels weird reading my file."

"It's better than reading other people's mail."

"Thanks," she says sarcastically.

The first few pages of health insurance forms are followed by notes on Samantha's medical history and a page of handwritten comments by Dr. Clay.

"What?" Samantha's jaw drops slightly.

Frank looks up.

"Listen to this. 'Samantha has responded well to treatment. This has improved her disposition, making her less resistant and argumentative.' He wrote that after my first day here."

"So?" Frank notices a wry smile on her face.

"My *disposition*? I am not resistant and argumentative."

"Yes you are."

"No I'm not."

He laughs, then adds, "Maybe he meant it as a compliment."

"That's not a compliment." She tilts her head sideways and raises her eyebrows.

Frank is silent for a moment as he pulls out a file from the bottom drawer and sits in the desk chair. "'Endymion's Circle,'" he reads the label, and holds it up for Samantha to see. "Why would he hide this away?"

Frank spreads open the file on Dr. Clay's desk. Samantha stands close behind him now, resting her hand on his right shoulder as she leans forward.

"Here's a list of the four participants in the study," Frank says.

"Gabriel Morgan," Samantha reads the fourth name.

Frank turns slightly to look up at her. "So that's how Catherine found out about the study. She must have met Morgan at the restaurant in Salt Lake and followed him to San Francisco."

"Because she was sick like Max." Samantha steps back and looks warily at the officer, who is picking at one of his fingernails.

"What do you mean?" Frank spins around in the chair to face her.

"That's how her roommate described it. Catherine was worried that she was getting sick like Max. If he cut her that night on the bridge—" She pauses, looking at Frank nervously. "After Max died, she couldn't sleep. Maybe she was becoming violent like him. She hears about this study from Father Morgan and thinks Dr. Clay can help."

"That doesn't explain why she ran away."

"Maybe it does. . . ." Her voice trails off, then she looks into Frank's eyes. "She may have run to protect her family and friends."

"From whom?"

"Herself." She almost whispers the word.

Frank stares, confused.

"Dr. Clay's study targeted people who were experiencing extreme cases of parasomnia."

"You said that was like sleepwalking."

"It can also result in violent behavior. I think the killer may be acting in a parasomniac or semiconscious state."

"That's ridiculous," he says with noticeable irritation. "First of all, Catherine didn't hurt anyone. Second, people don't commit murder in their sleep."

"During sleep, we go through various stages," she starts earnestly. "The most important is REM sleep. That's when we dream. It's an outlet for our anxieties and fears. In this state, your brain is active, but your body can't move. It's like a safety mechanism. It prevents you from acting out. But people who suffer from parasomnia don't reach REM sleep—that's why they can walk or even hurt someone."

"Look," he cuts into her explanation. "Somehow the killer knew about Catherine's connection to Father Morgan and this study. That made her a target. We need to find out who had access to this office and these files."

"I agree, but that doesn't mean that Catherine—" She brings her hand up to her mouth. "Maybe the curse manipulates people in their sleep. It would make sense."

"To a mental patient, maybe." Frank says, shaking his head. "Christ, Sam, enough with curses and disgruntled musicians. Catherine is a victim, just like Father Morgan, just like Dr. Clay, just like Phebe."

"Fine. But if the killer is acting in a parasomniac state, he might not know that he is the killer." She turns and walks to the file cabinet.

Frank watches her silently. For six months, sleeplessness has been her curse. The thing that has rendered her powerless, like a ship without sail or engine, tossed by waves and sharp winds. Moving only with some unseen current. He wonders if the Goldberg story gives her hope, the ability to blame something other than herself for so many relentlessly sleepless nights. Maybe she needs the fantasy.

Frank's phone rings. He uses an unmarked pad on Dr. Clay's desk to write down two addresses. Samantha turns.

"Well?" she asks.

"Snair has search warrants for Dr. Cooper's and Arty's homes. The police are already inside. We should probably go to Arty's place first. It's closer."

"All right."

Frank follows Samantha uneasily through the door and past the officer, certain that each of them is traveling alone.

# Parasomnia

Years ago, silence brought Veronica to the library. It made her want to learn more, talk less, and wear sexy clothing. For those who come only to check out and return books, the library is nothing more than a storage facility—a stuffy place where dust gathers on the things—books—we can live without. But for anyone who stays, passions burn in these uncomfortable chairs and temperature-controlled rooms. Surreptitious glances, the faint smell of perfume and sweat, skintight clothing, and the way someone's hand catches the light as he turns a page. Perhaps it's being in a place devoted to quiet concentration that ignites so much desire. Veronica isn't sure, but she knows one thing—coming to a library is never simply about the books.

For almost a year, the churchlike silence of the Durham Public Library has tormented her. Monday mornings are particularly bad. It's always slow, and the empty stillness gives her too much time to think. She can't remember when she last slept for more than a few hours, and every time she closes her eyes, violent images return—the kind that would make most people avoid horror movies and ice hockey.

She yawns and rubs her eyes. As if she's suddenly turning a corner and running into something, another vision flashes before her.

A dark man in ragged clothing waits quietly on a wooden bridge. Slowly, out of the dark, a figure steps into the faint light of a hook-shaped street lamp. Her eyes are a deep, piercing blue, and her face is flushed—not from the cold, but from crying. The man spins suddenly on one foot, like a dancer, and slashes into her stomach with a knife. She screams, reaching for his hand, but he quickly pulls the blade away. It cuts deeply into her palm.

The sound of an approaching train grows like a tremor, rumbling through the boards beneath her feet and up her body. Before he can take another step, she shoves him into the railing. He yells, dropping the knife, but the baritone of the train's horn mutes his cry. A jagged iron rod from the railing has lanced his lower side. She moves forward tentatively, then helps him pull free. She presses her hands on the bleeding wound, and he says something she can't hear. His eyes express an odd mixture of sorrow and gratitude, and this frightens her more than the pain. The train is practically beneath them.

He hurls himself over the ledge.

With a start, Veronica sits up. The screen saver shows a colorful fish swimming in circles; several yellow sticky notes surround the screen, and her book has fallen to the floor.

"I'm not closing my eyes anymore," she mutters to herself.

"Good; we're not paying you to sleep on the job." Mildred scowls a bit as she straightens a pile of "Story Time at the Library" pamphlets and walks toward the newspaper racks.

"Technically, you're not paying me at all," Veronica snaps after her.

Mildred has been assistant librarian for twenty-one years and acts as if she owns the place. For almost the same amount of time, she has been next in line for head librarian, but Caroline won't retire. At seventy-nine, she has the energy of someone half her age, and assures Mildred every day that she doesn't plan to die or step down anytime soon. So on Mondays, Caroline's day off, Mildred takes the opportunity to walk around the stacks like a drill sergeant, barking orders and making faces.

Veronica picks up the book and opens to Canto XX.

She's not sure when it started, but a few years ago, she began reading other people's books. Every few months, she picks an attractive man who comes in regularly, keeps track of his account, and reads each return. She likes to imagine what these stories say about him—his boyhood fantasies of being a superhero or crime fighter, the ideal women he wants to love, or at least have sex with, and his dreams for power and influence. But this one is different. He doesn't read what she expects. Tall, athletic, and with dark brown skin, his beauty arrested her from the start. He asked for a library card, and she handed him the form nervously. At the top, in large black letters, he wrote Maxwell Harris, then looked up.

"You can call me Max," he said with a charming smile, and they shook hands.

"So what brings you to the library, Max?" She couldn't believe she'd said something so stupid. It must have sounded like a bad pickup line, because he chuckled before answering.

"Books."

"Well, we're a little short on those right now. But we do have a good collection of silent films and country music."

"What?"

"Just kidding." Veronica stamped his temporary user card and handed it over. "Welcome to the Durham Public Library."

He has been her favorite reader ever since, not just because his body looks as if it were chiseled from marble, but because he writes lightly penciled notes in the margins. If Mildred finds out, she will cancel his card, but Veronica won't tell. She reads each note as if it were meant for her. In a few weeks, she has fallen in love with him.

He returned Dante's Inferno on Friday:

*For every visage had been clean*
*round to the loins, and backward they must go,*
*since looking forward had forbidden been.*

*Amphiaraus? Mark how his shoulders to a breast are made!*
*Because he wished to see too far before,*
*forever backward doth he look and tread.*

The handwritten margin notes add:

*Amphiaraus—a seer and warrior to whom Zeus granted*
    *immortality. He predicted the disastrous attempt to*
    *restore Polynices to the throne at Thebes.*
*How could someone who knows the future ever live in the*
    *present?*

Veronica wonders why he asks this. To her, it seems like the wrong question. Dante believed that the past was a much greater burden than the future. And like him, she can understand the endless torment in continually reliving it—knowing history without the outcome and looking back only to see mis-

*takes, lost loves, and missed chances.* Yes, *Veronica thinks,* this
is the wrong question. *Max must not know what it's like to
look behind and stumble backwards.*

JANUARY 5, 1999
3:02 A.M.

*He lies naked with his arms stretched out to his sides and his
legs tied together. There is no blood on the bed. The only colors
in the room seem to be the whiteness of his buttocks and the
ocean blue tattoo on his right shoulder—a modest-sized tear
hanging above the initials I. D. The quiet of the room feels
charged with anticipation.*

*His head has been twisted around, and his chin rests on the
tattooed shoulder, making the tear look as if it just fell from his
open eyes. Veronica reaches for it, but something is wrong. Her
arm isn't long enough. She stretches, but so does the room. Her
gestures become more frantic, and the gap widens. Somewhere
far away, music—almost too soft to hear—plays sorrowfully.
She knows it, but can't remember why or from where.*

*Her eyes open, and she recognizes the carpet on her living room
floor. She gets up and runs to the bedroom. Nothing.*

*In the bathroom, she turns on the light and looks at her
nightgown. No blood, bruises, or torn clothing. No wounds on
her chest or stomach. Too many times she has woken up with
evidence that something terrible has happened, but she can't
remember what. For the last eight months, she hasn't gone out
after work; she just locks herself in the apartment by sunset. She
has become terrified of nights like this.*

*She finds nothing this time—no clue to a mystery she can't
solve. In the kitchen, she turns on the overhead light, pours a*

glass of water, and opens a bag of oatmeal raisin cookies. She carries the bag with her to the bedroom. On the way, she stubs her toe on the living room table, dropping the bag.

"Crap."

She starts picking them up. One cookie has rolled partially underneath the couch and sits next to a book. She slides it toward her. The cover is soft and grimy. The upper right-hand corner curls up. She doesn't recognize it in the dark, so she walks back to the kitchen and turns on the light.

It's a Gideon's Bible, but not one from her collection in the closet. She stands there until her feet feel cold from the linoleum and her lower back is moist with sweat. Slowly, she opens the cover, and written in the upper left-hand corner is a name in her handwriting: Ian Dickerson.

She doesn't drop the book or move. She just stands there until she realizes that the stains on the page are from her tears.

## 25

# Five Thousand Feet

Artemus Beecher lives in a basement apartment that smells like rotting vegetables and barbecue sauce. Piles of newspapers line the walls, and a hazy yellow light glows from a lamp in the corner of the living room. A jaundiced crucifix hangs on the wood-paneled wall separating the two main rooms. The couch has been knocked over, and parts of the dirty gray carpet stick up like needles on a porcupine's back. At the top of the far wall, a window—the only window—is partially open, and Samantha notices the room reflected in its pane. Two officers move quietly and speak in hushed tones around the circular brown stain on the floor.

Another says to Frank, "Forensics is on the way."

Samantha walks into the bedroom, which is crowded with more newspapers, a small desk, and an unmade bed. She wonders how Arty found solace in the chaos of so many papers. At the clinic, he sat calmly with those large pages spread out in front of him. Samantha had never considered finding comfort that way. Would reading words that smear and fade with every touch make her feel better? She didn't think so.

Samantha notices a book on the comforter and picks it up. It has countless dog-eared pages and sticky notes: *The Metamorphosis and Other Stories* by Franz Kafka. The first sentence is underlined: "As Gregor Samsa awoke one morning from uneasy dreams he found himself transformed in his bed into a gigantic insect."

"Sam?" Frank walks into the room.

She looks up.

"The police are still trying to contact the landlady," he continues. "But it doesn't look like anyone has been here for a few days."

"I don't understand," she says, walking back into the living room.

"What?"

"Assuming that someone was killed here, why move the body?"

"Well, it slows down the investigation. It makes it more difficult to catch the killer."

"But why worry about that now? There was no attempt to hide anything before. Other than Catherine, it has been about the ritual."

A uniformed officer enters the living room through the front door and signals to Frank. They communicate in whispers, standing at a distance from everyone else in the room.

Samantha opens the story again, looking for the next underlined passage: "he fell down with a little cry upon all his numerous legs. Hardly was he down when he experienced for the first time this morning a sense of physical comfort; his legs had firm ground under them; they were completely obedient, as he noted with joy; they even strove to carry him forward in whatever direction he chose; and he was inclined to believe that a final relief from all his sufferings was at hand."

"Well?" She doesn't look up when Frank returns to her side.

"The police haven't found anything yet at Dr. Cooper's place, but Detective Snair just got a call from Saint Mary's Hospital."

"And?"

"Dr. Cooper was in a car accident."

"A car accident?" She turns to him.

"Yeah."

"Is she all right?"

"No. She's dead."

"No." Her eyes widen, and her voice sounds tight and dry. "I don't believe it."

"I'm sorry—"

"Have someone check out the car."

"The police are investigating—"

"No," she interrupts. "Someone from the corporation."

Samantha hurries to the front door and up the stairs without waiting for Frank to respond. The night air feels thin and hard, as if she's standing at five thousand feet. For a moment, she wishes there were more stairs—anything so she could keep moving, so she could climb far away from basement apartments, unanswered questions, and sleepless nights.

The church is still on Friday night. No choir sings in preparation for Sunday services. No priest hears confession. Only the candles glow steadily in the dim light. Samantha searches for the words to pray, but without music she can't find a starting tempo. Maybe true prayer is like crying, she thinks. Something that needs to well up inside until it breaks free like water from a cracked dam. She wonders how much longer she will have to wait for the tears of prayer. Her eyes stay dry.

She has always admired actors who can weep on cue, but she can never trust them. Some things shouldn't be easy to control.

Frank coughs, and the sound startles her. The church doesn't feel the same with him beside her. He's there because she insisted they stop. She's there for herself. Neither seems to be the right reason for coming. She knows Frank is impatient to leave, to take her home, then go to Dr. Cooper's, but Samantha wants to sit for a few more minutes. There is nothing like the silence that comes from the smell of faded incense, cold drafts, and uncomfortable wooden benches.

She looks up at the cross, studying the spikes through Christ's palms and feet. The historical inaccuracy never bothered her before. Spikes were driven through Christ's wrists, not palms, because the flesh there would tear too easily. In this sculpture, his writhing hands seem to struggle for freedom, each finger experiencing a separate agony. What is it about hands that makes artists want to paint and sculpt them? Is it the way hands communicate so much pain and tenderness without speaking?

Her body and mind ache. From fear, loneliness, uncertainty. Uncertainty about whether the sadnesses of life will keep her awake forever. Uncertainty about her connection to Endymion's Circle, the count, the crimes themselves. She feels as if she were spinning in the craziness of it all.

God. Fate. A curse.

For Samantha, they all seem to be part of the same desire. The desire to believe in something. To explain pain and suffering. To explain the mark carved into her own writhing body. To make sense out of the chaos of life. Frank thinks it's easier to believe in a curse than to live without answers. *But he's wrong*, she thinks. *It's much harder to believe in something we can't control.*

"I'm ready." Her voice echoes loudly.

"You sure?"

"Yeah. Let's go."

*    *    *

Samantha notices the squad car in front of her apartment as they turn the corner on Twenty-first Street. Frank pulls alongside it, and she rolls down her window.

"Hey, Frank," the officer in the driver's seat calls out pleasantly.

"Sam, this is Officer Chang. He and his partner will be keeping an eye on you."

"Hi. You can call me Wayland." He smiles. "Officer Brooks is in the building. He's posted outside your door. If you need anything, just let us know."

"Thanks."

"I'll walk you upstairs," Frank says as he pulls into the driveway.

On the third floor, a uniformed officer sits on a folding chair by her front door. He fills most of the narrow hallway and has to stand to let them pass. He introduces himself clumsily, and his lanky body, pale skin, and dark hair unfashionably parted on one side remind her more of a high school counselor than a cop. Once she unlocks her door, Frank walks ahead of her. To Sam, this extra precaution seems somewhat scripted, like something in a thriller movie.

"After I check out Dr. Cooper's place, I'll come back. Just to see how things are going."

"You don't need to do that."

"I want to." He smiles.

"We're missing something, Frank."

"I know."

"The change of pattern doesn't make sense."

"We'll figure it out."

As he turns, Samantha places her hand gently on his back. He lingers, and her mind races with reasons and excuses for him to stay. But she can't ask. Not now. Not with so many unanswered questions about the case.

"I'll see you later," she says, and her words rise in pitch, as if she is asking a question.

He turns and smiles. "Definitely."

Frank steps into the hallway, closing the door behind him. It leaves a hollow sound, a thud that echoes throughout her empty, lonely apartment.

## 26

# Mrs. Brinkmeyer

The muted trumpet of Miles Davis sings with hopeful melancholy, telling the story of someone who waits patiently for love without being afraid of loneliness. Samantha pours a glass of Napa Valley chardonnay and sits on the couch with her eyes closed. She's not sure if having a cop outside the door makes her feel more or less anxious, but it does make her self-conscious. She sits straighter, tries to make less noise, and wonders about what to wear for the evening. The music shifts seamlessly into a nostalgic stroll. She sips the wine.

The phone rings a few times before she picks it up. "Hello?"

"Samantha, dear, it's Mrs. Brinkmeyer."

"Hi."

"I haven't seen you in a while. Is everything all right?"

"Yes, I'm fine. I've just been really busy."

"Do you have a minute to stop by? I have some new cheeses."

"Sure, I'll be right down."

Mrs. Brinkmeyer, her seventy-four-year-old landlady, lives on the first floor. Every week, she invites Samantha for wine and cheese. They talk about books, music, the latest idiocy in the White House, education, current art exhibits, property value in the Bay Area. The list is endless. Mrs. Brinkmeyer calls Samantha intelligent, talented, eloquent—and her ego loves it—but in truth, Samantha learns more from listening to Mrs. Brinkmeyer than she could ever offer in return.

Grabbing her keys, Samantha steps into the hall. Officer Brooks has abandoned his post, leaving a folded newspaper on the chair and an open can of soda underneath. *I feel safer already,* she thinks sarcastically and walks down the hall. The back stairs lead directly to Mrs. Brinkmeyer's apartment, and by the second floor, piano music starts to paint the drab, unused space of the stairwell with color. As always, Mrs. Brinkmeyer waits with her door open and a record playing.

With a warm smile and a kiss on the cheek, Mrs. Brinkmeyer says, "Wonderful to see you, dear."

White wine is already poured, and the glasses have been chilled. Today's cheeses—Roquefort, chèvre, and Brie—are set out with crackers and red grapes. Samantha sits in her usual spot on the firm, pearl-white couch, and they raise a glass to each other. After a sip, Mrs. Brinkmeyer asks, "So?"

As part of their weekly ritual, Samantha tries to impress her by guessing the composer. "Bach, I think."

"His Second Partita." Mrs. Brinkmeyer moves to the edge of her chair, eager to listen, like an athlete ready to play. "Who's the pianist?"

"Glenn Gould." Samantha takes another sip. "Do you have his recording of the *Goldberg Variations*?"

"Yes. Would you like to hear it?"

"Sure."

As Mrs. Brinkmeyer gets up to find the record, Samantha quickly spreads some Roquefort on a sesame-seed cracker. She always feels guilty about eating other people's food, even at dinner parties and birthdays. Frank used to laugh at her for worrying about such things, but she was raised by a father who taught her to say no to anything she hadn't paid for or earned. "Just because someone offers you something," he said, "doesn't mean they really want you to take it." And, like so many other things her father had said, that was the final word on the subject. She looks at the cracker for a moment, debating whether or not to eat it, until her stomach growls.

"So why this piece today?" Mrs. Brinkmeyer asks, turning around to see the cracker halfway in her mouth. Samantha smiles like a child who gets caught with her hand in the cookie jar.

"Well—" She tries talking with a mouthful of cheese, then decides against it. The music starts humming through the speakers like a faint lullaby, and they listen to the opening while Samantha chews as quietly and inconspicuously as possible. Mrs. Brinkmeyer takes another sip from her glass.

"Well, for one thing," Samantha says after she's swallowed, "it has a very interesting history. . . ."

By the time Samantha leaves, they have listened to the entire piece. She has told her stories about the count, Goldberg, and Bach's commission to write the variations. She was worried that she might fall asleep at any moment, but the music had no effect on her tonight. Only the wine made her drowsy—and somewhat buzzed.

Samantha climbs the stairs slowly, light-headed from two glasses, and pauses to catch her breath on the third floor. She hasn't eaten dinner, other than Mrs. Brinkmeyer's cheese and crackers, and is too tired to cook. Then, remembering that there is nothing edible in the fridge, she considers sending Officer Brooks to pick up some Thai food.

Still smiling at the thought, she sees the empty chair in front of her door. More irritated than concerned, she fumbles through her crowded key chain, imagining all the disparaging things she could say to Brooks but never will. *He probably didn't even notice I was gone,* she thinks, putting the key in the lock. The door falls open as soon as she touches it. *Did I forget to lock it?* She considers going downstairs and getting Coffee-Break Brooks to check out her apartment. She can hear Miles Davis playing softly, and the CD must have repeated, because it's back to "Someday My Prince Will Come." She steps inside cautiously. The living room is empty and still. She doesn't want to seem as if she's overreacting, so she takes another step inside, leaving the door open.

With each step, the floor creaks. Everything seems the same until she turns off Miles. She expects silence, but another sound is coming from elsewhere in the apartment. A steady hum . . . no, running water. She walks to the bathroom door, which is closed. Her legs feel like blocks of cement as she reaches for the knob. She turns it slowly and pushes. The sound of rushing water gets louder.

Suddenly, the entire floor is covered with water. The light doesn't work, but a shaft from the living room illuminates the overflowing bathtub. She enters, and water splashes at her feet. Bending over the tub, she turns the faucets clockwise, then counterclockwise. The water stops. She stands up and looks around the room, unsure of what to do next. Through the window, she notices a strong wind rippling the trees.

Then she sees a dark bulky figure on the floor in the corner. It reminds her of a vision. Water covering a face. Her face? She's not sure. Without moving, she strains to see more clearly. It looks like a body curled up and turned away from the light.

She quickly backs away, to get help, to get out of the apartment. Suddenly, her legs slip out from under her. Everything seems to move with exaggerated slowness.

*   *   *

*As a child, she wondered if magicians could really levitate a body. Every time the fair came to town, she and Rachel begged Father to take them to the magician's tent. Samantha would go to every possible show, standing in the audience and waving her hand wildly in the hope that some magician would choose her as a volunteer. They never did. She wanted to know what it felt like to float several feet above the floor, to fly. For a moment, she remembers these magic men, with their red handkerchiefs, black capes, and silver rings. She remembers what it feels like to be in the audience, standing safely on the ground. And in that brief moment, with her body hovering parallel to the linoleum floor, she knows that, if ever given the chance, she'll never raise her hand again.*

Samantha's body slams against the water-soaked floor, and the sound resonates in her head like a drum that gradually fades with each beat until the lights go out.

# 27
## *Intermezzo*

*H*er face feels numb against the cold wet tile. She turns her head slowly toward the ceiling and rolls onto her back. Everything seems hazy. The sink, towel racks, hamper, and tub vibrate in and out of focus, and she tries to concentrate on one thing to stop the dizziness. Through the window, the trees are swaying more frantically, and the streetlights seem to reflect off their leaves like Fourth of July sparklers. She wonders how long she has been unconscious. Then she remembers the body. She tries to move, to see something, but her arms feel weighted down. She tries to touch her face.

Something is wrong with her arms. No, it's her wrists.

They're bound with rope.

She lifts her arms together, then lets them fall back into her lap. Once again, the room spins into darkness.

# *Parasomnia*

*Veronica watches him leave—not through the smudgy window of an anonymous motel room or the side-view mirror of a taxi, but from her bedroom. He slept here, in her bed, without sneaking off before dawn or forgetting a wedding ring on the nightstand.*

*He kissed her on the lips before leaving. His face wasn't tortured with guilt or preoccupied with excuses for saying goodbye and never looking back. He kissed her with desire. He kissed her like a man torn between leaving and making love to her again.*

*Yes, making love.*

*He carelessly left his library copy of Christoph Wolff's* Johann Sebastian Bach: The Learned Musician *on her dresser. Does Max play the oboe? Or did he say the clarinet? She will* have to ask when she sees him again. She repeats these last words out loud like lyrics to a favorite song—"when I see him again." Opening the book, she skims for margin notes. None. Just a bookmark about halfway through. The page describes a legend surrounding one of Bach's keyboard pieces, the Goldberg Variations.

She closes it abruptly, not wanting to read it before he does. She'll call to arrange a rendezvous as lovers do—for coffee or dinner or drinks. Just the two of them.

But he didn't give her his number. He called her. They met for dinner and came back to her place. Well, his number will be in the library database. She'll look it up and call under the pretext of returning his book. She wants so much to see his face in the glow of restaurant candlelight again, to hear his deep voice in the dark spaces of her bedroom. She imagines holding hands while stumbling along the uneven sand dunes of Wrightsville Beach. Or getting dressed up for the symphony and drinking a glass of champagne.

Is this what love does—make people long for stereotypes? She is a librarian, a lover of words, yet she has been reduced to clichés and images from romance novels.

What does it matter anyway, *she thinks suddenly. Angrily.* She can't love him. She knows what will happen if she falls asleep by his side. She will wake up and find him dead. She took that chance once. It was selfish, she knows, but she wanted to feel love.

What if it's true? *she keeps asking herself.* What if the most improbable thing in the world just happened, and someone fell in love with me?

She shouldn't see him again. She shouldn't call. She considers writing his name in a Bible and storing it with the others.

No, not him.

*For hours, for days, for weeks, she doesn't call.*
*Neither does he.*

*For months, it goes on like this. Weeks of silence, then a long night of passionate sex. After the first time, she doesn't let him stay, insisting that he leave, but this makes him oddly jealous and angry.*

*She loves him in spite of herself. She knows other women like this. Afraid of being alone. Taking whatever they can get even when it makes them feel like less than what they are. But she feels something with him that she has never known, and having him to think about makes the sleepless nights more bearable. She starts wearing makeup to cover the bags under her eyes. She uses eyedrops to take away the redness. Anything to appear attractive to him—to keep him, if only for a while.*

*Seasons change and more months pass.*
*She keeps forgetting to ask about the oboe.*
*She has never seen his apartment.*

APRIL 19, 2000
11:17 P.M.

*Max insists on staying, but not for love. Something is bothering him, and he wants to test her. He sits in front of the television in his boxers, another beer in his hand. Veronica wears only a white button-down dress shirt.*

*"Are you sleeping with someone else?" Exhaustion gives her the courage to ask. Time goes by quickly when you're living in denial—when you're afraid of the changes the truth might bring.*

*"Yes."*

*"What's her name—other than whore?"*

"Catherine." His eyes stay on the television.

"Get out."

"Like you're not sleeping with other people."

"I'm not, you ass. I'm in love with you."

"What about those Bibles?" He looks at her earnestly.

"How did you—this is about the Bibles? They have nothing to do with you or my life right now."

"Then who are all those men?"

"That was a long time ago."

He turns back to the television angrily.

"Hey, you don't have a right to be angry here. You're the one fucking someone else. How long has it been?"

"A few weeks."

"You bastard!"

"At least I'm honest."

"This is your definition of honesty?"

A loud hissing sound explodes from the television, and Max quickly presses something on the remote. It becomes silent.

"Get out." Veronica's voice has gone cold.

He looks at her again, then responds evenly, "I think I'll stay awhile."

"Why?"

Silence.

"You think someone else is coming over, don't you?" Veronica says, dumbfounded.

"Maybe."

"You have no idea what you just lost." Veronica turns, walks to her bedroom, and slams the door. Her face sinks into the pillow, and she feels the moisture of thick tears against her face. She shakes with each sob as if her tired body and broken heart have finally had enough.

Part of her hopes he will sneak in and start rubbing her back. Apologize. Kiss her. Call himself an idiot, a bastard, a piece of crap who doesn't deserve her love. But the room stays quiet except for her heaving breath.

Then she feels it happen. Slowly, at first.

Everything becomes darker.

The room fluctuates with the pulsing light of the television. Dark, twisted shadows climb the walls. An infomercial drones like white noise, and Max's body lies still on the couch. His snore is barely audible over the sounds. Her shadow grows with each step and covers his body as she stands over him. She hesitates briefly—dagger poised over his torso like something out of a Shakespearean tragedy.

She strikes.

He catches her wrist with surprising force and agility. He's been awake all along. Now he gets up, both hands still clasped around her wrist. He twists her arm, and the knife falls to the floor. He looks down, trying to decide what to do next. His grip weakens.

He feels her knee smash into his groin, and the pain surges up to his neck. As she reaches for the knife, he thrusts his knee into her ribs, sending her into the wall. Something about her eyes frightens him. They seem to shimmer. He steps forward, and the knife slices across his abdomen. He leaps back, bumping into the living room table. Instinctively, he grabs the glass bowl on top and swings at her. It shatters against her temple. She yells. Blood drips from her nose.

She stumbles forward—the knife clutched in her right fist, pointing down. They fall back onto the table; two of its legs snap, sending them to the floor. He rolls on top of her and immediately feels the blade slide evenly into his left shoulder. She turns it, but his grip overpowers her. He pulls it out, and his hand seems to swallow hers as he thrusts it into her chest.

*He hears the snap of her wrist breaking.*

*She twists and bucks more violently now, and he struggles to keep her hands away from the knife. He presses the full weight of his body on top of her, and she becomes more still. More quiet.*

*Exhausted, he rests his head on her left shoulder.*

*As the room gets darker, he remembers lying with her like this hours earlier. Just a few feet from here. Worlds apart.*

APRIL 20, 2000
2:47 P.M.

*Max wakes up sweaty. The sunlight pours through the window onto his naked back. He pushes himself off her body—half-crawling and stumbling away from her.*

*"Oh, my God!"*

*He looks at her pale white, red-stained body.*

*"Veronica?" He crawls to her, touching her neck tentatively. Her lips are purple-blue. He plugs her nose, tips back her head, and breathes into her mouth. The clock above the television ticks loud as a drum. He places one hand on top of the other and presses against her chest, as he learned to do years ago in a first-aid class. He stops and wipes the sweat from his forehead. He looks down at himself. A long mark of reddish brown runs across his abdomen. Dry, smeared blood. He touches the wounds gingerly.*

What am I going to do? *he thinks.* I've got to call the police.

*He stands up and grabs the cordless phone in the kitchen.* No one is going to believe me. They'll think I killed her. *He hangs up, then clicks again for a dial tone.* Brad's a sergeant. He and the other guys will help me out. Hell, I work for the police department. I keep them in business. *Max paces the kitchen for a fourth time.* I'll call him at home. *A pause.* First, I need a story. A break-in. I found her like this. She was a friend. She called last night and asked me to stop by today. To go for coffee or something. What about Catherine? She can't find out. Brad can keep things quiet.

*Max hurries into the living room and sees her again. The expression on her face makes him drop the phone. Her eyes are open. They stare at him, and he thinks—as he picks up his clothes and looks for anything else that belongs to him in the apartment—*What have I done?

## 28

## *The Faceless Man*

Something digs deeply into her ankles. Samantha opens her eyes, and the room shifts and spins. The lamp in the living room has been turned off, and the darkness animates the shadows. She can't see where things end and begin. A dark figure with no face appears suddenly, towering above her like a wave at its crest.

She knows this nightmare. It has been replaying in her mind for years, since even before such visions kept her from sleeping through the night. Just before sunrise, a faceless man rises out of the earth to steal faces from the living. His victims wake up in perpetual darkness with no ears to hear, mouths to eat, or eyes to see. They can't scream or call for help. Slowly, they starve to death. The sun rises, and the faceless man returns blindly to the darkness, alone.

At first, Samantha is just along for the ride, watching as he peels off the faces, but eventually, he turns to her. She can't move or make a sound. In the distance, a woman sings a long wavering note, and only when her lament stops does Samantha know for certain that he has succeeded. He has taken Samantha's face.

This time it's different.

The faceless man stands still. His gloved hands hold a taut rope attached to some type of pulley in the wall. He wears a long black coat that obscures the shape of his body, and there is something mechanical about each movement. He leans forward, then pivots. Her head suddenly smacks against the floor, and everything flashes white from a sharp pain in the back of her head. She can hear the pulley squeak from the weight of her body.

Her feet are bound together.

This is not a dream.

Another quick tug, and Samantha's body slides forward again—her legs stretched up violently at a ninety-degree angle from her torso. She twists back and forth, trying to roll over, but before she can get enough momentum, he kicks her in the ribs. Her upper body swings like a pendulum across the floor. A deep cough tightens the muscles in her abdomen, and a sticky, sour taste fills her mouth. He steps forward, then adjusts his grip on the rope. Through his legs, she sees the body in the corner. It is no longer turned away from the light but faces the ceiling. Long black marks stain Brooks's cheeks like dried tears.

The faceless man's back leg tenses for the pull, and just as his body pivots, Samantha grabs one of his ankles with both hands. As her body heaves suddenly into the air, his leg is pulled off the ground with her. Her back slams into the wall. He releases the rope, and they both crash to the floor. The entire room shudders. Several bottles of lotion and perfume shatter as they fall to the floor. Rolling sideways and bringing her knees close to her chest, she tries to grab the rope at her ankles, but her wrists are bound too tightly. Blood moistens the rope where it has torn into her skin. She then pushes and rolls onto her knees.

Before she can look up, he kicks her in the stomach with the point of his boot, sending her forward breathless, forearms slamming hard into the wet floor. He pulls her hair back and clasps her shoulder.

She bites his forearm savagely. Yelling in surprise and anger, he shakes her loose and thrusts his knee into her chest, knocking her back onto the floor.

She can't see him now. He seems to have disappeared, but without smoke, mirrors, and magic wands. His absence terrifies her.

Then, with a forceful grip on her ankles, he flips her over in one violent motion. She twists, squirms, and kicks as he drags her facedown by the rope at her feet. She can't turn over. Then, in what feels like one surging motion, he wraps his arms around her waist and lifts her off the ground. She is standing, but her feet are bound so tightly that she falls back toward him. He adjusts his grip and wraps one arm around her neck.

Samantha gasps, struggling not to black out. She needs to fight.

Pushing against the floor, she tries to knock the two of them backward, but he moves with her instead—stepping back and throwing her into the tub. Her shoulder and head crash into a wall of water and porcelain. Turning onto her back, she tries to lift her head above the surface. She breathes in quickly before he thrusts her against the bottom of the tub.

She throws her feet over the rim and grabs a side with both hands. She lifts, but he pushes back. One hand claws around her neck. The other presses against her chest. Samantha swallows a mouthful of water.

He releases her suddenly, inexplicably.

She breaks above the surface and breathes in loud, shallow pants. He now stands at the counter with his back to her. It's too dark to see any reflection in the mirror. She tries pulling herself out of the tub but struggles to find enough strength. She places her feet against the bottom for leverage. He turns around slowly, and she sees a long silver blade in his right hand. It faces downward.

As he steps closer, she can see that he does have a face. It must have been obscured by the darkness. His skin is sallow and jaundiced. His eyes black. The muscles in his jaw are taut and strained.

It's Arty.

"Stop." Samantha's voice sounds hollow. She's winded.

Silence accompanies each step.

"You don't want to do this." She pushes herself up, struggling to put her left elbow over the rim. "It's me, Samantha. Listen, your name is Arty. Artemus Beecher."

He towers above her, still, his face colder than the water surrounding her body. He swings the knife swiftly, slicing across the forearm protecting her face. It stings, burning.

He reaches down to grab her shoulders.

She can't see the knife any longer, but she is sure this vanishing act is only a temporary illusion.

"Goldberg," she whispers to his face.

He pauses qizzically, as if trying to translate something from a language he once knew.

"Goldberg," she repeats like an incantation. The word tumbles out of her mouth.

His colorless eyes tighten, and he moves for her shoulders once again. It didn't work.

Clasping her hands, she swings them into his groin. Air explodes from his mouth, and his head bends forward. She drives her forehead into his jaw, then pulls her body over the ledge on the opposite side of the tub. She falls clumsily to the floor.

He reaches for her over the length of the tub.

Samantha looks up at his arms, which dangle toward her like tentacles, and into the black eyes that peer over the ledge. She slams her clasped hands into his nose and rolls away, hitting the wall underneath the window.

He is already standing, somewhat unsteadily, as she gets to her knees. His face twists fiercely. The knife seems to reappear in his right hand, and once again she thinks of those magicians at the fair—men who could say the right words and disappear with flashes of light and puffs of smoke. She wants to do the same, but she just doesn't know the words.

He kicks her across the jaw. She seems to hit the wall and the floor simultaneously. He straddles her hips, presses his weight into her as he pins her wrists to the floor above her head. Her shirt has torn from the struggle, exposing her stomach. She tries to twist free, but the weight of his body makes it impossible to move. She starts to yell and groan.

"No!"

He points the knife steadily at her lower abdomen and stops. She can tell that he has seen the scar and is puzzled. He looks at her face, then back at the crescent moon on her skin.

His expression turns slowly from uncertainty to resolution, as if he has been waiting for this moment.

She sucks in her stomach. For the first time she realizes that she is going to die—but not yet. Not quickly.

First, he has to mark her. He has to complete the circle.

## 29
# Deus ex Machina

The blade stings like dry ice as he presses it into her navel. Samantha kicks and twists and squirms and groans. She won't let her body be a canvas, she thinks, and she convinces herself that if he can't complete the circle she will somehow be all right. She starts picturing shapes from tenth-grade geometry class—a trapezoid, rhombus, isosceles triangle. Anything but a circle.

In one swift, clockwise motion, he slices a half-arc into her stomach. As the weight of his body shifts, she bucks, almost throwing him forward. He has to wrestle her arms to the floor and lean back into her hips before pinning her down again.

"*Please.*" Strained and shaken, her voice sounds unfamiliar, as if someone else is speaking for her.

He doesn't look at her, and Samantha is relieved not to see herself reflected in his black eyes. More steadily now, he positions the knife to finish the circle.

"Wake up, damn it!" she yells.

He looks up.

Suddenly, the floor rumbles like an earthquake as Frank charges toward them. Arty turns, and Frank kicks his rib cage, sending him into the wall beneath the window.

"Sam—" Frank calls out, but before she can answer, Arty springs to his feet, holding his side. He immediately slices up and away from his body. Frank jumps back, but not before the knife cuts across his chest. Arty's arm continues, twisting in one half of a figure eight and slicing back down. Frank slips in the water and falls into a sitting position.

"Hey!" Samantha yells, thrusting her bound feet into Arty's ankle. He stumbles backward, hitting the wall and clutching the thin windowsill.

Frank gets up. He now holds a gun in his outstretched hand. "Don't move!"

Arty pauses for a moment. They look at each other, and something passes between them that hits Frank like a wave. It makes him look unsteady and scared.

"Turn around," Frank says. His voice is thin.

Arty obeys.

"Put your hands behind your head."

Arty lifts his arms into the air, then springs forward, smashing through the window with both forearms. Samantha covers her face and turns from the shattering glass.

A strong, icy wind whips into the room. Frank rushes to the window, then to Samantha. He touches her shoulders and looks down at her bloody stomach.

"Are you all right?"

"Get these off me."

Frank hurries from the room and returns with a serrated kitchen knife. He cuts the rope around her wrists and ankles. He drops the knife and touches the side of her face with his fingers. His eyes reflect the glow of the street lamp. Below, a dog starts barking wildly. Frank helps her stand, then steps over to the body in the corner.

"Officer Brooks." He checks for a pulse and briefly examines the deep wound in his skull. "Damn," he says to himself.

Frank stands quickly, angrily. He glances out the window, and in one stride he is in front of her again, touching her shoulder with great tenderness. "I can't see anything through the trees," Frank says.

Samantha inadvertently squeezes his arm for balance.

"I'll call an ambulance and the police—"

"No, I can do it. Go!"

Frank hesitates, pulling the broken cell phone from his coat pocket. "But—"

"I'll call. Go!"

He tosses the phone aside and runs out of the apartment. Samantha listens to his long strides thunder down the stairs and fade. Now her apartment, the entire building, sounds perfectly still, as if it were waiting to exhale. She leans on the counter. Her hands tingle painfully, and her feet are numb from the dampness. So much blood covers her stomach that she can't see the shape of the wound. A black duffel bag lies on the floor by her feet. Several pieces of metal clang together as she lifts it to the sink. Reaching inside, she pulls out a long iron spike. There are two more.

Samantha imagines her own crucifixion. The sound of metal being hammered through her bone and skin. Blinding pain. She drops the spike from her shaking hand. What if he had completed the circle? What if—The questions frighten her more than the pain.

Samantha pulls off what remains of her shirt and grabs a thin sweater from on top of the hamper. She staggers into the kitchen and picks up the phone. The room seems to vibrate, and her eyes struggle to adjust. She dials 911 in case one of her neighbors hasn't done it already, leaves the phone off the hook, and stumbles into the hallway. With each step, she fights for balance, as if she had just been spinning in circles and suddenly wanted to walk a straight line.

She clings to the rail in the stairwell and makes her way to the first floor. The back door is open, and the wind has blown leaves and dirt into the corridor. At the end of the small yard, the wooden gate is partially open. It leads to an alley that spills into a labyrinth of side streets and dead ends.

She pushes the gate, but it moves only a few inches. Something heavy blocks it, as if sandbags were stacked on the other side. She leans against it until there is enough space to squeeze through. A dog behind the corner fence barks sporadically. She steps into the alley and nearly collapses when she sees Officer Chang's face. All the color has drained away except for the black-red line where the wire cuts through his neck and holds him against the fence. She steps closer, touching his shoulder.

"Wayland? Officer Chang?"

His black uniform is soaked with blood.

*Blood*, she thinks.

He's dead. His gun missing. A nightstick lies on the ground next to him, and though Samantha isn't sure what good it will do or if she can even figure out how to use it, she grabs it before turning into the dark alley.

Her vision goes in and out of focus. Then she remembers biting Arty's arm during the attack. His blood was in her mouth. She leans against a chain-link fence for balance, and the pain in her stomach surges.

*What if it's in me now?* she wonders. The way it was in Catherine before him and Max before her?

She is running now, her legs and feet pulling a reluctant, damaged body.

She passes buildings and turns corners without knowing where she is going. Her heart races, and she imagines her blood pumping with each step, bringing her closer to some end.

# 30
## *Crimson Doors*

The narrow alley is congested with garbage cans, cardboard boxes, and recycling bins. The black brick buildings on either side ooze with moisture and stretch high into the cloudy sky. Fire escapes dangle like spiders above their prey, and the air howls with every gust of wind.

"Frank?" Samantha calls out tentatively, her voice flat against the indifferent walls.

She moves unsteadily to the other end, navigating through spilled garbage, rotten meat, and spoiled vegetables. She looks up through the ominous black grates and feels a fresh dampness on her face. A light rain starts to fall. She steps forward more quickly, struggling to keep her balance. She can't decide what is making it hard to concentrate—the dizziness, her bleeding stomach, or the fear that she might already be the count's next victim.

A dark brown wooden fence separates this alley from the next, and at the bottom, near the center, several broken boards form a hole large enough to crawl through. A dented Dumpster protrudes several feet from the building on her left. She freezes, eyeing the space between it and the fence. Someone could be crouching there, waiting, she thinks. Tightening her grip on the baton, she holds it so the bar extends along her right forearm. She takes a deep breath. Another step forward. She stands directly under another fire escape.

The metal groans, and she looks up. The platform above her wobbles briefly, but she can't see anything distinct in the shadows. The rain falls more impatiently now, and she focuses again on the space between the Dumpster and the fence. Her muscles tense with each step.

The noise above her sounds different this time, heavier, like something snapping and releasing. She shuffles backward just in time to see him leaping off the platform. His coat flutters at his sides like a crow's wings, and his body looks rigid. She braces herself as he lands a few feet in front of her.

At the same instant, they both kick. Their shins collide and snap back into place. Samantha swings the baton hard into his jaw and kicks once again. Her right foot crashes into the side of his knee. He buckles.

She aims the baton for his head again, to knock him out, but he ducks underneath her arm. An electric pain shoots through her body as the knife slices across her side. She stumbles.

He moves with her, and Samantha can see that he is about to swing his left hand. Like a poor fencer, he telegraphs the attack. She slides forward with her right foot, smashing the baton into his wrist as he swings, then pivots toward his body, whipping it across his face. He spins into a fall, landing on his left shoulder. Immediately, he thrusts his right foot into her shin. Samantha drops hard, the full weight of her body smacking into the ground on her right side.

The baton tumbles out of her hand. She struggles for breath, getting to her feet uneasily. He is already up.

Before she can react, his heel smashes into her ribs, sending her into the metallic face of the Dumpster. She spins away from him. The rain drops thick as sleet, and the walls around her seem to vibrate.

He marches forward. A blade appears in each hand.

Moving one foot forward, he lunges with both arms. Instinctively, she parries with her arms, stepping to the left. She ducks and steps past him. He swings his right arm backward, and she can hear the gust of air and snap of his clothing as the blade whizzes overhead. Two more steps, and she dives for the hole in the fence, slipping through in one motion, then pushing herself up on the other side.

This alley mirrors the other except for the building materials. By the fence, a pile of loose bricks and a few bags of lime are partially covered with thick sheets of plastic. She picks up a brick and waits for him to appear through the hole. The rain pounds against the pavement. She waits. Panting. Muscles strained with exhaustion.

*What the hell is he waiting for?*

The boards of the fence buckle, and Samantha moves just in time. He has pulled himself up and over the top. His right leg lands on an uneven stack of bricks, knocking him slightly off balance. He bends his left leg to steady himself.

She throws her brick at his face, snapping it forward like someone throwing a dart. He stumbles back. The dropped knife rings at her feet.

She grabs it and runs.

Each step aggravates the pain in her stomach and ribs. Samantha wants to look back, but she doesn't need to. She knows he's there. Somewhere. She turns one corner, then another. Uphill now. The strain in her legs intensifies. Rainwater gushes toward her, and she imagines him gaining, only moments from pouncing on her. She can't lose focus and fall. She tells herself not to look. She can't look.

With a few more strides, she gets to the top of the hill. Ahead, a car passes hesitantly. Samantha takes one more step, then another. She makes it to the road, away from the shadow of alleyways and Dumpsters. She rushes into the street. Lights glow from several street lamps, and cars fill every parking space. She turns around.

Nothing.

Samantha watches the entryway of the alley, straining to see something. Everything feels remarkably still in spite of the rain.

He isn't there.

She starts downhill, and the momentum keeps her from collapsing. She wraps her arms in front of her chest, hoping to stop her body from shaking—shaking from fear as well as the cold, she thinks. The wind surges violently, whipping rain into her face. She tries to shield her eyes but can't see through the wall of water. She needs to rest, to take cover, to get help. But she doesn't know where she is going. Gravity carries her more than her own will, and she worries that something has already taken control of her.

She runs up three steps to the entryway of an apartment. The dark porch feels wide, though she can't see where it ends. Two crimson doors with black numbers—12 and 14—seem to glow in front of her. Samantha knocks on the left, then the right. She tries again, louder. A chill ripples through her, and she hears water dripping off her body like a faucet.

"Come on!" She looks out at the storm through the stone archway.

Someone grunts in the corner of the porch. She spins toward the sound, but can't see anything in the dark.

"Hello?"

A figure lumbers forward without speaking. She winces at the stench of urine and sweat. He stops moving as soon as he sees the knife in her lowered right hand.

"Who are you?" His voice sounds tired and scratchy.

"Who am I? Who are you?" Even to herself, her voice sounds scared, exhausted.

"I'm the guy who sleeps here."

Samantha notices a crumpled sleeping bag in the shadows behind him. "It's raining. I need to get help. I—"

"You're dripping."

"Excuse me?"

"I have to sleep on this floor. You're making a puddle."

"What?"

He speaks more deliberately this time. "I'm going to have to sleep in that puddle."

Angry and exhausted with pain, Samantha shows him the knife. It rests loosely in her upturned palm. "I could be a killer for all you know, and you're worried about a damn puddle!"

"You don't have it in you."

"What!" she ejaculates.

He steps back into the corner and sits on the bag. "You're not a killer, and that's not your knife."

"How the hell would you know?"

"Because I know killers." He pauses for a moment. "Stay as long as you like. Just dry yourself off." He tosses her a hand towel that is monogrammed with an *H*.

"Hyatt?" she asks.

"Hilton."

Samantha doesn't remember sitting down or fainting, but when she opens her eyes, he is so close that she can smell his sweat, his onion breath. He has propped her against the wall.

"Hey, you're bleeding."

"What?" She sits up quickly, startled to see his face so close to hers. She pushes with both hands on the floor. "I've got to go."

"You need a doctor."

Before he can say anything else, she gets to her feet and runs into the rain. It is still falling heavily, but the wind has died down. She seems to be stumbling more than running, and halfway down the hill she realizes that she left the knife on the porch.

*"You don't have it in you."*

Samantha repeats the words, hoping that he's right.

She isn't sure where she is, but she thinks the upcoming intersection will cut back to the alley behind her apartment. The narrow street has cars on one side. It rises slowly and steadily, making each step more difficult. She passes four or five cars, then leans against the hood of another. She tells herself to keep going. She looks up at the long row of cars, and the climb seems overwhelming. She tries to move and stumbles.

Someone is walking toward her, and if it weren't for the steady sound of his shoes clapping against the sidewalk, she might think it another illusion. Then she hears a different sound. A voice? It sounds muted, like someone trying to speak underwater. She leans back against the hood of the car and braces herself. He moves faster now.

She needs to act, to do something. The cars and buildings and streetlights and trees spin. Faster. Faster...

She falls before he gets to her. Her cheek feels cold against the wet pavement. Her body's numb. Her heart beats like the wheels of a train coming to a stop.

*Thumpthumpthump*

She needs to keep her eyes open. If Arty's blood has infected her, she can't let herself be taken over by it.

*Thump, thump . thump . thump .. thump ...*

She can't fall asleep.

*Thump ... thump.... thump—*

# *Parasomnia*

DURHAM, NORTH CAROLINA
JUNE 8, 2000
4:27 P.M.

*Max rests the clarinet on his right knee and adjusts the reed. He looks up at the score blankly, tapping his toe against the stand. The second movement of Mozart's* Clarinet Concerto. *He has been relearning it for Catherine—as a surprise. But today the melody sounds uninspired.*

*He feels too tired to focus. Terrible nightmares have been keeping him awake for months. Images of Veronica mostly— her mouth moving soundlessly, the twisted body underneath him, her cold dark stare. Brad and another detective at the station helped him out. They conducted a swift investigation, filed reports quietly, and never asked too many questions. Did they believe him? Yes. But they also knew the value of such a favor, and things were never the same between them.*

\* \* \*

"I put my ass on the line for you, Max."

"I know."

"I mean, you owe me and Lucas."

"Whatever you need, Brad. You know you can count on me."

"I know."

Her death was easier to keep quiet than Max expected. She had no family or close friends. The story only made the paper for one day. A life erased. Why? For loving him. Was it worth it? Not a chance, he thinks.

Catherine hasn't found out but suspects something. She sees his insomnia as a reflection of what's wrong with their relationship. Fix one and the other will follow, or so she seems to be telling herself. She tries staying up nights with him, but he doesn't like having a witness to his troubled conscience. On her own, she started researching insomnia. Now all their discussions seem to revolve around sleep disorders, treatment, clinics.

"Some of the best clinics are nearby—in Georgetown and Atlanta," she reminds him. She reluctantly admits that the most renowned program is in San Francisco, if he needs to get away for a while.

Max knows that he is short with her, that he hurts her with his actions and words. But lately, he feels as if he is leaning over a ledge—too far to pull back.

"You know all that money you raise. Maybe you could raise a little extra without anyone missing it. Hear what I'm sayin', Max?"

"Yes, I hear you."

"You hear me? Well, what do you think?"

"I . . . I think I can manage that."

"Good."

\* \* \*

The doorbell rings. Catherine stands on the welcome mat. Her hands fidgeting, eyes darting. She is clearly anxious about why he asked her over so urgently.

"I have a surprise for you."

"Really?" She tries to downplay her shock.

"Close your eyes," he says. Max takes her hand gently and leads her into the bedroom. He helps her sit on the edge of the bed, then picks up the clarinet. "You can open them now."

She looks wide-eyed and smiles with the brightness of the sun. He fell in love with that smile and those misty blue eyes. She has never heard him play.

"This was Mozart's last concerto. And his best, I think."

Max closes his eyes and begins. The wistful notes fill every inch of the room, and he imagines the entire orchestra behind him. The saddest moments remind him of Veronica—the darkness she always carried with her but masked in front of him. As he plays, Max hears the melodies as a love story. One with pain and loss brimming beneath the surface.

He finishes and opens his eyes. He is surprised that he didn't need the music. Catherine's eyes are still closed, and a tear meanders down her face. He watches her in silence, and at this moment, he knows he loves her. The feeling makes him sink with the realization that it's too late. He has already destroyed everything with selfish lies and cowardice.

"This is a good start, Max."

"A good start?"

"Yeah, I think we're going to enjoy doing business together."

"I can't keep this up. There's only so much money—"

"Sure you can. See you around."

* * *

*She opens her eyes.*

*He walks to the bed and kisses her with feverish intensity, as if it were the last time.*

JULY 28, 2000
12:44 P.M.

*"It's an important date."*

*"Why?"*

*"Bach died two hundred and fifty years ago today."*

*"The composer?"*

*"I need to see you. Let's meet at eight. Our usual spot."*

*That was all he said on the phone, and Catherine was worried. His insomnia has only gotten worse in the last few months, making him increasingly miserable. She doesn't know what to do.*

*They always meet on the small wooden bridge where they first kissed. It arches over some railroad tracks near Max's favorite Italian restaurant in Durham. On their first date, he took her to Anthony's, and they held hands as they walked after dinner. In the middle of the bridge, he let go, wrapped his arm around her waist, and pulled her close. No one was around, and the fog made everything but his face look far away. He kissed her.*

*She waits in the middle of the bridge. At a few minutes after eight, he appears out of the fog, like a mystery man in a noir film, his untucked shirt and body-length jacket masking the shape of his body. He hasn't shaved today. His eyes are red.*

*"Max, you look terrible."*

*"Thanks."*

*"What's wrong, sweetie? Why did you want to meet here?"*

"I'm leaving—maybe for Salt Lake or Reno. I have some old friends out there...." His voice fades with each word.

"What are you talking about?" Catherine says urgently.

"Something terrible is happening to me. It's like I have some kind of illness or something, and it's getting worse."

"Your insomnia can be treated—"

"It's not just that.... I'm leaving tonight."

"No! I don't accept that. You can't just run away. We can work through this."

"Leave me alone."

"No."

"Go away!" He glares at her.

"You selfish bastard! For once, take some responsibility for who you are."

"I am." He looks down, then says with a rising crescendo in his voice, "Now get away from me." He shoves her into the fog, then turns, resting his hands on the rail and closing his eyes.

Catherine angrily walks toward him.

"It's not over that easily, Max."

He spins around and slices her stomach with a short kitchen knife. She screams, grabbing at his arm and the blade wildly. Her hand is bleeding, and the ground rumbles violently. Her legs rattle with the wooden planks. The train horn cries out. He stumbles, and she shoves him into the railing.

He screams. The pain and rage drain from his face. He is her gentle, loving Max again. A loose, jagged rod from the rail pierces his side, and she helps him off. Pressing her hands on his wound, she tells him that she loves him. She tells him not to leave. She pleads with him as the train gets closer. It's almost directly beneath them now.

"I'm sorry," Max says. He turns suddenly, grips the rail, and throws himself over.

She can't hear her own scream in the thunderous roar.

# 31

# A Pyrrhic Victory

The squeal of reluctant gurneys. Darkness. But the kind that borders on light, like standing in a well-lit room with your eyes closed. Pagers beep, phones ring, footsteps patter, mops swoosh, silverware clatters, television sets murmur.

It smells like disinfectant, sterility.

Other hands have been touching her body, but not tenderly, the way Frank's did so long ago. These hands are indifferent, cold. They probe and poke and pinch. They are not interested in the softness of her skin or the length of her neck. Samantha tries to move but feels trapped in the grip of stiff, cool sheets. Her breathing accelerates.

Someone turns off the lights....

Bright, burning-white light. Her eyes open to fluorescence. Shades of white surround her—stucco ceiling, walls, floor tiles, curtains, sheets. Samantha recognizes the hospital trappings immediately. She got used to them with her father. A metallic cart with a faux wooden tray for meals, a yellow plastic decanter for room-temperature water, aluminum bars surrounding the bed. She searches for the call button but can't find one. The bed next to hers is empty.

A dull pain throbs along the left side of her body, and through the hospital gown Samantha can feel bandages taped to her stomach. She peels off the sheets and sits up slowly. The room spins. She leans back for a moment to regain balance.

As her toes touch the floor, which is warmer than she expects, Frank walks in. He wears a tight white T-shirt that reveals similar bandages underneath. He carries a coat in his left arm. He smiles in a way that relaxes the muscles in his face.

"Sam, you're awake."

"Hi." She winces slightly from pain, then smiles. "What happened?"

"You have a mild concussion. The doctor says you'll be fine with a little rest."

"How did I get here? The last thing I remember is a homeless man telling me not to drip on his floor."

"What?"

"I was trying to get help, and this guy started talking to me. He said I didn't have it in me."

"Have what in you?"

"A killer's instinct."

"I don't understand."

"I was carrying a knife."

"So he thought you were a killer?"

"No, that's the thing. He could tell I wasn't. Despite the knife."

Frank wrinkles his brow. "I have no idea what you're talking about."

"I think I'm okay." Samantha looks down at her bare feet. "How did I get here?"

"In my car. You passed out in front of me, on the street. And I didn't want to wait around for an ambulance."

"How long ago?"

"Almost three hours."

Samantha is silent for a moment, still feeling somewhat dizzy and unbalanced.

"You shouldn't have left the apartment," Frank continues. "What were you thinking?"

"What happened to Arty?"

"The police are still looking for him." His voice is dry now. Exhaustion has replaced the warmth of his smile.

"We have to go back there."

"You're not going anywhere. You have a concussion."

"We have to find him, Frank."

"He killed two cops tonight." He steps closer as Samantha braces herself to stand. "The entire police force is looking for him right now. They'll take care of it. You need to rest."

"You don't understand. If I'm out there, *he'll* find *me*."

"Sam—"

"When you left the apartment, did you see him again?"

"What does that have to do with anything?"

"Did you see him again?"

"No."

"Well, I did. Do you know why? Because *he* found me. I need to be out there."

Frank lowers his eyes.

"Come on, you didn't really expect me to stay here, did you?" she asks with a weak smile.

"No." He reluctantly holds out his hands to help her up. "I was just hoping you wouldn't wake up so soon."

\* \* \*

The rain has stopped, leaving the black streets of Noe Valley slick and shiny. As they get closer to Samantha's neighborhood, police cars crowd the streets. She asks Frank to take her to the place where he found her. It's much farther away than she expects—in an area that seems unfamiliar at first. Frank's car squeezes by a narrow row of diagonally parked cars. He pulls into an open spot. One street lamp glows blue-green; the other is unlit.

"You fell right there." He points through the window, then turns off the engine.

Samantha gets out of the car. She can smell beer from an open can in the gutter.

"I was coming from this direction?"

"Yes."

She walks to the corner, with Frank following silently. The steep hill to her left seems to rise like a drawbridge. Steady streams of water race down each gutter. "I remember running from Arty, but not here. He didn't follow me to the street."

"You think he's still in the alley."

"I don't know."

"Where are you going?"

"Up."

"Why?"

"I'm looking for the homeless man."

"We can find just as many walking downhill." Frank looks in the other direction as Samantha begins the climb.

The bandages around her ankles have become loose, and they rub against her skin like sandpaper. She thinks about taking them off but doesn't want to give Frank a reason to turn around. They walk in silence. She can hear skepticism in the plodding thud of his footsteps, but he is quiet for the time being.

A siren wails several blocks over, fading quickly. Most of the apartment windows are dark, but she can see clearly. The gray clouds seem to glow, as if reflecting the city lights. Samantha is aware of the thinness of her clothes with each gust of wind. A flimsy, worn sweatshirt and jeans. No jacket. She sweats from the climb, and the moisture makes her feel colder. She begins wondering if the icy air signals another storm. Then she sees the red doors. They seem to glow magically in the darkness. Attached to nothing. Each opening to a different path, a different world.

Instinct brought her back here, but what if she's wrong. About Arty? Goldberg? The curse? Don always tells her that a true historian is not led by what he wants to be true. He creates a narrative for the truths he discovers.

With each step, she is reminded that she is no historian. She replays Frank's stabbing words: *I know you've always wanted an explanation for what happened to you. But this curse isn't the answer.*

The red doors stare at her like bloodshot eyes, and she freezes under their gaze, afraid to go any farther, feeling as if she has lived her entire life choosing the wrong door, following paths that go nowhere, that leave her alone.

"What is it?" Frank asks.

Samantha doesn't respond.

Frank pulls a small flashlight from his pocket and walks cautiously up the steps. His skin appears red under the glowing eyes.

"Sam!" he cries.

Like the snap of a magician's fingers, his voice wakes her from the trance. She leaps up the steps. Frank is crouching over a body, a sleeping bag crumpled in the corner. The floor is saturated with a thick wetness. Frank turns, his eyebrows tight with confusion.

"This is the guy I was telling you about," she begins.

"What are you talking about?" Frank responds sharply.

"I was running from Arty, and I came here."

"This isn't some homeless guy."

"What?"

"Look."

Samantha hadn't gotten close enough to look at his face until now. Arty's throat has been cut from ear to ear. Looking around the alcove again, she realizes that the floor is covered with a mixture of water and blood.

Frank is already calling the police from a new cell phone, but Samantha isn't listening. She walks down the steps and looks into the sky. Several clouds stretch out like torn, dirty gauze.

"Arty must have followed me after all." Her voice is quiet, a monotone. "I dropped my knife and started running."

"You're saying the homeless guy used your knife to kill Arty?" Frank has followed her to the sidewalk, holding the phone to his ear.

"He was protecting himself."

"I'd say he did a pretty good job."

"He'll be bleeding."

"How do you know that?"

"Arty wouldn't have gone down without a fight." Her words are not entirely true, Samantha thinks as Frank nods.

Through the receiver, a voice suddenly says, "Hello?" Frank turns away to speak.

*Yes, there would have been a fight, but that's not why he's bleeding*, she thinks. *He's next, not me.*

Frank closes the phone with a snap. "The police are contacting hospitals within a ten-mile radius. In a few minutes, Snair should have a list of everybody who has received medical attention for a knife wound tonight."

"There are a few shelters nearby," Samantha points out. "He may have gone to one of them."

"All right."

The cry of sirens gets closer, and an ambulance turns the corner. This time it's for them. The flashing red lights hurt her eyes. A police car follows close behind. Two EMTs get out of the truck quickly. The officer lingers.

"He's up there," Frank says, then turns to her. "Let's start with the shelters."

The blue and red lights pulse in syncopation against each other, and the entire street seems bright with color. At the bottom of the hill, Samantha looks back. The three men are talking at the curb now. None of them look at Arty. The officer casually smokes a cigarette.

The EMTs have other calls to make.

The cop has a family to get home to.

They must stand around like this every night, she thinks. A different street. A different body. A different time. But for them, every night is just like the one before.

Samantha and Frank have checked three homeless shelters. Nothing. All of them have been locked and closed for hours. Back at her apartment, Detective Snair tells Frank that only two knife injuries were reported. Both at the same ER, both women.

A uniformed officer packs up cases with the fingerprinting equipment and evidence bags. He looks uncomfortable as Snair watches. Water stains darken the living-room carpet, and dozens of damp footprints lead from the bathroom to the front door. *Mrs. Brinkmeyer won't be happy*, Samantha thinks.

Frank asks Snair to post officers at several local shelters for the rest of the night and to inquire about new arrivals in the morning.

"We need a better description to put out an APB," Snair says with restraint.

Samantha knows that she has been vague, but she doesn't

remember much—Caucasian, no facial hair, thin face. His eyes seemed white.

"All right, I'll try."

Snair is about to make a call when his phone rings.

"Yeah...Uh-huh...Where?" He hangs up. "We just got a call from the bus station at the Wharf. A security guard found some bloody clothing in the men's restroom."

The shack of the Amity Bus Depot looks like a small island surrounded by a sea of empty parking spaces. Inside, there are a few seats, two bathrooms, a broken water fountain, and a desk for selling tickets. At 2:47 A.M., it looks abandoned except for several pieces of luggage in the far corner and a tired, anxious-looking man behind the desk. Snair shows his badge, and the man, smiling briefly and clearly excited, leads them to the bathroom.

The fluorescent lights above the mirror buzz loudly, and the painted walls are yellowish green. The only stall is missing a door, and lines of rust mark the back of the urinal. A few paper towels have been stacked on top of a broken dispenser, and the faucet leaks. It drips slowly onto the blood-soaked, torn shirt.

"Do you recognize it?" Snair asks.

"It's a garden variety T-shirt. I've got several like it at home," Samantha replies.

Snair's lips tighten.

"There's something over here." The manager, whose name tag reads *Aristotle Valdez, Supervisor,* points to the open stall. Samantha, standing closest to the opening, steps inside. A bloody white towel has been left on top of the tank.

"Frank, hand me some paper towels."

"What are you doing?" Snair asks as Samantha lifts the towel and turns it. The underside shows a monogrammed *H*.

"This is his. He let me use it to dry off."

"It sounds like you two were real close," Snair says suspiciously. "What does the *H* stand for?"

"Hilton."

"Like the hotel?"

"Yeah." Samantha turns to Aristotle. "Did this man buy a ticket?"

"I don't know. My shift started at midnight. I haven't seen anyone use the bathroom since I got here."

"You haven't sold any tickets?"

"No, the last departure was at one-fifteen. We're just waiting for one more arrival."

"Where was it going—the last departure?"

"Reno. But it sold out earlier today."

"Christ!" Snair explodes. "Get the last guy who worked here on the phone!"

"Wait a minute," Samantha says to Aristotle, whose hand is already gripping the doorknob. "How many buses left between nine and one-fifteen?"

"I'd have to check."

"Please."

He opens the door, eager to get away from the crammed room and stench of urine. "We'll also need to know where they were going," Samantha adds.

Six buses had left in that time period: to Chicago, Salt Lake City, New York, Denver, Las Vegas, and New Orleans. Except for the last, all of them have made at least one stop already. The Fresno police are waiting for the New Orleans bus to pass through. They will be looking for a white man with a missing front tooth.

It takes until four-twenty for Aristotle to reach the early-evening supervisor. He had gone to a strip club after work. He vaguely remembers a man fitting Samantha's description but isn't sure what ticket he bought. "It might have been the line going to Chicago or New York. Possibly Denver."

Frank asks if Samantha wants to stay at his hotel for the night. She says no.

He takes her home.

Her place feels strange. Filled with the echoes of strangers' footsteps and conversations. She looks at the closed door, too afraid to open it. Lying on the couch, she stares out into the obsidian darkness of her apartment. A clock ticks.

She can't fall asleep.

In truth, she doesn't want to.

# *Parasomnia*

*Blue pendant lights hang from the ceiling, making the dark brown wood of the bar seem black. The only empty stool is next to her, and the restaurant is mostly full. She orders a gin and tonic and watches the bartender scoop ice into the glass. A rectangular mirror magnifies the bar-length row of colorful bottles behind him—bright green, azure, honey brown, red.*

*The front door of the restaurant opens, and she turns. A man with short black hair and small eyes enters. He glances around the room, then walks toward the bar, toward her. His body moves sluggishly, and his face seems to droop with exhaustion. He sits next to her, clasping his hands neatly, almost prayerfully, in front of him. He smells strongly of soap and aftershave.*

*"I'll have the same,"* he calls out to the bartender, who seems unimpressed and slightly annoyed. *He must see this act every night of the week,* she thinks.

The man turns to her, and she pretends to study the napkin that she has been folding into smaller and smaller triangles.

"Origami?"

She looks at him, surprised by his sarcasm, and a sudden pain from the wound on her stomach startles her. She grimaces.

"Are you all right?" He reaches out with his hand to touch her shoulder but stops halfway.

"Look, I'm not interested."

"Interested in what?" He looks confused.

"In being picked up on or whatever it is you're doing."

He smiles. "Nothing personal, but I'm not hitting on you."

"Let me guess," she says sarcastically. "You're gay."

"Close. I'm a priest. My name is Father Gabriel Morgan." He extends his hand and they shake. "You can call me Gabe." His skin is soft and smooth. She notices a silver cross hanging from a chain around his neck.

"Catherine Weber." She smiles apologetically.

The bartender places two funnel-shaped glasses in front of them, and Father Morgan reaches for his wallet. She touches his arm.

"I've got it." Catherine hands a credit card to the bartender.

"No, I can't—"

"I insist." She smiles. "Really."

They toast, and the ice in their glasses rattles. She watches as he twists the lime into his drink and takes a sip.

"So," he begins, "tell me about yourself."


OCTOBER 10, 2000

11:25 A.M.


Catherine looks over at Father Morgan—his arms crossed in front of his chest, eyes closed. She turns down the music from *the tape deck and listens to his breathing. Its rhythm seems to keep time with Bach's music.*

*Part of her can't believe that she is driving him—both of them—to San Francisco. But since Max's death, nothing in her life has made sense. She can't sleep for more than two or three hours at night, and when she does, the nightmares make her wish she hadn't. Violent, hateful visions.*

*But they're not just visions, she thinks.*

Andrea would never talk about what happened, but Catherine could tell that she was afraid.

They had spent the day on a hike and returned to Andrea's small one-bedroom apartment, exhausted. They drank chilled white wine while sitting on her purple couch, and through the living room window, they watched the sun set behind the mountains. In the sky, the lines of color—red, orange, yellow—looked like a rainbow on its side. Catherine was surprised by the brightness of the Boulder sun. It seemed almost white.

They talked inconsequentially, as they had been all afternoon—about weather, family, shoes, slipcovers, showerheads, long hours at work. But Andrea was too polite to ask why. *Why are you here? Why the surprise visit? Why won't you tell me what's wrong?* She would wait for Catherine to bring it up.

Catherine had never told her about Max, and she couldn't start now. She didn't have the right words for her pain. So she listened to Andrea's voice. The rise and fall in pitch. Her light, skittish laugh. The way she unconsciously ended sentences with a conjunction, which kept her talking even when she had nothing more to say.

*and ... but ... so ...*

Just after two in the morning, Andrea's emerald eyes started to dim. Her white teeth seemed unnaturally straight as she smiled one last time before suggesting that they go to sleep.

They shared her queen-size bed.

Catherine closed her eyes and waited.

Warm fingers brushed against Catherine's thigh. An accident? No. They slid around to her stomach, avoiding the bandage, falling lower. Hot lips pressed on her shoulder. Teeth pushing lightly into the skin.

Catherine rolled onto her back and pressed her elbow into the throat beside her. Harder and more aggressively, she leaned the weight of her body into the soft skin. Then, with her right index finger, she drew a quick circle on Andrea's chest.

A muffled yelp. "Stop!"

Andrea scratched and pushed and squirmed. The side of her knee hit Catherine's stomach, and the pain jolted her. Catherine felt as if she woke abruptly. She sat up and retracted her arm without speaking. Her hands were trembling.

Andrea slipped away, crying, muttering apologies, scrambling for her clothes beside the bed.

For the rest of the night, Andrea stayed on the couch. She was silent the next morning.

Catherine wanted to talk. She wanted to understand what had happened last night. Andrea had touched her like a lover. She never knew Andrea felt that way for her, for other women.

But there was only silence between them, and Catherine could tell that she was afraid.

At that moment, Catherine realized that she needed to run. From her family and friends. Until she knew what drove Max to kill himself, until she knew what was driving her now, she wasn't safe.

*   *   *

*"How are you doing?"*

Catherine jumps slightly, startled to hear Father Morgan's voice. *"Oh, fine. I thought you were asleep."*

*"Very funny,"* he says with a smile, and they both laugh.

*"Sorry, I wasn't thinking."* She pauses, tapping the steering wheel repeatedly with her index finger. *"Last night, I meant to ask about the guy who put you in touch with Dr. Clay. How do you know him?"*

*"Oh, Arty,"* he says, sitting up straight. *"I actually met him in an insomnia chat room."*

*"On the Internet?"*

*"Yeah."* He clears his throat. *"Most nights, when I can't sleep, I get online. There are so many people out there. On the Net, I mean. Lost. Just looking for someone to talk to. Anyway, I found this chat room for insomniacs a few months ago. I became a regular, actually. One night, this guy Arty mentioned several sleep clinics in San Francisco and a specialist named Dr. Clay. I did some research and found out that he was not just a specialist, but* the *specialist. Eventually, Arty and I started e-mailing each other. We've become friends, I guess."*

*"And he's the one who told you about the treatment?"*

*"Yeah, about a month ago. He contacted Dr. Clay, who invited him to participate in a new study. Arty gave me the doctor's number."*

*"And . . . you think Dr. Clay will help me?"* She can hear the desperation in her voice.

Father Morgan nods encouragingly, then says, *"I do."*

But Catherine isn't convinced. She can't believe that she's pinning her hopes on a man she just met and some guy from cyberspace. She and Father Morgan don't speak for the next few miles. Nothing but dry, seemingly empty fields line both sides of the highway, and the air smells of manure. Even the road signs look tired. Faded, unfamiliar names for quiet towns. She doesn't know exactly where she is going, except that she is heading west. And for the first time, she realizes that she too is lost.

8:53 P.M.

Catherine follows Father Morgan down the steps to Arty's apartment, but before they can knock, the front door opens quickly. Yellow light fills the entryway.

"Arty?" Father Morgan asks with a smile.

Arty shakes Father Morgan's hand, then Catherine's, awkwardly.

"Come in, come in." He mutters and doesn't look at either of them directly.

They step inside.

The light comes from a floor lamp in the corner with an old shade. A crucifix hangs on the wood-paneled wall behind the couch, and Catherine wonders if Arty is Catholic, if that too is something that Father Morgan and he share.

Several newspapers cover most of the space on the couch and coffee table. A small microwave dinner has been placed on one stack, still steaming. It is pasta sprinkled with something green, broccoli, perhaps, and Catherine thinks, I'm glad we stopped for dinner.

"Sorry about the mess," Arty mutters and starts collecting the papers. He looks mostly at the floor when he talks. His tall, lanky body moves clumsily as he shuffles back and forth between the living room and kitchen, removing the dinner and placing the papers in one of several large piles throughout the *apartment. He steals glances at Catherine's body with each pass, and she wonders if she is the first woman to set foot inside his apartment.*

*When the couch has been cleared, Arty gestures for them to sit. He pulls up a chair. Catherine notices the dark lines around his eyes, his pale white skin, and a chipped tooth.*

*Father Morgan starts talking. In fact, he carries the conversation for the next couple of hours, telling them about his childhood in Salt Lake City, the small Catholic community there, his church, and his forced leave of absence for participating in a gay rights parade.*

*It's getting late, Catherine thinks, and eventually, they have to rest. To turn off the lights and struggle for sleep.*

*"I'm a bit tired," she says impatiently.*

*And Father Morgan adds with a weak smile, "Perhaps we should get to bed."*

*This is the moment that they dread every night, but no one suggests an alternative. A game of cards. Watching television. More awkward chatter. None of these distractions will change the fact that they ultimately have to face their inability to sleep.*

*Arty brings them several pillows and blankets from the hall closet. He covers the couch with sheets, then unrolls a sleeping bag for Father Morgan. He leaves the room without saying a word and closes his door.*

*Father Morgan turns to Catherine. "Are you all right?"*

*"Yes." Catherine watches as he unbuttons his shirt and drops it to the floor. "I'm just . . . everything is happening really fast, that's all."*

*"Well, for what it's worth, I'm glad you're here." He climbs into the sleeping bag and adjusts his pillow.*

*"Thanks." She turns off the light and waits for her eyes to*

adjust in the darkness. Lying on the couch, she tries to avoid thinking about Max, about the life she had hoped they would have together. When they were in love, she used to play a game with herself, imagining their wedding, where they would live, how they would greet each other after work, what they would name their children. If they had a girl, Catherine would name her Isabella. She has always loved that name. Isabella. Isabella Harris.

Stop. She has to focus on herself now. On the future.

If she is going to do this, to stay away from family and friends until she gets some answers, she will need to start over. In the morning, she'll look through some of those newspapers for a job and a place to stay. She isn't comfortable here. She doesn't trust Arty. In the last hour, he has opened the bedroom door and walked to the bathroom three times. She can tell that he is watching her.

There's nothing she can do about that right now. She reaches into her bag and takes out a portable CD player.

*The* Goldberg Variations *start playing through her earphones. It's the last CD Max gave her. She plays it at night to block out the memory of the approaching train. The rattling wood. The blaring whistle. Her own silent scream.*

OCTOBER 19, 2000
11:34 P.M.

Her new, unfurnished apartment is in the misty hills below Coit Tower, and she is happy to be away from Arty's probing eyes and awkward body. Father Morgan hasn't found a place of his own yet, but he isn't surprised. She was lucky to find something so quickly, he keeps reminding her.

*The nights have gotten worse for Catherine, and she is anxious about meeting Dr. Clay on Monday. He isn't sure about bringing her into the study, but she hopes to convince him.*

*Her eyes are tired from reading, and she closes the Bible, putting it next to her copy of Kafka's* The Metamorphosis. *These are her only books; Father Morgan gave them to her a few days ago as a gift. Right now, she is reading the Book of Job for the second time. Job, the great sufferer. Job, who cannot sleep because God made a wager with the Devil.*

*She gets up from the mattress on the living room floor and walks to the bathroom.* Maybe a bath will relax me, *she thinks and starts running warm water. Standing at the sink, waiting for the bathtub to fill, she looks at herself. Her skin appears pale and lifeless in the fluorescent light.*

*A figure emerges like a phantom through the doorway behind her, just as Max did from the fog. She feels his breath on her shoulder, and it takes her a few moments to recognize Arty's face in the mirror, his chipped tooth.*

*She turns to face him. His body is almost pressed against hers, and she is certain that he can hear her heart pounding erratically.*

*"What are you doing?" Her words sound weak and fearful.*

*Arty lifts his hands slowly like someone about to surrender, then grabs the back of her head. Before she can react, he slams the side of her face into the glass. Two large sections fall into the sink, shattering into dozens of smaller fragments. Her face and nose drip blood onto the basin. She can feel him rubbing his lower body against hers.*

*Everything seems to move more slowly. The light flickers, and her eyelids feel heavy. She grabs a triangular shard.*

*A sudden jolt. Something passes between them.*

*Looking down, he sees her bleeding hand pressed against his abdomen. He pushes her angrily, knocking her into the tub. He* then removes the jagged glass from his stomach, and it slices into his palm and fingers. He looks at the wound, then at her. There is more blood on him than he expects.

With one long stride, he is above her, clamping his hand forcefully around her neck. He shoves the broken glass into her stomach. She gasps.

Arty steps back, blood dripping from his hand, and he rushes out of the room.

Catherine can't move. She feels tired, incredibly tired. The cool rushing water covers her body, and the sound reminds her of a train. But this time its steadiness is calming.

She closes her eyes, grateful for the darkness, and sinks slowly into sleep.

Arty feels drowsy as he looks over the nearly empty apartment—the small mattress on the floor, the boxes of Chinese takeout, the books by her pillow. He takes another step, then falls, slamming hard against the wood floor. He closes his eyes to stop the spinning. The room becomes still and black as he listens to the moving water.

When he wakes, he stands in the kitchen, unsure of the time or how much of it has passed. He scrambles through the mostly empty drawers until he finds a set of knives. He walks to the bathroom more steadily now. He must finish what he has started.

THURSDAY
OCTOBER 26, 2000
8:32 P.M.

The newspapers in his room seem to grow like weeds. Arty inhales deeply. The smell of the paper, the feel of black ink rubbing off on his fingertips, he loves everything about newspapers. Most people don't appreciate them. They read only parts and then throw the rest away. But Arty reads every single word. He saves them too. He saves them to preserve the past.

He has watched for news of Catherine, but nothing has been reported all week.

He wasn't planning to kill her. To fuck her, yes, but not to kill her. He remembers her body lying in the bathtub, and the anger in him surges. From the moment she walked into his life, she looked at him with revulsion and disgust. She wanted nothing more than to be miles away from him. Now she'll never have to see him again, he thinks.

No, he wasn't planning to kill her, but now it feels right. She should thank him, thank him for finally enabling her to sleep.

Arty closes the paper and puts on the earphones he took from her apartment. He presses P lay on the portable CD player and inhales again, as if the sounds of the Goldberg Variations were air. He opens the book Father Morgan has been reading, Martyrs and Saints.

A large image of Saint Peter fills the page. His body nailed to a wooden cross—feet raised, blood rushing to his head. The muscles in his face are tight with agony and the painful knowledge that death is coming.

He saw that expression on Catherine's face.

"Hey, Arty." Father Morgan walks into the room and sees him at a small desk with his back to the door. Most of the floor is covered with newspapers, and there is little light. Arty doesn't move at the sound of his voice. "I haven't been able to get ahold of Catherine for a few days now. She hasn't called, has she?"

"No." His voice is flat. He doesn't turn around.

"Is that mine?" Father Morgan asks, somewhat surprised, as he steps closer and points to the book.

"Yes." Arty turns slightly. "I saw it in the front room. I didn't think you'd mind."

"I don't," Father Morgan says, looking at the image of Peter. "The father of the church. Did you know that he asked to be crucified upside down?"

"Apparently so." Arty looks back at the image.

There is a moment of silence between them, then Father Morgan says, "I'm going over to Catherine's place. I'll see you later."

"No," Arty blurts out.

"Why not?" Father Morgan looks at him, puzzled by the outburst.

Arty is silent again. Lost in the image of Saint Peter, he hasn't lifted his eyes from the page.

"Arty," Father Morgan begins again, "what's wrong?"

Arty stands up and slowly removes one of Catherine's kitchen knives from the desk drawer. "I'm sorry, Father, but we're all martyrs."

"I don't understand."

"It's time for your suffering to end."

Father Morgan stumbles back. His shoulder slams against the doorjamb as he pivots and runs into the hall. The yellow light of the living room engulfs him. He turns, and Arty is there. At first, Father Morgan is confused, unaware of what has already happened. He grabs his own throat involuntarily and gasps. Blood pours over his hands, spraying away from his neck.

He falls backward, over the couch and onto the floor. He is staring up at the wall behind him, and Arty follows his gaze. The crucifix. From down there, it must look like Saint Peter, he thinks. Upside down and unworthy.

*Arty stands over the body for another moment without moving.* I will have to get rid of him fast.

*He looks up at the cross and suddenly knows what to do. Like an artist overcome by inspiration.*

*He starts to hurry now. Tomorrow is a big day. Tomorrow he starts treatment with Dr. Clay.*

*Tomorrow he'll start to sleep again.*

# 32
## *Aria*

SATURDAY

The doorbell rings, followed by two quick knocks.

Samantha hasn't spoken with Frank since that night a week ago. He called once and left a message saying that there were no new leads. She didn't call back. She needed time away from the case, from him.

She reads the paper every morning, afraid of the possibilities, but has found no reports of similar killings. Not yet.

"Hi, Sam. It's been a while." Frank stands with his hands tucked into his pockets, and he forces a quick smile.

"Yeah."

He shifts his weight uneasily from one foot to the other. He can't read her face. The straight lines of her eyebrows. Closed lips without a smile. "How are you?"

"All right. And you?"

"Good." Frank walks into her apartment with a folder tucked under his arm.

"Any news?"

"The police still haven't found him, but we finally came up with something on that partial print from the bus station bathroom. May I?" Frank motions toward the couch.

"Of course. Sorry."

He sits. She pulls up her desk chair.

"We think his name is Jack Hansen. He was arrested five years ago for assault, then paroled after serving two years. Surprise, surprise, no current address." He hands her a mug shot. "Look familiar?"

*The small black-and-white photo could be anyone,* she thinks uneasily. *It could have been me.* "Not really." She returns the picture. "I never saw him closely. I ..."

"I know." Frank notices the stillness of her body. Head bowed slightly to the floor. "The important thing is that it's over, and you're safe."

"It's not over, Frank. The trail has just stopped. It'll pick up somewhere else."

"This guy was a transient, Sam. You said it yourself. He probably killed Arty in self-defense." Frank stops, uncertain how to read her silence.

"What if it's not that simple?" she asks.

"Sam," he says with a steady voice, "Arty had a record."

For the first time, she looks directly at his face.

"He was arrested for sexual assault in 1997. Apparently he attacked a coworker in the parking lot of her apartment, but the charges were eventually dropped."

Samantha shifts in her seat and leans back.

"We got the right guy," he says conclusively.

"We still don't know exactly how Catherine was involved. And how did the killer find out about Father Morgan?"

"By searching Dr. Clay's office. That's what we did. Arty could have done the same thing. And maybe he was setting up Catherine to take the fall, and something went wrong."

"That explains it?" Exasperated, Samantha crosses her arms.

"What more do you want?" Frank leans forward, one hand pressing down on his left knee. "We caught Arty trying to do the same thing to you that he did to three other victims." He accentuates the last three words, then inhales audibly. "So all the pieces of the puzzle don't fit. They never do. Mostly we're left with unanswered questions, doubts, fears—the things that keep us up at night. And . . ."

"And?" Samantha pushes.

"The others are dead now. We'll never know for sure, but at least the killings have stopped."

"What if they haven't, Frank? Something is happening here. Max, Catherine, Arty, and now this homeless man."

"Jack Hansen," Frank adds.

"All of them lost the ability to sleep. They all experienced a sleeplessness that left them so exhausted, so terribly lonely and frustrated and desperate"—Samantha shudders at the word—"that they became violent."

"And none of these people had the *will* to stop themselves?"

"Not if they were acting in a semisleep state. Maybe they only realized what was happening gradually, through their nightmares. Or at least what they thought were nightmares. Horrible night visions that overpowered them, that made them feel like victims. A kind of curse," she says the last part softly, more to herself than Frank.

"Sam, I don't believe that we're all potential victims. I can't."

"Because you don't know what it's like to be desperate."

Frank looks at her eyes, which seem far away. "Desperate?"

"Yes, desperate to the point where you'll do anything to regain control, to fight the fear that you'll never sleep again."

"Even to kill."

Samantha lowers her face and closes her eyes. "It changes you, Frank."

They are silent for a moment, and Frank picks up the deep blue folder in his lap. For the first time Samantha notices a design. In the center, the profile of twin faces is outlined in silver.

"I flew to Washington yesterday, to report back to the corporation." The frustration has left Frank's voice. "I talked about your help with this case. Yours and Don's."

Samantha doesn't respond.

"They gave me a new assignment, and I asked to bring you on—as a consultant, if you're interested. This is the case file."

She reaches for it, then stops herself. Frank stands and puts it on her desk. "Look it over and let me know what you think."

"I—"

"Just look it over before you decide." Frank smiles tentatively, then checks his watch. "I have to run to the station and see Snair about a few things. I'll call you later tonight. Maybe we can have dinner or something."

"I don't know."

"I'll call you regardless."

"I need some time. I'll call you in the next few days."

He looks at her skeptically.

"I promise," she adds and reaches for his hand.

Everything in the apartment feels still. Their clasped hands fill the space between them, and Samantha smiles.

Frank squeezes her hand one more time before letting go. He turns, walking slowly, almost soundlessly, out the door.

Her eyes open suddenly in the darkness. At first, there is only panicked breathing and the tympani of a pounding heart. She struggles to lift her arms and legs but can't move. Car tires screech on the street below, and she turns her head toward the window. Moisture beads on the inside of the pane. She tries again to move, straining until her body rises like an anchor from deep waters. One at a time, her feet touch the floor, and she begins to feel safe. Sweat bleeds through both sides of her T-shirt.

The bedside clock reads 3:20.

She wipes sweat from her forehead and gets up for a glass of water.

Standing at her desk, Samantha looks out at the cloudy haze covering the street. Even the sky is tentative, drizzling instead of raining. Not sure what it wants to do.

She turn on a lamp, and the blue folder glows like a jewel. She touches the cover with her fingertips, sliding them along the silver outline of faces. Inside, the letterhead on the cover page reads *The Palici Corporation*. She closes it—unsure if she wants to accept the responsibility for what's inside.

She turns off the light to wait, preferring the misty darkness. She is afraid to check the clock, to start thinking about how few hours she has left before sunrise. Looking at her hands, she can't remember the last time they touched someone else's face. Frank's face.

She tastes the salt with her tongue before feeling the moisture on her cheeks.

A drop falls onto the back of her right hand, then the left. The storm clouds have been building in Samantha for too long; the water finally falls. A hot, angry pain lessens, slowly becoming relief.

The waiting is over.

# Coda

*A*nother bus. His third in as many days.

He has to keep moving. Some nutball attacked him, but that doesn't matter now. Not for an ex-con.

The girl at the ticket booth is chewing gum and looking through a glossy magazine. He uses cash, and she slides the ticket underneath the Plexiglas without looking at him.

"Teenagers," he mutters.

Sitting on an uncomfortable metal bench, he waits, head in hands. For the first time in his life, he has become restless at night. He has never been one to dream, but something leaves him feeling uneasy in the mornings. Quick flashes—images he can't quite make out and doesn't remember.

A bus pulls into the station with RALEIGH, NORTH CAROLINA printed on a digital sign above the driver's window. He steps inside, hands his ticket to the driver, and sits in the back. Very little is in his wallet: $87.65, a few stolen credit cards, three driver's licenses, a library card for the San Diego Public Library, and one document with his real name—a faded Social Security card.

*A lot of good that'll do, he thinks.*

He takes one last look at the name—Jack Hansen—and puts it away. He closes his eyes but knows immediately that he won't be able to sleep. Something is haunting him. Not his past. Not the death of that man. Something much greater. Something much more terrifying.

# Acknowledgments

My agent, Elaine Markson, and my editor, Sarah Durand, have my heartfelt gratitude for their enthusiastic support and dedication. Their feedback and hard work have made this book a reality.

Several dear friends read early drafts of this manuscript, and their encouragement gave me the confidence to keep working. Many thanks to Sara Frane, Victoria E. Johnson, Christina Nelson, Manel Kappagoda, and Joshua Archibald. I also wish to thank Caitlin Hamilton and Jennifer Roche, who have invested a great deal of time and energy in promoting this project.

I have a number of friends whose unfailing support and love make everything possible: Ryan Losey, Daniel Kurtzman, Laura Garrett, Kirstin Ringelberg, Fiona Mills, Jessica O'Hara, Lilah Morris, Nina Yamanis, Satish Gopal, Robert and Jennifer Spirko, William Loewe, Brian Byrdsong, Jennifer Meltzer, Michael Everton, Pamela Cooper, Townsend Ludington, Kimball King, the Taha family, and David Ziring.

I have been fortunate to have exceptional teachers throughout my life. I particularly want to thank my mentor and friend,

Linda Wagner-Martin. Her boundless intellectual and emotional support has been staggering.

I am also indebted to the English and Music Departments at the University of North Carolina at Chapel Hill and the University of California at Davis. They have given me incredible opportunities to grow and develop as an artist, teacher, and professional.

My mother, father, and brother have always supported me without question and believed in me without doubt. They have kept me grounded through their laughter, compassion, and generosity.

Lastly, Susann Cokal wins the award for reading the most drafts of this manuscript. A generous friend, dedicated editor, and consummate professional, Susann has challenged me to be a better writer at every stage of the project, and her efforts and remarkable talents are evident on every page.

To all of you, I am, truly, grateful.